POETIC JUSTICE

POETIC JUSTICE

USA TODAY BESTSELLING AUTHOR

H.B. MOORE

Mirror Press

Interior design by Cora Johnson
Edited by Haley Swan

Cover design by Rachael Anderson
Image Credit: Deposit Photos #19065491, by Peshkova

Published by Mirror Press, LLC

ISBN-13: 978-1-947152-20-5

Also by H.B. Moore

The Omar Zagouri Thrillers:
Finding Sheba
Lost King
Slave Queen
The Killing Curse
Beneath: An Omar Zagouri Short Story
First Heist: An Omar Zagouri Short Story

Esther the Queen
Daughters of Jared
Eve: In the Beginning
Ruth
Deborah
Hannah

Writing as Heather B. Moore
The Paper Daughters of Chinatown
The Slow March of Light
In the Shadow of a Queen
Under the Java Moon
Love is Come
Condemn Me Not: Accused of Witchcraft

POETIC JUSTICE

Justice might come in different forms,
but justice always comes.

Claire Vetra is looking for two men. The first man she'll destroy. The second man she'll also destroy—after she makes him watch everything he's ever built crumble in front of him.

This is only the start of her revenge against the World Alliance Order, which held her hostage for a year and subjected her to live human testing in the name of medical science.

But when Claire begins to unravel her past, she discovers that unlocking the memories of what happened to her might destroy the remaining shreds of her sanity.

PROLOGUE

THREE YEARS EARLIER

SHE'D ALWAYS BEEN the good girl. Straight A's, no boyfriends, no sneaking out. So when the letter arrived at her mother's flat, Bethany saw her ticket to freedom.

"Do you know what an honor this is?" her mother had said, tapping her long cigarette on the crystal-cut ashtray. "An internship is almost unheard of for a kid in high school."

Bethany could only stare at the red design on the top of the letterhead that said *International Student Alliance*. The interlocked hands of the logo gave her a fleeting sense that she'd just shaken hands with the devil, but that was ridiculous. Her mother had always criticized her for her wild imagination. Plus, Bethany didn't believe in devils, or God.

Her mother had cured her of any notions of deity by the time she was six.

"Do you think a god would allow so much suffering in the world?" her mother had told her, standing in their front room and pointing at the massive TV, where ambulance lights flashed on the screen as a reporter detailed the massacre of an entire family.

A little girl had been murdered, along with her older brother and both parents.

Bethany had spent weeks wondering about that little girl and what it had been like when she knew the bad man was going to kill her. Had she screamed? Had she cried? Had she tried to run or hide?

"They had no security system," her mother had said during the newscast.

If there was anything that Bethany's mother believed in, it was security systems.

Her mother had waved her long, elegant fingers. "If there was a God, there would be no need for security systems, and I wouldn't have a career."

Bethany had nodded, had agreed, as she always did.

When she was eleven, her mother enrolled her in a self-defense course. Bethany was the only child in a class of adults, and she'd come home bruised.

"Never trust anyone," her mother had told her. "Especially strangers."

She might as well have told Bethany to stay locked in her room. The world was full of strangers.

Now, at eighteen, Bethany was doing something completely on her own. As she left their flat and walked outside to climb into the waiting taxi, her mother said, "You can change your mind anytime. Just call me."

Bethany nodded. "I will." She wouldn't.

"Well then," her mother said, bringing up a hand to smooth her long dark hair that was pulled into a severe knot at the nape of her neck. It was a rare show of uncertainty and hesitation.

Bethany was a miniature of her mother but without the makeup. Her mother's green eyes and dark hair were made even darker on her ghost-pale skin. She emphasized her coloring contrast by applying thick eyeliner and the deepest red lipstick.

Now, her mother leaned forward and gave Bethany a light kiss on the cheek.

Bethany could only remember three times her mother had ever shown affection. This was the third.

"Don't trust anyone," her mother said. "And remember the list. Memorize it."

"I have it memorized."

A rare hint of a smile touched her mother's lips. "Good girl."

Good girl.

Once, Bethany had lived for those words. Had excelled on her exams and kept her school uniforms perfectly cleaned and pressed.

Good girl, echoed in her mind as Bethany rode away in the taxi. The list was in her small suitcase, but Bethany would have happily left it behind if her mother hadn't been watching every item she'd packed.

The list started with the taxi ride. *Have the taxi driver drop you off a block from the dorms. You don't want him to know where you live.*

Bethany leaned her head back and closed her eyes. She didn't want to see the passing stores and homes as the taxi took her into the heart of London. The next time Bethany opened her eyes, it would be to her new life.

When the taxi slowed, Bethany had nearly fallen asleep. She blinked her eyes open to see the driver pulling alongside the curb that was the location to which her mother had given him directions.

Bethany leaned forward in her seat. "One more block please. I'll get off at the Biomedic Centre."

The driver glanced at her in the rearview mirror. "Are you an intern there?"

Her heart thumped, but she did not hesitate. "Yes."

She'd done it. She'd revealed her destination and her purpose to a stranger.

Her mother would be furious. The thought made Bethany smile.

She didn't stop smiling until she'd climbed out of the taxi and thanked him. Her mother had already paid him, plus the tip.

"Good luck," the driver said before driving away.

Bethany stood on the sidewalk for a moment, watching the departing taxi. He hadn't tried to kidnap her. He hadn't molested her. He hadn't asked for more money. And he was a stranger.

Slowly, the other sights and sounds of the street came into focus. People walking, cars driving. A bicycle. Laughter.

This was what normal was like. This was how people lived.

Bethany couldn't wait to join them.

Once she'd checked into her dorm room—one that she alone would use, at the insistence of her mother—Bethany unzipped her suitcase. There, on top of her folded, dark conservative clothing, was the laminated list.

The words were a jumble before her eyes, with items such as securing her dorm room, what to say and not to say to the other students, how to maintain her nutritional diet, all the way to her bedtime routine.

Bethany pulled out her makeup case, something she'd been adding to over the weeks, taking small things from her mother. She found the cosmetic scissors and stood over the trash bin as she cut the laminated list into fingernail-size pieces. She watched as each bit of paper floated into the bin.

When she dropped the last bit into the trash, Bethany released a breath. It was done. The list no longer existed.

A knock on the door startled her, and she quickly buried the scissors into the makeup bag.

"Hello? Anyone there?"

It was a man's voice.

Bethany's heart about stopped.

"I'm here," Bethany called out, her pulse drumming as she reached for the door handle and opened it.

The man was in his twenties, Bethany guessed. He had shockingly blond hair, almost white, and his blue eyes reminded her of the color of her school uniform.

"Beth?"

She almost corrected him to Bethany. "Yes?"

"Hi, I'm Jasper," he said, extending his hand, a gleam in his eyes.

Had she ever had someone's eyes gleam at her? Definitely not.

She shook his hand and was soon enveloped in a warm, strong grasp.

And he smelled good.

Her mother had not put this on the list—what to do when a gorgeous college student knocked on your door and introduced himself?

"Welcome, Beth," Jasper said and grinned.

Was it possible to fall in love at first smile?

"We're all getting together tonight at the pub," he continued. "Sort of an orientation for the newcomers. Coming?"

Bethany inhaled. "Yes."

"Great," he said, those blue eyes of his sliding down below her face a bit, then back up. "Should I stop by to pick you up?"

"That would be great," Bethany said. "I don't know where anything is."

He chuckled. "That will change soon. All right, then, I'll see you later on."

Bethany set to work immediately by shortening one of her skirts, then taking in the sides of a rather boxy blouse. She went to the mandatory new student orientation during the afternoon wearing her creation, and no one looked at her like she was odd. She was hardly stylish, that she realized, but she didn't stick out either.

She was too anxious to eat dinner, so she just grabbed an apple from the cafeteria line. She hadn't seen Jasper at the orientation, which meant he probably wasn't new, and as she hurried back to the dorm room to get ready, she hoped that he wouldn't forget about her.

Bethany had spent hours watching online videos of how to put on makeup, and she'd even experimented a little on the nights that her mother worked late. But as she began her makeup routine, her hands shook, and she messed up on her eyeliner more than once.

She didn't want to look like a little girl playing with her mother's makeup.

It was dark by the time she'd finished her makeup and used a flat iron on her long dark hair. Then it was time for her next indulgence. She took out the pair of jeans she'd bought at a vintage shop without her mother's knowledge. She'd been hiding them for two weeks and had stuffed them into her suitcase at the last moment when her mother left the room to take a call.

The jeans fit her slim build like one of those waif models, and as Bethany posed in the mirror, her blood raced through her body. She was really going to do this. She was going out with a whole group of strangers, to a pub, at night, and she was wearing jeans. Next, she pulled on a blouse that she'd previously altered by cutting off the sleeves and sewing tucks at the waist.

Not bad. She took a cigarette, stolen from her mother of course, from where she'd hidden it in a pencil box, and lit the end. She inhaled, then burst into a violent cough. After catching her breath, she inhaled again, and again.

A knock on the door sent her into another cough. She stumped out the cigarette in the pencil box, then waved her hand frantically to clear the air. She grabbed her purse, which contained her phone and dorm keys and a couple more cigarettes she'd stashed inside.

When she opened the door, she saw that she had more than one visitor. Jasper and another man—the second one was sandy haired with a generous spread of freckles across his face.

"Beth, this is Randall."

Randall stuck out his hand, and Bethany shook it with a lot more confidence than when she'd shaken Jasper's earlier in the day.

"He's tagging along with us," Jasper said, his blue eyes focused on Bethany. "You smoke?"

"Sometimes," she said, trying to sound more sophisticated than she felt. She stepped into the hallway and shut the door, then locked it with her key.

"You're ready?" Jasper sounded surprised.

Bethany had been ready for a long time. Eighteen years to be exact.

The walk to the pub was a riot of sounds and color and conversation and laughter. The longer Bethany was with Jasper and Randall, the more comfortable she became. She could tell they were both brilliant in their biomedic fields of study from their random bits of conversation, but they also knew how to have fun. And that's what Bethany had been missing her entire life. The fun part.

The outside of the pub looked like it had been around for a hundred years, with its cracked stonework and creeping ivy. Perhaps it had. The music was thumping, and the place was half-filled. Most of the patrons looked like college students, and a couple Bethany recognized from the student orientation.

Jasper led her around the room, introducing her to a few people. Then he got caught up in a conversation with a pretty redhead. Bethany tried not to be envious, so instead she wandered to the bar and sat down.

The bartender was busy with someone else, so Bethany waited her turn, debating what to order.

"What are you having?" a man said, sliding onto the stool next to her.

She turned to see a pair of nearly black eyes watching her. His face was lean, almost hawk-like, and he was good-looking in the classical way. In other words, he probably had an easy time meeting and picking up women. His dark eyes scanned her face as if he were appreciating many things about her.

From Jasper, Bethany had gotten the "I'm interested, and we'll have fun together" vibe. From this man, it was a different vibe entirely. More of a "You're interesting, and this night will be unexpected."

Bethany dispelled the wild thoughts running through her mind and tried to relax. She'd been meeting and talking to strangers all day. None of whom had been on her mother's list. This man definitely didn't make the cut, and Bethany sensed he was no student. He was older, for one thing, at least thirty, and the depths of his eyes had many layers in them.

A slight shiver passed through her as he leaned close and said in a low voice, "I hear the beer is decent."

"Sure, that sounds good."

The man signaled the bartender, and just like that, they were served.

The man tipped his open beer bottle against Bethany's, then took a long swallow before setting it down.

Bethany had had beer a couple of times, but never in a pub, and never with music pulsating around her and a pair of dark eyes watching her intently.

She lifted the bottle and took a couple of swallows. The beer went down cold and happily settled in her stomach, giving her another layer of determination which she hoped would turn into confidence soon.

From across the room, she spied Jasper, who was laughing now with the redhead, his hand on her shoulder. They seemed to be getting more intimate. Bethany took another drink of her beer. There couldn't be a lot of alcohol in it, but just a few swallows had made her feel significantly relaxed and warm. Too warm.

"I haven't seen you here before, Bethany," the man said.

Her eyes snapped to his.

"I'm Paul," he said, holding out his hand.

She looked down at his hand, and a sudden sense of vertigo slammed through her. She gripped the edge of the bar. "Hi, Paul."

She took his hand, but it wasn't really a shake—more of a caress. When he let go, his gaze stayed focused on her.

Trying to remember how he knew her name without her telling him, she took another drink of her beer.

"You're very pretty," Paul continued, leaning toward her again. "Just like your mother. It's not often that beauty and brains go together."

Bethany wanted to laugh at him—was that a pickup line? And how did he know her mother? She looked into his eyes but couldn't quite seem to focus. He was saying something else, but she couldn't make it out above the music.

His hand went to her waist, and she could only think of how good his touch felt as he helped her stand. She swayed against him, and she thought he said something like, "Easy, sweetheart. We need to get you some fresh air."

When she tried to hold onto the beer, Paul removed it firmly from her fingers and set it on the bar.

She wanted to protest, but no words came. Leaning against Paul, she wondered what it would be like to kiss him. She must be drunk, she decided, because she felt like she had to wrap her arms about his waist to walk a straight line.

But instead of leading her out the front entrance of the pub into the cool night air, he led her through a door she hadn't noticed before. The darkness of the room made it hard to see, and she turned her head to look where Paul was taking her. He said something, but it sounded so far away and muted that she didn't understand.

"Where are you taking me?" she asked, although her words came out so slurred.

And then a sharp burst of air hit her face, and for a moment, her head cleared.

They were behind the pub, she guessed, and a sedan was parked there. Two men stood by the open back door of the car. It was too dim to make out their features, but Bethany's one impression was that she wouldn't want to meet these men in an alley alone.

The irony hit her too late because her knees buckled, and her numbness returned with force.

Dimly she was aware that Paul had scooped her up like a doll. And then his words vibrated against her body as he spoke: "Payback's always sweet."

Her last thoughts echoed through her mind before she gave way to complete unconsciousness: *Mother was right. Never trust anyone.*

CHAPTER 1

PRESENT DAY

CLAIRE VETRA SET the envelope stamped with the dark-red hand-in-hand logo of the ISA on top of the folded clothes. Her suitcase was packed, and she zipped it shut. As if called by the sound of the zipper, Lance appeared in the doorway of her Columbia University dorm room. He folded his arms and leaned against the doorframe, his hooded eyes telling her everything that she'd already heard in the past couple of weeks.

"So, you're really going?" he asked, his voice hard and clipped.

Claire held in a sigh as she dragged her suitcase off the bed. There was no use asking Lance to carry it for her. He was trying to stop her from leaving, not help her go.

"We've already talked about this," Claire said. "I can't pass up this opportunity." The moment she'd ripped open the letter from the International Student Alliance and scanned the words, she'd known it was a game changer. Now, five weeks later, she was leaving to spend the summer in London interning at the Biomedic Centre along with six others.

Students who completed internships through ISA were almost guaranteed a straight ride to the best job offers out of college. The biomedics industry was actively looking for the brightest and most competent students, but the competition for the limited job openings was fierce. Claire Vetra didn't come from a long line of who's who, and she had no connections outside of her professors, so this opportunity from ISA could be seen as a small miracle.

Thankfully the beast of a suitcase had wheels. She shouldered her satchel that would act as a purse while she traveled, then grabbed the suitcase strap and wheeled it across the dorm room toward Lance.

He was a tall, athletic guy—blond, blue eyed, wealthy parents, naturally smart, two years her junior. Perhaps that had been the chink in their relationship all along. He was young, and he could be as moody as hell.

Claire didn't have time for moody. She'd fought for everything she had since she was orphaned at the age of ten. Bounced between relatives' homes until she graduated from high school at sixteen, she then worked for two years before getting into Columbia University. She could have been accepted at the age of sixteen, but she needed to be completely free of her guardians and any power DCFS, the child protective services, had over her life.

She liked Lance, but he'd become a drain on her time, and she couldn't afford it any longer. Once she started the biomedics master's program in the fall, she had no intention of indulging in keg parties, and if that meant leaving the frat boys behind, they would just be a casualty.

Claire had received top honors in her classes and was now on full academic scholarship. This London internship would put her résumé ahead of other applicants, and she couldn't afford to dismiss such an opportunity.

"Claire," Lance said, grasping her arm as she tried to pass by him. "You really don't want to do this."

Was that a threat? She turned to look up at him. Lance's size made her petite five-foot-three frame feel even smaller, but she was hardly intimidated. She could walk circles around him any day in the classroom, and she'd kept herself in top physical shape, running in the mornings and lifting weights during study breaks.

Claire said nothing, just held his gaze as she waited for the ultimatum she knew was coming. She'd expected it, so that's not what hurt; it was that Lance didn't think she was worth the wait.

"I might not be here when you get back," Lance said, his hand still wrapped around her upper arm.

"You're dropping out?" she asked just for spite.

"You know what I mean, Claire," he said, lowering his voice as a couple of students passed by in the hallway. "I might not be *here*. Waiting for *you*."

Claire drew her arm out of his grasp and moved through the doorway, pulling her suitcase behind her. She felt Lance's gaze on her as she walked down the hallway. She could have said a million things to him. Instead she'd said nothing.

By the time she reached the Uber waiting for her in the dorm parking lot, she was smiling.

CHAPTER 2

"YOU LOOK *SO* American," a woman said, walking into the room and eyeing Claire up and down as if her ratty jeans and fitted T-shirt were an anomaly in the UK.

A nice introduction. This must be Riya, her roommate. Claire wrestled her suitcase into the miniature closet. Who would have thought a dorm room could be so small, especially one she was supposed to share with another student? She'd been handed her key, dorm number, and roommate's name upon arrival at the Biomedic Centre.

She looked over at Riya as the woman settled onto the edge of her bed. She appeared to be in her early twenties, and her skin was a to-die-for-smooth caramel color. Her thick black hair and smoky brown eyes added to her mystique, but the red dot in the middle of her forehead gave her away. Hindu. Not to mention her wraparound black shirt and flowy pants.

"And you are so . . ."

Riya laughed. "I'm Indian, from *India*. Not like the Indians you keep corralled in America."

Claire raised a hand. "Easy. I'm just here for the internship, not to start an international debate."

Riya's sculpted brows lifted. "You do know we're the only two female interns this summer?"

Claire picked up the set of sheets folded on her narrow twin bed. "Is that unusual?"

"Not in and of itself," Riya said. She rose from her perch on her bed, crossed to the door, and locked it.

Surprised at Riya's action, Claire turned to look at her roommate. "Is there a security issue in the building?"

Riya said nothing until she settled once more on her bed, sitting cross-legged. "Three years ago, a female intern from the Student Alliance group disappeared. She was only eighteen."

Claire stared at Riya. "Disappeared, as in never heard from again? Or was there a crime—"

"Never heard from again."

"Really," Claire said. "How did you find this out, and why is the Student Alliance still operating if something like that happened on their watch?"

"Great questions," Riya said. "Of course, I couldn't pull up the police report, but I did read the obscure news that found its way to the internet. The Alliance claims that the woman ran away—that she used the internship as a way to escape her family. Apparently her mother was extremely overprotective."

Claire stared at Riya. She'd heard of such a thing during the Olympics when a couple of athletes claimed political asylum during the games. But the interns chosen by the Alliance were at the tops of their classes. Its ideology was to provide top students a summer internship in Europe, after which they could then take their global knowledge back to their classrooms. Thus the hand-in-hand logo that represented countries sharing education and knowledge.

Claire smoothed the sheets she'd just tucked in and settled onto her bed, across from Riya. "What do you think happened to her?"

"That's what I'm trying to figure out," Riya said. "I doubt that Bethany—that was the girl's name—was a runaway."

"If someone kidnapped her, wouldn't there be a ransom or something?" Claire asked.

"All kinds of bizarre things happen out there," Riya said with a shrug that wasn't exactly comforting to Claire.

"And you came anyway?" Claire asked.

"I can take care of myself," Riya said. "A girl from a city in India has to learn to protect herself in all situations." She hopped off the bed and crouched on the floor to pull something from beneath her bed—it looked to be a small version of a boxer's punching bag.

"Kickboxing bag," Riya announced.

Claire watched her set the thing upright, then Riya backed up to the door and charged across the room toward the bag. She leaped into the air, spun, then sent the bag crashing against the far wall, almost taking out the lone window in the room.

Claire jumped off her bed. "You almost broke the window."

Riya laughed and grabbed the bag again to set it up in the middle of the room. She did another running leap, and this time the bag flew directly at Claire. She dove out of the way.

Riya crossed to where Claire had landed on the floor and extended her hand. Claire grasped it, and Riya hauled her effortlessly to her feet.

Riya might be a thin lithe woman, but she had a lot of strength. Still, against a determined man, how would she fare? A man like Lance was a mountain compared to Riya.

"You think kickboxing is going to save you if you get attacked?" Claire asked, truly curious. She'd taken a self-defense class at the university her first semester, but the instructor had been clear that half of self-defense was out-witting your attacker. That and having a concealed weapon.

"Of course not," Riya said, then reached into the waistband of her flowy pants. She withdrew a metal tool, which she pressed, and a blade emerged.

"How did you get a knife through security?"

"I can't tell you all my secrets on the first day." Riya turned to her nightstand drawer and pulled out a small case. "I'll give you one to practice with."

"Practice?" Claire asked, her mouth dry as Riya produced six more switchblades, each one ornate and beautiful.

"I'm not staying cooped up in the dorm every night," Riya said. "The London nightclubs are said to be raging."

"I'm not really a nightclub person," Claire said. "This internship is pretty important to me, and I plan to excel at it."

Riya sifted through her knives without saying anything for a moment. When she finally raised her gaze, she said, "So what is it? You're a whiz kid or something?"

"Excuse me?"

"How did you get the internship?"

"I applied and got in," Claire said with a shrug. "How about you?"

"I have an eidetic memory," Riya said.

Claire stared at her.

"And so do some of the other interns. The ones who don't are just freakishly smart." Riya tossed one of the closed knives at her. Claire had no trouble catching it. "So, what is it really?"

"I . . ." Claire looked down at the closed switchblade in her hand. Was she about to tell something to Riya that she'd never shared with another living soul? "I have an eidetic memory too."

"Ah." Riya gave her a triumphant smile. "I should have guessed. You cataloged everything about me in about ten seconds."

Claire opened her mouth, then closed it. "How did you know?"

"Takes one to recognize it, I guess," Riya said. "Now, we need to get started on your first lesson. If we're going to go out into the wilds of the London streets, you'll need to know how to use that thing."

Claire shook her head. "I've never carried a weapon. I'll just stay out of dark alleys."

Riya laughed. "You're not at Columbia anymore. Besides, that missing eighteen-year-old I told you about? Eidetic memory too."

CHAPTER 3

PAUL RAINE HAD been sitting in the back of the parked sedan so long that the temperature inside now matched the cold drizzle outside. It was early summer, and the British spring weather had yet to release its cool grasp. A car accident had tangled the traffic, and Paul had missed Claire Vetra's arrival at the airport.

He had yet to see her in person. He had her face and her background memorized, as well as Claire's roommate Riya's. But Paul wasn't here for Riya. He'd been waiting for Claire for years.

As the lead recruiter for the World Alliance Order, Paul had a lot riding on selecting the right young women to bring into their program. The previous team lead had screwed up a few years ago when he got greedy and brought in three women from the same internship group. WAO ran dozens of internship companies under different names, so it was a major faux pas for the recruiter to triple dip.

That recruiter was no longer with WAO; in fact, he was no longer breathing. Handel Raine could be a tough boss.

Two women exited the front doors of the building, and

Paul watched as they walked beneath a streetlight. Neither woman was Claire, although one of them was Riya. Paul's hope deflated. If Riya was going out without her roommate, that meant Claire was likely staying in for the night.

And then the door opened again, and Paul straightened when the woman he was waiting for emerged.

Claire was petite, but her presence made up for her small stature. Although he was watching her from across the street, Paul sensed her confidence. Despite the fact that Claire had been orphaned as a ten-year-old and had bounced between different relatives' homes, she'd managed to stay at the top of her class and had graduated summa cum laude.

She'd earned her associate's in a year through an online university program in New York, and then at the age of eighteen she started at Columbia University, using Pell Grants and student loans. By her second year of college, she'd been granted academic scholarship status.

One might consider her a smart woman and diligent studier, but Paul knew better. She was careful about her talents and hid them from her professors. Paul guessed it was to stay out of the limelight. Nowhere in any of her school transcripts was any acknowledgement to her eidetic memory. Many people had various types of photographic memory, but through his undercover work, Paul suspected that Claire not only remembered text but images as well.

And nothing in her school transcripts mentioned that her parents had also been brilliant prodigies. Claire was a rare find.

Paul watched her catch up with her roommate and the other woman, who must not be part of the intern program or else Paul would have recognized her. He watched Riya sling an arm around Claire's shoulders and laugh. Claire smiled back. It added to her appeal, Paul admitted to himself. Yes, he knew Claire was beautiful from seeing her images, but seeing her in person was a different experience. Her hair was a thick, lustrous brown, and her hazel eyes could definitely pull a man into their depths. She was petite but athletic, which made her sexy and definitely Paul's type, if he were to indulge in a type. But Paul never indulged. He couldn't get lazy or careless. Employees of WAO had died for less.

Paul shrugged off his assessment of Claire's physical features. Beauty was only skin deep—that he knew better than anyone. It was the mind that fascinated him. And right now, he was fascinated with Claire's.

It was the one part of his job he liked: investigating those who looked to be promising recruits. The family business was supposed to be an option for Paul, but it seemed he'd always been groomed to work for his father. He never felt he had a choice, not really. He was the one link to his mother, who'd died when he was a young boy.

"Time to go," Paul murmured to himself. Before exiting the sedan, he slipped his Glock into its holster and hooked his trusty Taser to his belt. Not that he expected to use either of them. The bartenders of the nearby pubs had proven to be easily bribed cohorts and slipped the right drug into whichever drink Paul ordered for a young lady. Most of the women had been flattered that someone of Paul's suave demeanor would order them a drink.

It was all routine now, and once in a while he wondered what it would really be like to pick up a woman at a pub—for fun, not for work.

Paul shut the door of the car and strode across the street, following Claire and the other women at a respectable and innocent distance.

Predictably, they entered the first pub they came to. Paul was almost disappointed, hoping that tonight he'd have a better chase. Claire held no surprises so far. Not that she was exactly making any of the decisions in this group. It was clear that she was a sheep tonight.

When Paul stepped inside the All Hails Pub, he made his way toward the far side of the bar, skirting the main dance floor where people were already moving to the music, their clothing flashing light and then dark in the strobe. Jordan was bartending tonight, and after a brief nod, Paul took a seat and settled in to watch.

Claire and Riya had found a table, and they'd already drawn the attention of other men. It wasn't hard to catch the interested gazes being cast in their direction.

Paul almost smiled to himself as he watched a twentysomething man approach the table full of the newly arrived women and set his hands on the back of Riya's chair. His blond spiked hair caught the multicolored lights strobing through the room. He leaned forward and said something that made the women laugh.

Paul signaled the waiter and ordered his usual beer. Then he took a sip and settled in to watch the show.

As the next hour wore on, the blond man seemed to connect with Riya and joined them at their table. What Paul didn't like was the blond man's friend, a dark-haired guy with one of those heavy, brooding faces. He'd dragged over another chair and squeezed himself next to Claire.

By the expressions crossing her face, Paul could see she was being nice to the guy, but she was also keeping a wall up. Paul, of course, knew about her boyfriend Lance, and he knew that once Claire disappeared, Lance wasn't the type to head up an international search. Paul refocused on the new guy. There was something about him that Paul couldn't place.

Brooding Guy wasn't just trying to flirt with Claire—he was trying to draw her way from her friends. Claire had barely touched the beer in front of her, which told Paul she intended to stay completely sober and alert.

Brooding Guy stood and held out his hand to Claire. He was tall, thick about the shoulders and neck—really, a brute of a man. Paul watched as Claire hesitated, but then she grasped Brooding Guy's hand and followed him to the dance floor.

Paul took another swallow of his drink.

Brooding Guy put his hands on Claire's hips, and she looped her arms about his neck. They weren't dancing to the rhythm of the music but instead moved slowly, as Brooding Guy seemed to be asking her a series of questions.

Then he pulled Claire closer, but she slid her hands to his shoulders and kept the distance between them. She was flirting but still wary; Paul could see that. He wasn't worried that Claire would leave the pub with the man. Her background held all the indicators that she wasn't a one-night-stand type of woman. She'd worked too hard to get where she was to fall prey to something so reckless.

Brooding Guy moved in again, sliding his hands across her back and dipping his head toward her neck as if he intended to kiss her. His size dwarfed Claire's petite frame, and Paul idly thought that she'd be better matched with someone his size: just under six feet and lean.

Paul watched with interest as Claire pushed against her dancing partner's chest, causing him to lift his head in surprise.

Paul scoffed. Brooding Guy would certainly get the hint and back off now. Paul wondered if the guy would start looking for another girl to pick up before he even got off the dance floor.

The guy's arms fell away from Claire's waist, which was good, because Paul wasn't in the mood to get into a bar fight. It would bring too much attention to himself and Claire.

It was then that Paul saw Brooding Guy glance over his shoulder and give a quick nod. Just as quickly, he'd turned back to Claire and raised his hands, saying something that Paul guessed was along the lines of "I'm only trying to have some fun."

Paul looked where Brooding Guy had glanced. That's when he saw the blond man with spiked hair standing near the back entrance of the pub. The door was painted black, and there was no exit sign above it, but Paul was familiar enough with the place to know all ways in and out.

Were these men tag teaming women?

Paul straightened, pushing aside his beer.

No one was going to move in on his job.

First, he had to get rid of the blond man. Then hopefully Brooding Guy would follow. Paul didn't need Claire catching on.

He rose and walked to the front of the pub. More people had arrived since the time he'd entered, so he maneuvered through the healthy crowd while staying on the outskirts of the dance floor.

He kept an eye on Claire's location. She said a couple more things to Brooding Guy but was headed back to the table of friends now. Brooding Guy was following her, keeping his distance, but it was clear he wasn't ready to give up.

When Paul reached the entrance, he slipped one of the broad-shouldered bouncers a couple of fifty-pound notes and said, "Can you send the blond guy at the back entrance on his way? He's been harassing a couple of ladies."

The bouncer moved off, a little richer, and Paul started toward the table where Claire had rejoined her friends.

Brooding Guy had noticed his blond friend being escorted out of the pub by the bouncer. Paul watched as Brooding Guy did something unexpected. He took a couple of quick strides toward Claire and grasped her arm, spinning her toward him.

Claire's mouth fell open in surprise, and she shouted something at the man.

Paul was there in seconds. Plans had changed.

"Release the lady's arm," Paul told Brooding Guy. He was taller close up.

"We're in a private conversation," he said, his brown eyes narrowing under his thick brows.

And it was from that expression that Paul remembered this man. He'd grown his hair longer, had his gold tooth recapped, and he wasn't wearing glasses anymore. Paul couldn't believe he hadn't recognized him sooner.

At that same moment, it was clear that Gerrard recognized Paul as well.

Gerrard let go of Claire and stepped back.

Paul folded his arms. "You're bothering the wrong woman."

Gerrard glanced at Claire, then back at Paul. He turned and started for the entrance.

Paul followed, and before Gerrard could get very far, Paul grabbed his arm.

Gerrard stopped but didn't look at him.

"So this is what you've stooped to?" Paul hissed. "Trafficking?"

Gerrard's sad face twisted into a smile. "You're pathetic," he said. "What you're doing is no different."

"You're lucky to be alive," Paul continued, glancing about the crowded pub. "If I see you or blondie anywhere near here again, you're dead."

Gerrard scoffed. "You can't have all the women, Paul."

"I don't want *all* the women."

"So this woman is priority one, huh?" Gerrard continued, his dark eyes burning up.

As much as Paul wanted to flatten this man right in the middle of the pub, he couldn't afford the scene. Besides, Gerrard was right. Claire *was* priority one.

"I'm not trafficking," Gerrard added. "I have a new boss."

"Who is he?" Paul asked, studying Gerrard's face closely for signs of lying. He didn't see any.

"She." Gerrard's gaze shifted away. "I'm just the grunt worker. I'm only following orders, nothing more."

Paul froze. "Who's your operative?"

"You'll find out soon enough," Gerrard said. "These women don't mess around. Especially the boss lady. They also don't reveal their identities." He spread his free hand. "They send out disposables first."

"You?"

"Yes."

"Who are they?" Paul said.

Gerrard released a low laugh. "I might be disposable to my new boss, but I still value my own life."

Paul had never liked or trusted Gerrard. But Paul's father had hired him, and when Gerrard slipped up with a confidentiality clause, Handel Raine had requested a private conference. Gerrard had run. Which had been smart of him if Paul were to be honest, but Handel Raine never buried a grudge and always got his due. "Why are you telling me all of this?" Paul asked.

Gerrard's face transformed into a smile.

Paul released Gerrard's arm. "You're bugged, and you're setting me up."

"It only took you three minutes to figure out that you're the real target. Getting sloppy, Paul." He took a step back and lifted a hand. "Have a good evening." Then he hurried toward the entrance.

Paul watched him leave, disbelief pulsing through his body. If he didn't have a mission to complete tonight, he'd go after Gerrard and beat the truth out of him. But it was too late. Whoever the guy's boss was, she had just moved a step ahead.

CHAPTER 4

CLAIRE LET THE conversation, laughter, and music buzz around her as she watched the two men talking. Riya had brought her to the All Hails Pub, and apparently it was the same pub where Bethany—the girl who'd disappeared three years before—had last been seen.

When Riya told her, Claire had felt a bit creeped out. But then she told herself she was being ridiculous. History didn't repeat itself in that way. Nonetheless, Claire was determined to do some of her own research on the missing student once she got back to their dorm room. Maybe Riya had missed something in the news reports that Claire would pick up on.

For now, she watched Gerrard talking to some guy. Gerrard had been coming on to her all evening, and at first Claire didn't mind in the least. It felt good to have some fun, forget about Lance, and embrace the new opportunities facing her. But Gerrard had gotten a little too handsy, and that's when the new guy had stepped in.

The two men appeared to be in a pretty focused discussion. The second man wasn't as tall as Gerrard, but the way he held himself spoke of his strength and intensity. He looked ready to pounce, reminding her of a lean leopard. His hair was dark and skimmed the collar of his button-down shirt with rolled-up sleeves that showed off tanned skin, as if he'd recently spent time in a sunny province.

And he'd been watching her all night. He'd been discreet, but Claire had felt his eyes on her. So when she'd been dancing with Gerrard, she took a few glances to where the man was sitting at the bar watching the crowd. Claire could say that she'd felt flattered, gaining the attention of two men almost as soon as she entered the pub that night, but all she felt was uncomfortable and exposed.

It wasn't that she exactly missed Lance, but she missed having the security of a relationship and not feeling so vulnerable when meeting new men.

Yes, pubs were pickup joints, and it was all part of the evening. But she wasn't interested in a hookup, so when Gerrard started putting his hands on her, she told him to back off. Gerrard might be good-looking, but he seemed a bit too aggressive and intense.

On the other hand, the second man was a different intense. He seemed quiet, where Gerrard was more gregarious. The second man also seemed more classy and more of a gentleman, if interfering with Gerrard was any indication.

Now, Gerrard turned from the stranger and hurried out of the pub. *Interesting.*

Claire waited, wondering if she should approach the man who'd stood up for her and thank him. Or if she should wait for him to come to her table.

When he turned toward her, their gazes connected for a brief moment before one of the dancers blocked the view. By the time the dancer moved, the man had moved as well. Claire scanned the pub and soon found that he'd returned to his place at the bar and the beer he'd been drinking.

He was scrolling through his phone, seeming unencumbered by all that had taken place—as if it were something he did every night.

Yet Claire sensed he was still aware of her. In fact, she sensed that he was aware of everything going on in the pub, as if he were some sort of an overseer.

Another glance at him, and she tried to guess his age. She placed him as early thirties. He wore no wedding band or other type of jewelry. His two- or three-day scruff made him look like he wasn't in one of those jobs that required a clean-shaven face.

Gerrard had told her he was a house renovator, and she could believe it by his strong and calloused hands. It made her wonder what this other man did for a living.

"Go over and say hello to him," Riya said, leaning close and nudging her. "I think he's hot, for an older guy."

Claire's pulse jumped. "He's a good Samaritan, that's all. Doesn't want to be bothered."

"He's sitting at a bar by himself—of course he wants to be bothered," Riya said with a laugh. "It's not like you have a boyfriend waiting for you back home."

Claire wasn't sure why she'd told Riya about Lance and his ultimatum. Maybe it was because Riya was so open with information and it had rubbed off on Claire a little.

"Ooh, he just glanced over here," Riya said.

Claire had noticed it too. It was only polite to tell him thanks. "All right." She took another swallow of her drink, then stood. "I'll be back in a second."

"Take your time, honey," Riya said.

Claire started to weave through the crowd, still holding her beer, since she planned to nurse the same one all night.

The man glanced up as she neared, and instead of looking past her, he held her gaze. And the way he was looking at her made her feel like he'd been expecting her. He didn't smile, but his gaze was appreciative, as if he was a man who knew a good thing when he saw it.

Claire swallowed back the uncertainty as she continued toward him. Another woman bumped into her, and Claire almost spilled her beer. But she managed to keep her balance and keep the bottle upright. The seat next to the man was open, so instead of hovering over him and telling him thank you, she decided to sit down.

It was bolder than she was typically, but she only planned to stay for a minute, then make her way back to her new friends.

She slid onto the seat and leaned one arm on the counter, then turned toward the man.

"What are you drinking?" he asked, with no preamble.

Before she could answer, he'd signaled the bartender, who came right over.

"Your best for the lady," he said, and the bartender set a cold bottle of beer—a brand she didn't recognize—in front of her.

Claire saw that it was the same brand he was drinking.

"Thank you," she said, although she hadn't intended for him to buy her a drink. "For the beer, and for helping out earlier."

"Not a problem," he said, looking past her.

He wasn't even looking at her directly, but she had the sense that he didn't miss many details and was hyper aware of his surroundings, although he was careful about his body language. In fact, this man reminded Claire of herself. She knew she wouldn't forget anything about Gerrard, or this man, or anyone else she encountered, which meant that sometimes she purposely stayed oblivious to her surroundings in order to reduce the noise that would plague her mind later.

"You're American?" the man asked, finally moving his gaze back to hers.

"Yes," Claire said, deciding that being cryptic was always the best approach with men in a bar. Even the smallest bit of encouragement could lead to someone like Gerrard thinking she was more interested than she was.

"It's really good," he said, tilting his head toward the beer.

Claire flushed. She was being rude not to at least try the drink he'd ordered for her. She picked up the narrow-necked bottle and took a drink. The taste was more refined than what she'd already been drinking, but beer was beer. She set down the bottle after only a couple of swallows. "Nice."

Something in his eyes flashed, but it was so quick that Claire decided she imagined it.

"I'm Paul," he said, slipping his phone into the inside pocket of his jacket.

Claire noticed there was a deep scar that ran the length of his index finger. She also caught a bit of his scent at his movement. Clean, yet woodsy, as if he wasn't exactly a city dweller. That interested her.

"Claire," she said.

He extended his hand, and she shook it, momentarily caught in his grasp. His hands were cool, a marked contrast to Gerrard's sweaty palms.

He released her hand after only a quick handshake, but it had been long enough for Claire to feel the collected strength in his hands. She also noticed that his nails were clean and short, and his skin wasn't particularly soft, but not calloused either.

"What brings you to London, Claire?" he asked in a low voice. The way he spoke her name was strangely familiar, in a way that someone who knew her well would speak. He closed his mouth, and his jaw clenched as if he were holding back another question. Reaching for his own beer, he rotated the bottle but didn't seem to mind the wait.

"I'm here on a university internship," she said, giving a shrug as if it wasn't something she cared to go into detail about. "Are you a local, Paul?"

His gaze shifted then, moving past her. "I suppose I would call London home," he said. "It's a beautiful city, and you can't beat the nightlife."

Claire nodded, and even though she had no intention of drinking much more, she took another swallow of the beer. It was mellow and made her feel calm. Perhaps she'd found a new favorite. She turned the bottle to examine the label again and was surprised to see that the words seemed out of focus.

She blinked, but the label was still unreadable. Perhaps it was the dim lighting and the flashing lights coming from the dance area that made her vision blur.

"Are you all right?" Paul asked.

Claire tried to brush off her concern. "I have major jet lag," she said. "I should get back to my friends."

"Sure," Paul said, and watched her stand up.

Her mind spun, making her feel light-headed, and she grasped the bar to steady herself.

"Claire." Paul was next to her in an instant, his arm coming around her, supporting her.

The dizziness passed, and her mind refocused. Paul was staring at her, his face only inches from hers. His scent was stronger now. Too strong. Like a warning.

"I'm all right," she said. "Just felt light-headed for a moment."

Paul didn't move, and he didn't release her.

She wanted to tell him to stop touching her, but she couldn't seem to muster the words.

"I'll walk you back to your friends in case you feel dizzy again, Claire," he said.

Why did he keep saying her name like that? Like he knew her? "No," she pushed out.

Paul's gaze didn't leave hers, and his tone became more insistent. "I'm walking you back to your table, Claire."

What was wrong with her? Paul grasped her hand, and Claire decided he wasn't much better than Gerrard. The men at this pub were too forward for her taste. He led her through the pub, skirting around the dance floor. She followed because she really had no other choice. Her mind and body didn't seem to be on the same wavelength.

When they arrived at the table where Riya had been, Claire was surprised to see another group of people instead. She tugged her hand from Paul's and turned to scan the pub. "Riya," she managed to get out. She was surrounded by strangers talking, laughing, and dancing. But she couldn't see Riya or any of the others who'd shared their table. The room wobbled and then sharpened again.

"Maybe she's in the ladies' room?" Paul suggested.

Whatever had been messing with Claire's senses seemed to have lifted. She looked over toward the restroom door and watched the women going in and out. She didn't recognize anyone. The tables had all filled, and when Riya came back, her table would be gone. But another scan of the dance floor and the bar area told Claire her roommate wasn't in sight.

The music had slowed to a low pulse, and the couples on the dance floor had their arms wrapped around each other as they swayed to the sultry beat.

"Do you want to dance while you wait?" Paul asked, his low voice vibrating against her ear.

Claire turned to look him. Standing this close and with the lights of the dance floor surrounding them, his dark eyes weren't nearly as dark as she thought they were. They were brown with gold in them. The room seemed to shift behind him, and Claire felt as if she'd missed a step, although she wasn't walking. Paul grasped her arm, as if he knew she needed steadying.

She'd dance with Paul, and as soon as Riya appeared, Claire would tell her she was heading back to the dorm to crash. This jet lag was worse than she thought.

"Sure, I'll dance with you," Claire found herself saying to Paul.

He gave her the slightest smile, and his eyes seemed to lighten. It was kind of fascinating to watch.

He led her to the center of the dance floor. In the middle of all the swaying couples, Paul rested his hands on her hips, keeping a comfortable distance, and Claire rested her hands on his shoulders.

They moved to the music, and Claire tried to ignore her pulse, which had increased at Paul's closeness. His hands were like an anchor at her waist, keeping her steady when she started to feel dizzy again. Why had she said yes to dancing with Paul? Maybe he'd expect her to go back to his place with him. She wasn't sure how London hookups worked, but it couldn't be too different than in the States. Riya still hadn't come out of the ladies' room, and Claire didn't recognize anyone else in the pub.

A couple bumped into them, pushing Claire against Paul. His hands slipped behind her back as he pulled her closer and drew her away from the drunk couple at the same time. They escaped the intrusion, but Paul still held her close. And Claire found that she didn't mind. She looped her arms behind his neck, her hands brushing the edges of his hair.

Goose bumps broke out on her skin at the feel of his breath against her neck. Their bodies were touching now, and although Paul was a complete stranger, Claire fit against him as if they were in a much more intimate relationship.

Her mind started to spin again. She clung to Paul, wondering if she was going to faint, and his arms tightened around her in response, holding her up.

"Claire," he whispered in her ear, his voice a low caress. "Are you all right?"

She didn't know. Her body was responding to this man. She wanted to be closer to him, have him hold her tighter, but she felt light-headed, and everything around her seemed to mute. The music, the conversation, the people.

"Let's get you some air," Paul said, drawing away.

She wanted to protest and tell him not to let her go, but then his arm came around her waist, and he was practically holding her up as they walked around the dancers and toward the back of the pub.

"We can go out the back," he was telling her.

But Claire wasn't really paying attention. She was focusing on putting one foot in front of the other and trying to figure out why she felt the way she did. Even fatigue shouldn't incapacitate her this much. And she couldn't help clinging to Paul, both of her arms wrapped around his waist.

He opened a door at the back of the pub, and for a moment Claire wondered if it was a restroom. But the room they entered was nearly dark and looked to have a couple of tables with chairs—a private dining room?

The door shut behind them, and the music faded. This room was so much cooler, and Claire let go of Paul, embarrassed that she'd been hanging on to him for support. She just needed to sit down, to have some water. And then she'd be fine.

"I'm sorry—" she started to say, but then her legs gave out, and her vision blurred to gray.

The last thing she remembered was Paul catching her and effortlessly picking her up before he pushed his way out of another door into a cold and drizzly night.

CHAPTER 5

CLAIRE COULD HEAR the whispers above her, but she didn't open her eyes. She wasn't sure if she should. Because the voices were speaking about *her*. Two men, one woman. The woman sounded as if she were in her fifties at least, perhaps older. The men—one had an accent, British, the other man spoke at a rapid clip as if his sentences were trying to keep up with his thoughts.

None of them were Paul.

Paul. What had happened to him? Where had he brought her? Who was he?

Memories of the night at the pub had marched out in succession as soon as she became conscious. In exact detail, of course, thanks to her ability. It also allowed her to recall details that she might not have completely paid attention to at first. Such as the scar on Paul's index finger. Yes, she'd noticed it when she'd first thanked him, but now she remembered other details about the scar. It hadn't been a clean cut, as if made by a knife or razor. It had been jagged, like his hand had been caught in some type of machinery.

When he'd looked at her, his gaze had been intense. Not like a man who was trying to get her attention, like she'd first thought, but like a man who was analyzing and cataloging her features and expressions.

"She needs to be moved today," the woman's voice said. "Raine's bringing in another tonight."

The younger man spoke up. "Claire's listed as priority one. We can't move her until she's awake."

"Tell Raine to hold off then," the woman said. "It's our only choice. And keep the IV drip in until she wakes. I'm guessing it's been more than twenty-four hours since she's eaten. The drugs should have worn off by now, although Raine said he had to give her an extra dose. Stubborn, it seems."

Who's Raine? Claire wondered. She focused on keeping her breathing steady and slow. She didn't know who these people were; she didn't know where she was. And she didn't know what they were talking about. But she could pretend she was asleep with little effort. A mirror of her teenage years, she realized. As she moved from one relative's home to another, she'd been put into foreign situations time and time again. She'd learned to adjust and change to whatever would most benefit her. It had also been easy for her to disassociate with people and events around her. Nothing ever lasted, so there was no reason to allow herself to become connected.

Her aunt Lynne had been a chronic complainer. Lynne's tightly permed hair only emphasized her pear-shaped body, and her large doe-like eyes could convince the harshest cynic that she never had a cruel thought in her head. To neighbors and PTA mothers, Lynne had given off a benevolent persona—she was caring for her dead brother's daughter, after all. But at home, out of the public eye, Lynne had harped on Claire constantly. If Claire didn't have dinner ready on time, she'd be sent to her room without food.

Claire learned to sneak granola bars and crackers, things too "healthy" for her aunt to miss. Even if Claire had dinner ready at her aunt's deadline, something else would be wrong— the rice too watery, the chicken too dry, the carrots under-cooked—and Claire would miss a meal again.

This punishment wasn't the worst that Claire could imagine, or experience, but it was the worst Lynne could justify. Lynne was a sugar addict, and to miss a meal, or a snack, was paramount to torture.

The sharp concave feeling in Claire's stomach now didn't bother her. She'd felt this on a daily basis for two years when living with Lynne. Claire had lived with Lynne for three months before her aunt brought home a man. At first, Claire was pleased. Jimmy was the peacemaker in the home. He contradicted Lynne when she wanted to send Claire to her room. "She's just a kid, Lynne," Jimmy had said, then winked at Claire.

At first, Claire glowed in Jimmy's praise. But then he came into her room one night when he thought she was asleep. He watched her for a few minutes, then left.

The next morning before school, Claire told her aunt what Jimmy had done.

She would never forget the look on Lynne's face. Her eyes rounded, and she staggered forward, almost dropping the platter of reheated cinnamon rolls she carried. Lynne's mouth opened, then closed, and opened again. Her face slowly moved from its pale yellow to a deep orange.

Claire took a step back, and another, then she hurried out the door and made it to the school bus stop with about ten seconds to spare. Later that afternoon, she walked slowly home from the bus stop, thinking about her options. She needn't have worried. A car sat in the driveway, one that Claire recognized as belonging to her DCFS caseworker.

Lynne had packed Claire's things into a scuffed mustard-yellow suitcase that was duct taped along the bottom. The bulky form of her aunt watched through the front room blinds as the social worker climbed out of the sedan in the driveway.

Ms. Breinholt extended her chapped hand. "Claire? We've had some changes happen."

Claire didn't take the woman's hand; she just picked up the suitcase. It felt lighter than she thought it should, but she wasn't about to go inside her aunt's house again. She opened the back door of the car and lifted the suitcase into the back seat. Then she walked around and climbed into the passenger seat.

When Ms. Breinholt got back into the driver's seat, Claire said, "Now where?"

The door of the room clicked shut, and the voices of the men and woman faded down the hallway. It was only then that Claire opened her eyes. Her imagination of what the room might look like wasn't too far off. Overhead fluorescent lights faintly buzzed, illuminating the stark medical machines that lined one wall. A scan of her body told Claire that she was hooked up to an IV and a blood pressure wrap. What had happened. She remembered not feeling well at the pub. Had she fainted?

She was obviously in some sort of medical facility, but why, she couldn't imagine, since she didn't think she was sick enough for a hospital. Lifting her arm, she felt a rush of urgency to get the IV out. She only hoped there wasn't any sort of alarm that would alert others. She lifted her head and reached for the tape on her arm to peel it off. But her left hand wouldn't budge. In fact, her entire arm seemed to be numb. And that's when she realized she couldn't feel anything from the neck down.

Claire exhaled, letting her breath out. Surely if she could breathe, if her chest could expand, she could move her body. She tried to move again, focusing on her left hand, and attempted to lift her fingers. Nothing.

Her breathing went shallow as she looked down her body. She was covered with a sheet from her chest down, and only her arms were exposed. Although she couldn't see her legs, she knew she was strapped to the bed. They were in too perfect of a position. Her legs and feet felt numb too, but at least she could move her toes a little.

She turned her head to examine the path of the IV line. The IV bag was positioned in such a way that she couldn't read the printed label.

All she knew was that she had to get the IV out of her arm. Then she had to get out of this facility. She had no idea what time of day it was or if she was even still in England. Why had Paul brought her hear? She could only assume he'd done this?

She turned her head from side to side and wriggled her feet, hoping that she could somehow stimulate the nerves in the rest of her body and fight whatever intravenous fluid was pumping through her system.

And then she felt it. A tingling sensation had started in her right arm, near the site of the IV entrance. Claire focused all her efforts into moving that arm, and after several moments, she was able to lift a couple of fingers. She closed her eyes, concentrating on moving her hand. Perspiration broke out on her forehead as she worked. But soon she was able to move both hands. It felt as if she were lifting hundreds of pounds with her arms as she raised her hands over and over.

Finally, she was able to gain enough sensation to reach the IV drip with her left hand. She tugged out the line and watched as beads of blood bubbled up along her skin. Her head fell back on the bed again, and she tried to catch her breath after the effort of so much movement. The tingling continued and spread across her stomach. Feeling moved from her feet up her legs, similar to how it felt to have a numbing shot wear off at a dentist's office.

Voices sounded outside her room, and before Claire could think of what to do, the door swung open.

Her first impression of the approaching people was that she'd guessed wrong. She wasn't in a medical facility at all. The people who'd just walked into her room weren't wearing lab coats or scrubs. They wore all black, as if in uniform.

"She's awake," the woman said, her short red hair smooth against her head. The woman's intense gaze didn't miss that Claire had pulled out the IV. "Strap down her arms," she commanded.

Claire raised her hands to block whatever the two men were about to do. Before she could, the man with steel-rimmed glasses gripped her wrists. He had an angular build, but his grip was stronger than Claire could resist. Besides, it was three to one, and the woman was quick to plunge a needle into Claire's arm. Everything went dark within seconds.

CHAPTER 6

Paul watched Claire sleep. It had been twenty hours since he'd seen her. The IV in her right arm pumped in a sedative, keeping her in a dream state until the testing was over. She'd passed every one so far. Physically, she had no illnesses or defects. Mentally, she'd already proved her superiority. Emotionally, she was a wild card. She hadn't grown up coddled. She'd had to fight every step of the way for what she'd achieved. But Paul could deal with that. What he couldn't deal with was if his father took Claire on as a pet project.

Paul knew that his father had tagged Claire for years as a possible recruit.

Once she neared eighteen, Paul had been assigned to bring her in.

Paul shoved his hands in his pockets, tamping down the growing anxiety. Claire had been immune to the 302 drug, but when the guards had injected her with a stronger sedative of a different drug class, she'd finally gone down. He hoped that Claire would tolerate the injections she'd been given; he didn't want to lose a recruit on his watch.

Right now, Claire looked too pale for his taste. She was mostly covered with a blanket, but he could see the paleness of her neck and upper chest and arms. Her dark lashes rested on her cheeks, fluttering just barely when she breathed. Her dark hair, instead of lustrous and smooth, was tangled behind her neck. Paul was just about to brush it away from her skin when the door opened.

"You shouldn't be in here," Raymond said, coming into the room.

Paul lowered his hand and stepped back from the bed, relieved to see the doctor. Paul had been starting to feel remorse—something he couldn't afford in his line of work. Get the girl, get out, deliver her, move on to the next project. This pattern had been working for Paul ever since he officially joined the Order.

Raymond didn't dress like a doctor but instead chose to wear khakis and a polo shirt. Today, his white shirt was a stark contrast to his dark skin. Raymond carried an electronic tablet, and he peered at Paul over his reading glasses.

Paul knew the doctor didn't need reading glasses, and the ones he wore were not prescription. It was all part of the persona that Raymond presented to the Order.

"The medics record all visitors," Raymond said. "That's how I knew you were in here."

Paul swore under his breath. "Has my father reviewed her file?"

"Yes, he logged in last night," Raymond said.

"What do you think?" Paul said. "Can we move her to training without my father getting involved?"

"I don't think so. You know he's had Claire on his radar for years." Raymond turned his tablet around; it was opened to an email app. "He's on his way down here."

"Now?"

Raymond nodded. "Be careful, Paul. If he thinks you have an added interest in this woman, he'll use it against you."

"I can't be here when he arrives." Paul's phone buzzed, and he pulled it out to check the incoming text. "He just texted me to meet him in an hour."

Paul left Raymond in Claire's recovery room and navigated through the hallways of the lower level of the Order's compound. His father would come down the main stairs, so Paul headed to the back ones. Since arriving at the compound and turning Claire over to the medic, he'd been searching for information on Gerrard and who he could possibly be working for.

Paul couldn't stop thinking about how Gerrard had targeted Claire, which meant that Gerrard somehow knew that Claire had been *Paul's* target.

That meant that someone out there was interfering in his business.

"Paul?"

He froze. This couldn't be happening. His father should have come down the main stairs.

Slowly, Paul turned.

"You brought her in last night?" Handel said.

"Yes."

"How is she?"

"Recovering from being drugged," Paul said. He refused to give his father information that he could find out for himself.

"Well done."

It might sound like a compliment, but Paul knew better. His father's eyes were as hard as black marble.

Paul folded his arms in a casual gesture, although he was keeping his eyes on his father's hands, knowing that he was packing a concealed weapon.

Handel licked his lips. "Does she . . . Does she look like her mother?"

"I'd say that she looks more like her father," Paul said, knowing that the observation could cut straight through Handel's conceited and very black heart. Then Paul turned and walked away. His father might choose to stop him at any moment, and Paul wouldn't be surprised if it was with a bullet.

CHAPTER 7

CLAIRE HELD STILL as Robert DeStefano slid his hands around her waist and pressed against her from behind.

"Do you really have to go to London, babe?" he whispered in a voice like silk against her ear.

She released a small sigh. "I do." He knew the answer, but they continued the cat and mouse game that was perfectly satisfactory to Claire. The more that Robert wanted her, the more he'd trust her, and the more information she could steal from him. Robert owned the accounting firm that handled the books for the World Alliance Order. Claire had been watching Robert's personal emails and company emails on his DeStefano Financial accounts for several weeks, and when she found out he was going on an executive officers' retreat to Park City, Utah, she booked a reservation at the same hotel.

Only a handful of days ago, on that first night, she'd worn a short black dress that left just enough to the imagination. Robert hadn't been difficult to pick out in the hotel bar and grill. He sat with his vice president and one of his lead accountants. It was clear that Mr. DeStefano liked to travel in style and that he liked others to be witnesses, if anything was to be assumed by the expensive wine he'd ordered. More significantly, he'd left his wife and two children at home in Palo Alto. Which meant, for Claire, he might as well have had a bull's-eye painted on his forehead.

She sat three stools away from Robert and his coworkers at the bar, ordered a dry martini, and leaned her elbows on the counter while she scrolled through her cell phone. Out of the corner of her eye, she saw Robert look over, followed by the other two men. They'd definitely noticed her. Now she had to zero in on Robert's attention.

Ten minutes passed as conversation buzzed around her. The men had looked their fill, yet none of them had approached yet. It was time to push things ahead. Claire slid off her stool, carrying her half-filled martini glass, and walked toward the three men.

Their conversation faded as she neared.

"Hello," she said.

The three men greeted her in unison.

Claire glanced at each man but then settled her gaze on DeStefano. He was the one with the power and the knowledge she sought. That he had deep-blue eyes and sandy blond hair didn't hurt either.

"What are you gentlemen drinking?" she continued, although she already knew. She kept her open gaze on DeStefano, and he gazed back appreciatively.

"We were just leaving," one of the men said. Not DeStefano.

"I might stay a little longer," DeStefano said, his eyes dipping to Claire's neckline.

It was at that moment she knew she was in. Not that she entirely doubted, but she never called a victory too early.

The other men said something about having to make

phone calls; Claire wasn't really listening. She'd remember enough later. For now, she needed DeStefano to know that he had her undivided attention.

"Another glass of wine," she told the bartender as she slid onto the stool next to DeStefano.

He lifted his brows, a slight smile on his face. Claire could see how his wife had fallen for him. Strong jaw, inviting lips, elegant hands.

"I'm Claire," she added, extending her hand.

He shook it, slowly. *Good.*

"Robert DeStefano."

"Nice to meet you, Robert," Claire said, tilting her head. "Do you ski?"

They chatted for a few moments at the bar, and then he asked if she was hungry. They shared a long dinner while Claire encouraged Robert to do most of the talking. After dinner, she invited him to join her in one of the hotel Jacuzzis. Shortly after midnight, Claire sat in the bathroom, Robert's laptop perched on her lap while she hacked into it and he slept soundly in the bed they'd just shared.

It took her only three minutes to get past the password prompt on his laptop, then six more minutes to find his password for his World Alliance Order email account.

She logged in to the email server. Her breath hitched as she saw the subject headings. *From: WAO. Subject: Confidential Q4 Earnings.*

Claire had spent one year, two months, and four days at the WAO compound after her abduction at the London pub. She hadn't been an intern recruit for the Biomedic Centre. She'd been a WAO target all along. She'd endured months of invasive procedures and psychological conditioning. When she'd finally escaped, she'd found temporary reprieve with the Amazon Sisterhood, a private organization of women who help other women recover from trauma. But she couldn't stay there, not after she found out the truth about her parents.

Once she found the WAO compound, she would shut it down. She'd stop Handel and his business partner Bethany from operating ever again. Then she'd take out Paul Raine, the man who'd stolen her dreams.

Claire scanned Robert's account for any email subject lines that were marked *Priority*. Clearly, Robert didn't organize his emails, so everything was in order by date.

Through DeStefano's accounting firm, she hoped to locate the WAO compound. Clicking on one of the emails, she looked for any sort of signature that might include an address or phone number. She wasn't too surprised that there wasn't anything listed. The sender was a woman, though: *Bethany*.

Ah, Bethany. Claire found herself feeling nauseated all of a sudden. She set down the laptop and moved to the sink, placing her hands on either side of it. After taking a few deep breaths, she splashed water on her face, then dried her clammy skin with a towel. When she felt more composed, she made her way back to the laptop, passing by Robert sound asleep in the bed.

Claire read through a series of emails, all about quarterly financial reports that included revenue from dozens of companies, none of which she recognized. It seemed that WAO acted as an investment broker for various companies. Did WAO have insider trader information? Were the names of the companies listed code names? She forwarded several emails to her own account, then deleted the Sent file and the Deleted file. Claire emptied the Recycle Bin on the laptop. More leads, more work, more promises.

Claire did a search on the hard drive for documents that contained the words *World, Alliance, Order*. Over fifty pulled up, and she quickly dumped them into her Dropbox account, then deleted all trace of her history. She shut down the laptop, then picked up her phone and opened her Dropbox app. One by one, she started skimming through the documents, looking for anything she could add to her growing arsenal of information on the WAO.

By the time Robert woke up a few hours later in the early morning light, Claire was snuggled next to him, feigning sleep with her even breathing.

"You're still here," Robert murmured into her ear as he tangled their limbs together.

"Where else would I be?" she teased. Then she kissed him, letting him know that for now he was her entire world.

The next forty-eight hours were filled with stolen moments as DeStefano ditched out early on his meetings. They skied the Park City slopes and drank champagne in the Jacuzzi, and while Robert slept, Claire continued sifting through files on his laptop and copying them.

Now, as the snow fell in large swirling patterns outside the hotel suite window, DeStefano's hands were making their way to the snap on her black skinny jeans. Claire exhaled as if she was regretting that she had to leave him for any length of time. She turned to face him and looped her arms about his neck.

"It's only for a few days, sweetie," she told him.

"You'll come to Palo Alto?" Robert asked in a low voice, his blue eyes intent on hers.

"Of course," she said, pressing her mouth against the jawline she'd come to enjoy quite a bit. But Robert was only a stepping stone. He thought she was a trust fund kid who lived life on a whim. She'd told him she was going to London to meet her father for his birthday.

In truth, going to London would be no celebration, and Claire had no father. Somehow she'd find Paul—the man who'd taken her from a life of promise and offered her like a sacrifice to his father.

She remembered her first encounter with Handel Raine like it had been only a few hours before.

He'd come into her room, and the first thing that Claire noticed was his dark auburn hair, his square features, and the cruel depth of his eyes. She was just coming off the most recent injection the medic team had given her, and her left arm throbbed with the side effect of burning pain. She'd spent weeks in isolation after she woke up and then weeks being experimented upon with injections followed by various IQ tests.

Handel's eyes missed nothing as he scanned her body, then settled on her face. "Hello, Claire. I'm Handel Raine," he'd said in a gravelly voice like that of a former smoker. "You're our most promising recruit. Yet you refuse to cooperate with our testing."

If he'd stepped closer, Claire would have spat in his face. As it was, he kept his distance from the chair that Claire had been strapped to. Her body was crisscrossed with injection scars from the shots she'd been given by the WAO medical team. More like a terrorist team, if anyone thought to ask Claire. But she was in a place where people didn't want her opinion. They only wanted her obedience.

"When my son told me you'd accepted the internship for the Biomedic Centre," Handel continued, shoving his hands into his pockets, "I agreed that you were going to be an excellent addition to our team."

Claire kept her mouth shut.

Handel's mouth curved into a sardonic smile as if he enjoyed standing over her while she was strapped to a chair. Claire couldn't help but notice more details than she cared to. His thinning hair was almost auburn, and his features were squared off as if his nose and jaw had been broken a time or two. His nose wasn't quite lined up right, and his deep-set eyes seemed to be focusing on more than one thing at a time.

Handel stepped forward, close enough that if Claire had the strength to kick the man, she could have driven her heel into his shin. But she was at a distinct disadvantage, with the intravenous medication keeping her limbs too heavy and numb to lift.

"We have opportunities that will enable you to change the world, Claire," Handel continued, his black eyes scanning her from head to foot. "Doesn't everyone want to have an impact? I know you do. And I've been patient so far, but that won't last much longer." He braced his hands on the armrests of her chair and leaned close, his face stopping only inches from hers. "You're an intelligent woman, Claire. Use that intelligence to make the right decision."

He smelled like antiseptic and cinnamon, if such a combination was possible. Apparently it was for Handel Raine.

"Once you pass security level one, you'll never want to look back," he said in a much quieter voice. His fingers traced a line from her jaw to her collarbone.

Claire lurched forward and sank her teeth into his forearm.

Handel cursed and struck her across the cheek. Claire's head snapped to the side, but then she lunged for him again. This time Handel was too far to reach. He must have pressed the alarm, because the door flew open, and two medics rushed in, faces red, eyes determined. Another injection was stabbed into her shoulder, and Claire sank into darkness.

"You're somewhere else again, Claire," Robert whispered against her ear.

Robert had teased her a few times when she'd become lost in her thoughts.

"Already counting down the days until we can hit the beach," she said.

He chuckled and pulled her tightly against him.

Claire let him hold her for a moment, then she drew firmly away. "I'll see you later?"

"I'll be counting minutes," Robert said, his blue eyes bright.

She kissed him one last time on the cheek, then stepped away. He opened the hotel room door for her, and she walked out into the hall. Although she could feel Robert's gaze on her as she walked to the elevator, she didn't turn back. When his door quietly clicked shut, she stepped past the elevator and entered the stairwell.

She'd never forget Robert, but she had no more use for him if things went as planned. She'd never forget Paul Raine either. His dark eyes, the slope of his nose, the way one side of his mouth lifted when he smiled, the furrow between his brows when he'd injected her with drugs. She'd make him pay.

CHAPTER 8

THE NICE THING about Robert DeStefano's little vacation in Park City was that Claire hadn't needed to travel far in order to meet up with him. She lived only a handful of miles away on a private estate on the side of the mountain. She drove the winding road that cut through the quaking aspens and the snow-laden pine trees.

She left off the car heater so she could breathe in the crisp mountain air. It was better than any therapy session or self-help book she could read. Once Claire arrived at the private turnoff blocked by a heavy gate, she clicked the app on her phone that would open it. Moments later, she pulled through the gate, knowing that her own security cameras were logging every movement of her car.

As the gate shut behind her, she continued to drive the next half mile along the gravel lane. This area too was left heavily wooded. It prevented those satellite pictures from picking up the formation of a road.

One more bend, and her single-story home came into view. At first glance, one might think it was a sophisticated warehouse of sorts. The outside was made of thick concrete interspersed with large windows—windows that happened to be bulletproof. But the inside was anything but plain.

Another click on the app opened the door to the garage, which sat only halfway above ground. The descent into the garage was steep, which was why the concrete driveway was also heated. Claire didn't have time to shovel snow from her driveway, and she wasn't about to hire a snow removal company. No one had entered her private gates since the place was completed the year before.

Claire pulled into the garage, parked, and turned off her engine. The garage door closed silently behind her. The garage stayed lit since the lights were always on, permanently. Claire had spent thousands on the top-of-the-line LED lights that not only conserved energy but burned long-term. She changed them all out every six months just in case.

The dark was not her friend.

Claire climbed out of the car and entered her house by typing her code into the keypad. It was just an added precaution. No one could get into the garage in the first place. The Teflon steel of the garage door was impenetrable.

The lights in the kitchen were already on, as usual. And the large kitchen window let in the gray afternoon light. Claire pulled out a precooked meal from the deep freezer and put it into the microwave. Then she walked into the living room, which looked more like an office. In the center of the room was a long table where she kept her main computer. On the opposite wall hung a flat-screen where she could project larger images if needed.

Her client work was caught up for a few months, and she had no pending contracts. In her downtime, when she wasn't researching the WAO, she built security software for the banking industry. She charged them exorbitant fees, of course, but they could afford it. Thanks to her training at the Amazon

Sisterhood after her escape from WAO, and her apparent natural ability to hack into computer interfaces, she found that she was a natural for building software.

Knowing how to break code was a useful skill when building code.

Claire powered up her computer and set the monitor to project onto the flat-screen on the wall. Being away from her mainframe for a few days always raised her anxiety—she wanted to be home to monitor all her research requests that were surely starting to bounce back by now. She inserted the thumb drive with the downloaded files she'd taken from DeStefano's laptop and started the uploading process.

Next, Claire checked on the links she kept active to see what her old roommate Riya was up to. After escaping the WAO, Claire had discovered that Riya had started a major search to locate Claire. Riya had involved all the police and government agencies. She'd sued the Biomedic Centre, won the suit, and used the money to continually put out alerts on Claire's disappearance.

Now, Riya ran a missing persons' database out of her hometown, and she'd had amazing success. She'd found runaway teens and abducted kids. Whatever detective skills Riya had developed, they had been too late for Claire. Regardless, every few months, Claire made a sizeable donation to the company. Anonymous of course. Claire logged in to her fake Facebook account and looked up Riya. There was a recent post from Riya about an outing at a zoo with her two children. The smiles on their faces were sweet and innocent. And Claire intended to keep it that way.

As DeStefano's files continued uploading, Claire logged off Facebook and walked down the hallway to her bedroom at the back of the house and unpacked her small suitcase.

Everything inside her bedroom was a soft yellow with

mellow blues mixed in. Nothing like her stark room at the WAO compound. The throw rugs were thick and plush, and she had more than a dozen pillows on the queen-size bed. The two large windows let in the light all year round, creating a sunny oasis in the summer and a calming retreat in the winter.

Claire moved into the bathroom, also fitted with a large window, although this one was of mottled glass. She hurried through a shower, since her meal would be cooked soon and she wanted to eat it warm.

Once she toweled off, she picked up a tube of skin cream. The cream cost ninety dollars an ounce, but Claire hadn't found anything better for making the scars on her body fade. She rubbed it vigorously over her inner arms, then below her breasts and at the top of her hips—where the scars were the deepest. Finally, she rubbed the cream along the mostly faded scar that decorated the lower part of her stomach. If asked about the scars, she made up a story about an intense bout of chicken pox as a child. The orange fragrance was strong and would last for a couple of hours. But she wasn't going any-where, not yet.

She twisted on the lid to the cream tube, then entered her bedroom. She pulled on a comfortable pair of yoga pants and a stretchy sweatshirt. She kept the inside of the house to a constant seventy-two degrees Fahrenheit.

Claire walked back to the kitchen and carried the hot tray into the living room, where she pulled up a website and ordered a couple more tubes of the cream to be delivered to a post office box. The last thing she wanted was for someone like Robert DeStefano to notice her injection scars and think she was an addict. He would have dropped her instantly. Men like Robert didn't take risks.

They also didn't like to be put out of business.

Unfortunately for Robert, his luck had run out.

Claire took a bit of her rice-and-chicken meal, clicked on a software program she'd built, and logged in Robert's phone number and SIM card number that she'd memorized when he'd fallen asleep.

She watched the software sync up with his phone; he'd just arrived at the airport.

Next, she pulled up a file that contained her spreadsheets. On the flat-screen, the spreadsheets looked like a spiderweb of color. There was a method to her color-coding system, and certain cells were linked with other cells on subsequent spreadsheets.

The first column contained the list of subsidiaries linked to WAO and their respective parent companies. So far, she'd discovered that three of the companies WAO supposedly had holdings in were simply fronts for other companies. And as she traced those secondary companies, she found legitimate names. None of them had captured her interest yet.

Now, she performed a sync on the newly uploaded information from DeStefano. The linking engine was fast, and in less than two minutes, she had several matches.

According to DeStefano's financial statements, he was receiving a biannual bonus from an organization called Hughes & Ross. Claire stared at the screen, her chicken-and-rice meal forgotten. She already knew that Hughes & Ross was one of the top biomedics firms in the world. They were also the parent company to the International Student Alliance, which offered her the internship in London . . .

Claire lowered her head and rubbed her temples. There was a connection that she wasn't seeing. Somehow, Hughes & Ross was integrated with WAO, which made sense considering that the testing that Claire had been forced into at WAO had to do with medical advances.

She located the routing number from the bank that had deposited the money. Opening another screen, she entered it into her encryption software. A match came up for a bank in Switzerland. Of course.

Her next search was for the Hughes & Ross corporate headquarters. It seemed they had offices all over the world, including US offices in Chicago, Salt Lake City, and Minneapolis. Both ironically and conveniently, Salt Lake City was only thirty minutes away from her Park City home.

She Google searched the office location and phone number, dialed, and pressed Send. After the second ring, the phone went to voice mail. A red flag, Claire decided. It was two in the afternoon, and a company the size of Hughes & Ross should have a receptionist answering phones.

She called the Chicago number. It would be later in the afternoon, but the same thing happened. The messaging system kicked on.

Next Claire scanned the international office locations and decided to call London, fully expecting the same result.

A woman answered, "Hughes & Ross offices."

Claire barely composed herself in time to say, "I'm calling with a donation offer from my boss. Are you the person to speak with?"

"This is an answering service," the woman said. "But I can take a message, and someone will get back to you during business hours."

Claire was about to give a bogus number, since she knew that her cell would show up as Unknown on caller ID. Instead, she changed her mind and gave out her number, then said, "This is Shelly Anderson with Alpine Mutual."

The woman didn't ask for any more information. She thanked Claire and hung up.

"Huh," Claire said to herself. She returned to her research and found a press release stating that Hughes & Ross was in negotiations for a buyout by . . . Her phone rang.

For a moment, Claire stared at it. The number was blocked. No one had this number except for the office she'd just called. Perhaps it was the answering service.

"Yes?" Claire answered.

There was no sound, but Claire knew someone was on the other end of the line.

And then she heard a faint exhale. Her skin went icy. Was it possible to remember the sound of someone's breathing? It had been six years since she'd heard from Handel Raine.

Her mind raced as she tried to figure out how he got her number from a secretary in London who answered phones for Hughes & Ross. And, if it was Handel calling her, why wasn't he speaking? The last time she'd seen Handel Raine was when he'd grabbed a chunk of her hair and yanked her head back, then told her that she would complete the testing or he would kill the rest of her family.

What had he meant by the *rest* of her family? Her parents had been killed in a car accident. She hadn't seen her aunt in years, and they didn't keep in touch.

But she hadn't been able to question him because Handel trailed a disgusting hand down her body, causing her to start shaking.

"Release her," someone had said, coming into the room and interrupting Handel. Relief had flooded through her like a waterfall in a desert until she saw who it was. Paul was no better than his father.

Handel had turned, facing his son, and she could only imagine the look on Handel's face.

Paul's eyes had narrowed as he gazed at his father with the same disgust that Claire felt toward both men. It was the first time she'd seen Paul since the abduction, and he looked different in the garish fluorescent lights. He looked older, and harder, and his eyes were darker.

"This is none of your business," Handel had ground out.

It was then that Claire saw Handel reach for a gun in a holster strapped to his back.

"Watch out!" Claire had screamed out of reflex. Except she wasn't quite sure if she was trying to warn Paul or if she just didn't want to see someone shot right in front of her.

Paul dove to the floor and kicked out his feet, crashing into Handel. Handel slammed to the ground, knocking his head. He stopped moving.

Paul didn't even check on his own father—instead he strode to Claire and looked her over. "Are you all right?"

What kind of question was that? She nodded mutely, when she had wanted to spit in his face.

Something in Paul's eyes shifted. He leaned close, like his father had, but it wasn't threatening. "Be patient," he whispered in her ear. "I am going to get you out of here."

He drew away, and Claire's eyes stung as she looked at him. How could she believe him? She didn't trust him . . . It was because of him that she was here in the first place.

And then he was gone.

Two medical aides rushed into the room and revived Handel. They helped him to his feet. Handel didn't say a word to her. He only wiped the blood from his mouth and chin and limped to the door.

The sound of someone hanging up the phone clicked in Claire's ear. Whoever had called had just hung up on her. Claire hadn't even heard a voice, but somehow she knew. She'd been foolish to give out the number.

Her breathing went shallow, and she brought a trembling hand to the scar along her scalp. The one that she kept covered with her hair. The one that Handel had given her during one of his interrogations.

She couldn't move. It was as if she were back in the compound and he had strapped her to a chair again. She leaned forward, testing her invisible bonds. Her body moved. She wasn't tied down. Claire pushed to her feet.

With a slow exhale, she removed the SIM card and powered down her phone. Had she already been tracked to her Park City location? She hurried to the kitchen and tossed the SIM card into the incinerator.

Had she just given away the fact that she was still alive?

She was breathless thinking about it. But if Handel sent someone to Park City, she'd be long gone. Next, she pulled out a reserve SIM card from a locked drawer in the kitchen. She inserted the new card and set up the basics on her phone. She'd do the rest later and sync up with her main server. Clicking on the backup run application, she'd let that complete itself while she packed.

Claire hurried to her bedroom and picked up the carry-on she kept packed for emergencies. She unzipped it and double checked that everything was in place. Then she moved into the bathroom and repacked her toiletry bag, which she zipped into the outside pocket of her carry-on.

Less than five minutes later, she walked out of the bedroom. She powered off her computer and put it into lockout state. She'd take only her laptop, which was stripped of everything, but it was handy to access her server through it. She couldn't take any chances that Handel had already traced their call.

Claire grabbed her carry-on and opened the door to the garage. After climbing into the sedan, she opened the garage and slowly pulled out. Once the garage door was shut securely, she took a final look at her mountain hideout and wondered if she'd ever see it again.

Her hands were already shaking, and she couldn't even confirm it was WAO who'd called her. But just the thought of it had sent her body into a panic. As she drove along the gravel lane back to the gated entrance, she rolled down the window. An icy wind slapped against her face as she breathed in the fresh air. She couldn't seem to get enough oxygen.

Snow had started to fall in large, lazy flakes. By the look of the heavy blackness to the east, a storm was on its way. She hoped she could reach the Salt Lake International Airport before any real storm hit. Thankfully her car had all-wheel drive.

Claire drove as fast as she dared down the windy road until she hooked up with the steep mountain interstate. The snow intensified into harder flakes that battered the car. Even though the towering pine trees on either side of the highway looked like a picturesque winter scene interspersed with mansion mountain homes and their cheery glowing lights, Claire's mind was anything but peaceful.

Her head throbbed with worry and probably from hunger too. But as she entered the darkening Salt Lake Valley, with its twinkling lights from homes and statuesque business buildings, she wondered what life would have been like for her if her parents had lived. Would they have ever taken a vacation to a ski resort like Park City? Would they have lived in a valley home where family and friends gathered for special occasions? She could only guess at the lives behind the walls of the homes and businesses she now passed.

Reaching the bottom of the canyon, Claire merged onto the 215 interstate exchange, and after a few traffic slowdowns, she finally reached the parking garage at the airport.

After parking, she walked into the airport and stopped, staring at the row of airline desks—airlines that would take her anywhere in the entire world. Her flight to London wouldn't leave for several hours. But she now had to change her flight, because if the caller had been Handel Raine, he'd have discovered that she was heading to London tonight.

She'd have to change her route; she couldn't let them find her. And she needed more information about Hughes & Ross.

Claire approached the airline desk, and with her regular ID, she canceled her flight.

"It's nonrefundable, ma'am," the attendant said, fixing her with a brown-eyed gaze.

"I understand," Claire said.

She then walked to another airline desk. Pulling out another ID she'd created for herself, she asked the tall man with a pale scar near his ear, "What's your next available flight to Chicago?" She didn't know why she was curious about the man's scar. A lot of people had scars. Some could be hidden like hers, others couldn't.

"There's room on a flight that leaves in two hours," the man named Ray said.

"Is it direct?"

"Yes," Ray said. "There's an aisle on row fourteen, or a middle on row nine."

"I'll take the aisle seat," Claire said, pushing her credit card that linked with her fake ID across the counter. She'd be Kelly Anderson today.

Ray swiped the card, then handed it back. A moment later, he handed over a printed boarding pass. "Enjoy your flight, Ms. Anderson."

She thanked him, then hurried to the security check-in.

As she walked, she caught a few people looking at her. But as she made eye contact with each one, they looked away. She was being paranoid. That was all. The phone call had been a wrong number. Six years had passed without any contact with Handel Raine or his son Paul. Handel thought she was dead. So why would he have a system in place to track her?

He wouldn't, which was why Claire needed to relax. Her London flight was canceled, and if Handel had found out she was alive, he'd have a lot of catching up to do.

After getting through security, Claire bought some chamomile tea that she hoped would calm her down and help her relax on the flight. She couldn't take one of her pills right now. She needed to stay alert and to figure out what damage she'd done.

She had to keep moving, keep thinking. If she sat down, she'd start to panic. Claire paced in front of the large terminal windows, watching planes landing and taking off. Hundreds and thousands of passengers were funneling through this airport. She was just one person in a crowd, insignificant. Not a target.

An argument broke out behind her, and Claire tensed. She turned her head enough to see a man and a woman, who was probably his wife, bicker about something their teenager had texted them. The argument was swift, harsh, and then over. Claire exhaled and refocused on the window.

It wasn't until the flight was announced as boarding that Claire noticed a man sitting at the end of the row near her. He looked away as soon as she caught his gaze. Her heart rate rose, and she talked herself into ignoring him as she walked toward the boarding line. He stood soon after she passed and hoisted a duffel onto his shoulder.

When he stood behind her in line, he said, "Are you from here?"

She turned to look at him. Sandy hair, hazel eyes, generous mouth. "I'm not. You?" Small talk wasn't really her thing, at least not in this setting with a stranger she didn't want anything from.

"Layover," he said, his assessing gaze clearly interested. "I live and work in Chicago. I'm Jeff."

"Kelly," she said, and left it at that. She knew she should ask him about where he worked. He was being friendly, flirting a little.

"What's taking you to Chicago?" he asked.

"I'm doing research for my employer." She kept it vague.

He nodded. "Sounds interesting. Maybe I can help if you're new to the area."

"I don't . . ." She tried again. "I think I'll be fine. Thanks, though." She turned and moved forward with the line.

She could feel the surprised gaze of the man behind her. He seemed nice, was probably available, definitely good-looking, but she was too broken for normal. The Raine men had made sure of that.

CHAPTER 9

CLAIRE'S AIRLINE SEAT was several rows behind Jeff. Perhaps he would have tried to switch seats and sit by her if she'd been more welcoming. Claire strapped on her seat belt and winced at the shape of the airline seat as she leaned back into it. The width and stiff cushion reminded her of the chair she'd been strapped to at the WAO.

She powered off her phone and glanced over at the two passengers next to her. They seemed to be strangers since they weren't interacting at all. The man sitting in the window seat was reading something on a tablet, his reading glasses perched on his nose. The woman next to her held open a mass market paperback—looked to be a romance.

Claire reached for the magazine in the seat pocket in front of her and flipped through the pages, scanning the titles of duty-free products.

An airline attendant spoke into the intercom system at the front of the plane. She made a few jokes as she ran through the safety features. Claire only half paid attention because two rows in front of her sat a dark-haired man. She couldn't make out his profile since his head was turned toward the opposite window. But the color of his hair, the shape of his shoulder beneath his fitted jacket . . . Claire's throat tightened.

He looked like Paul. And then the man turned. Nose angled wrong, eyebrows too heavy, lips thin. It wasn't him.

Claire closed her eyes against the image of the not-Paul man, and the image of the actual Paul filtered through her memory. How he'd left her to face Bethany and Handel. When she'd been brought out of isolation, she'd been a ghost of her former self. But she'd still been determined to fight. The testing room consisted of a desk, a computer monitor, and a keyboard, all bolted into place. Claire had been strapped to a portable chair.

Bethany was the woman who appeared on the monitor. She looked perhaps twenty or twenty-one, not much older than Claire at the time. Bethany's eyes were fully focused on Claire, unwavering, yet had depths that Claire could only guess at.

"Welcome, Claire Vetra," the woman had said, and that's when Claire knew it wasn't a recording, but some sort of video conference. "My name is Bethany, and today I'll be explaining what WAO's mission is and how you will become a key contributor. Are you following me so far?"

Claire had stared at the woman's green eyes. The name Bethany was familiar to her for some reason, but she couldn't place it. With her memory, Claire was surprised. Whatever they'd done to her in the isolation room has messed things up. Claire finally nodded.

"You will need to answer any questions I ask you," Bethany continued. "We are recording your sound waves."

"Yes," Claire said. Her mind was saying no, but she was curious. The more she knew about WAO and its operations, the sooner she could escape. She was still weak from her weeks in isolation, but she was determined to grow stronger.

"For every progress made in the world and every new law and regulation passed, something else suffers," Bethany said. "Jobs are lost, city infrastructures lose balance, cops become the bad guys and criminals the good guys. WAO's mission is to keep the two sides of every equation balanced."

"Like an accounting balance sheet?" Claire asked.

"I will ask the questions," Bethany said. Her green eyes seemed to pierce Claire right through the screen. "Have you ever wondered why, when millions of dollars are sent to alleviate poverty in Africa, there are still starving people?"

Claire thought it was a rhetorical question, but Bethany paused as if waiting for a response. So Claire said, "Corrupt governments and organizations pilfer most of the goods and money donated so that the people don't receive the full donations."

"Thousands of charities are set up worldwide to stop poverty," Bethany said. "The totals for the last year in donations have exceeded a billion dollars. If that kind of money can't stop poverty, then why do people keep donating?"

Another pause.

Claire ventured, "Maybe it can't stop all poverty, but it can at least help some." Where was Bethany going with all of this? Surely WAO wasn't a major charity organization.

Bethany continued. "It's fundamental to human nature to want to think we are helping someone, making a difference, doing 'good.' When in fact, if there was nothing to 'fix' in our world, nothing to fight for, eventually the world would give up hope and cease to exist."

Claire felt a smile push its way to her mouth. She repressed it, of course. Bethany sounded like an old-school philosopher who was throwing out ideas to see which one the wind picked up.

"WAO gives the world something to fix," Bethany said, her expression absolutely bland, almost robotic. "We make sure the corrupt governments stay funded while at the same time we donate money to the Red Cross."

Claire said nothing. She had too many questions to come up with a first one.

"Do you remember the Brussels protest last year over the cloning lab?"

Claire started to nod, then said, "Yes."

Bethany's expression went from bland to almost triumphant. "We funded the lab from its infancy, and we fed information to the journalist who wrote the article about the cloning experiments, and then we sent our operative to organize the protest rally."

WAO was trying to simultaneously take down what they were building? Claire had to ask a question. "But citizens and cops were killed in that protest."

"Yes," Bethany said, conceding the question. "And it enraged people. It gave them something to share on their social media statuses and talk about at work. Reporters had stories to chase and victims to interview. The cops secured their jobs by claiming they needed to hire more cops to better monitor any upcoming riots. A dozen arrests were made, and those arrested had to hire lawyers, who then had to appear before a judge for sentencing. The judge handed down a mixture of sentences from therapy appointments to community service. Therapists and psychiatrists benefited, filling their office hours with new clients. Nonprofit organizations gained free volunteers. The judge had a fuller docket, and the court collected new penalty fees. The pharmacy dispensed more antidepressant medications as prescribed by various psychiatrists. The families of the deceased had to hire funeral directors, pay for burial plots, hold fundraisers for expenses, then pay grief counselors. And don't forget the money the florists all made on the three funerals. By staging a single protest, that may or may not have gone bad, depending on your perspective, we kept the wheels of humanity turning."

Finally, Bethany took a breath, and Claire realized she was staring, openmouthed, at the woman.

"Now you may ask questions," Bethany said in a smug voice.

"Who . . . who are you?" Claire asked.

Bethany's face went rigid.

And then Claire remembered. Bethany was the woman who had gone missing from the Biomedic Centre three years ago—the woman Riya had told her about. If Claire's hands had been free, she would have clutched her stomach to stem the nausea that tightened it.

A slow chill crept through Claire. "You're the student who was kidnapped."

Bethany's eyes narrowed. "You do not have permission to ask me *personal* questions. You're lucky to be alive in the first place, Claire Vetra."

The tone of the woman's voice reminded Claire of a disembodied robot. Whatever had happened to Bethany, the woman had become totally absorbed into the WAO system.

Bethany had been abducted too . . . Did that mean that Bethany had chosen to stay at WAO, or had she been forced like Claire?

"Is that what happened to you, Bethany?" Claire asked in a quiet voice. "Did they take you too? And did they force you to test?"

Bethany ignored the questions. "I have told you about one of our very small operations, almost insignificant in comparison to our higher-profile projects." Her gaze flickered for just an instant. Claire had just seen the first almost-human response in the woman. "WAO has recently entered the biomedics research field. And with your talents, Claire, you are a prime subject to test. The results of your testing scores could lead to a medical revolution."

Claire exhaled, feeling as if she were too hot and cold at the same time. "What testing are you talking about? And what if I don't pass your testing?" Not to mention, she didn't want to be associated with WAO in the first place.

Bethany didn't seem phased by the questions. Surely she'd heard it before. Who were the other 'test' subjects? "Well, Claire, I can tell you this. You will learn information as needed, and you must keep in mind that you are a security risk. You will not be leaving the WAO compound until you have security clearance."

And Claire was soon to find out that everything Bethany said had a double meaning. The WAO never intended for Claire to step one foot outside of the compound. The testing would not only wreck her mind but her body and soul.

Claire flinched as the airline attendant's voice cut into her memories. "What would you like to drink, ma'am?"

She blinked up at the woman with dark-red lipstick and chunky mascara. What was she smiling at? Claire wanted to look behind her to see what the woman could possibly be looking at. But it seemed she was looking at Claire.

She'd been naïve to think that chamomile tea would help in the airport. Yoga and tea and meditation might work for some people. "I'll have water," she said, although she craved something stronger. But she couldn't let her senses dull.

The attendant poured bottled water into a cup.

"Thank you," Claire said, and took a sip. Her hands had started to tremble. She closed her eyes and concentrated on how the liquid cooled a path down her throat. *Relax*, she told herself. *Breathe. I'm on a plane, and Paul's not here. His father's not here. My memories are what happened before. I escaped. I am free.*

Free was the operative word. She might be free of the compound, but until she shut down the WAO, she'd never be free of what they did to her. Or what they were doing to the world.

CHAPTER 10

CLAIRE CHECKED INTO a hotel only a block away from the Chicago address of the Hughes & Ross office. She needed a shower; she needed sleep. She undressed and stepped into the steaming water of the shower and used the hotel soap, shampoo, and conditioner. The hot water was always a sure way to stop her trembling muscles. It had been a long time since she'd needed to take more than one shower in a day.

She closed her eyes and schooled herself to take deep, even breaths. The phone call had shaken her up more than she'd let herself admit, and she'd gone through the motions at the airport and on the plane. But now, her hot tears blended with the hot water cascading over her body. She needed a pill, but she couldn't let herself go into oblivion just yet.

After her shower, she toweled off. The hotel mirror didn't do much to soften the lines of scars across her hips and beneath her breasts. Despite the application of her ointments, the scars were permanent. And they stood out like welts after contact with the hot water.

Claire knew that sleep would be impossible, so she took a pill, and let herself drift into oblivion.

She awakened hours later when her phone beeped. A sliver of morning light filtered in from between the closed drapes, and Claire guessed it was around 7:00 or 8:00 a.m. She picked up her phone to see an alert in her inbox from the email app she'd downloaded.

She'd hacked into the Hughes & Ross server and logged in to one of the executive's email accounts. It seemed that Gregory Felt had a stack of meetings that day and would most definitely be in the office.

Time to get ready. First, Claire took her black suit out of luggage and ironed it with the hotel iron. She dressed and pulled her hair back into a twist, then clipped it into place. Claire put on light makeup, wanting to look both professional and appealing.

Then she left her hotel room, her briefcase in hand and a fake donation check inside. She stopped at the hotel's business center and pulled up a fake contract that she'd used on occasion. She changed the company names, then printed it off and tucked it into her briefcase.

Outside, the wind was brisk, and by the time Claire arrived at the office complex, her clothing and hair had been wind whipped. She opened the doors and walked into an expansive lobby as she smoothed back her hair. She checked the floor listing and glanced at the elevator, deciding to bypass it even though the office was on the third floor. She didn't care much for small, enclosed elevators with heavy doors. The stairwell was well lit. Excellent. When she reached the third floor landing, she reapplied her lipstick and became the picture of perfect calm and confidence. Then she opened the door and strode into the hallway. She located the office right away.

"Good afternoon," she said to the receptionist as she

pushed open the glass doors across from the elevator.

The young woman looked up and met Claire's gaze.

"I've brought the donation check that I discussed with Gregory Felt," Claire continued, in a British accent. "Is he in?"

"He is," the receptionist said, adjusting the bright floral scarf at her neck. "He's in meetings all afternoon, though. Did you have an appointment, Ms.—"

"I'm Kelly from the Global Alliance department," Claire said, then lowered her voice. "I've just arrived from London, and I can't keep this one-million-dollar donation overnight." She gave the receptionist a wink. "I don't exactly trust the hotel's security box, if you know what I mean."

To the woman's credit, her eyes widened only slightly.

"I, uh, I think I can squeeze you in for a minute," the receptionist said, clicking the keys on her computer. "His next meeting's in just a few minutes. But perhaps he can be a bit late."

Claire smiled and tapped her briefcase. "You're such a dear."

"I'll be right back," the receptionist said. "I'm sure there'll be no trouble working you in."

Only two minutes passed before the receptionist returned, all smiles. And just like that, Claire was walking down the corridor, led by the receptionist into a conference room.

Gregory Felt was well into his fifties, but his eyes lightened with warmth when Claire walked in. One look and she knew he was a player. That, and he wasn't about to turn away a woman with a one-million-dollar check, even if he had no clue who Global Alliance was. Gregory Felt's brown hair was thinning, and his tan looked a bit baked. His white dress shirt and dark-purple tie did little to conceal that he had a bit of a paunch.

"It's wonderful to finally meet you, Mr. Felt," Claire said, extending her hand.

Gregory rose from his seat and shook her hand as the conference door clicked quietly behind the receptionist.

Claire stepped back but not too far. Her expensive perfume would certainly help her cause. She set her briefcase on the table, and Gregory's gaze strayed to it. Undoubtedly the receptionist had told him the amount of the check.

"Before I hand over our donation," Claire started to say, tilting her head and holding his gaze, "I want to make sure you understand all of our conditions."

"Uh, of course," Gregory said. "Can you remind me—?"

"Haven't you been cleared by Samuel Gentry to accept large donations?" Claire dropped the name of the CEO of Hughes & Ross. "Your receptionist assured me you were the man to talk to."

Gregory smoothed his tie. "Yes, I can accept the donation on behalf of Hughes & Ross."

"Oh, that's a relief," Claire said. "I'll just need your signature on a couple of pages, and then I can hand over the check." She opened the briefcase and pulled out a manila folder. "And your company ID as well—it's just a formality, of course. I'll take a picture of it, and it will be downloaded securely into our database."

Gregory hesitated for only the briefest of moments. Then he produced his ID card. Claire snapped a picture on her phone, then looked up at him and smiled. "You're much better looking in person," she said.

Gregory chuckled. He had a nice, deep laugh.

"Sign here," Claire said, sliding over the page and pointing at a line at the bottom of an official-looking letter on letterhead.

Gregory signed his name, a smile still on his face.

"One more," Claire said. "Then I'll never bother you again. I know you're a busy man."

"Oh, I don't mind the interruption," Gregory said, signing his name a second time without even reading a word of the fake contract.

"You're a generous man," Claire said, touching his arm briefly. Gregory Felt had the decency to actually blush.

"It's been a real pleasure, Kelly," Gregory said.

She gave him a nod and a lingering look, then handed over the envelope. "Go ahead, you can open it to verify the agreed-upon amount."

"All right," Gregory said in a slightly elevated voice. He slit open the envelope and pulled out the check. He blinked, then smiled. "Your company is very generous."

"We appreciate all that you have contributed to our interests." She set the signed papers into the briefcase and snapped it closed. "Thank you for working me into your schedule. I'm afraid I have a plane to catch . . ." She acted as if she were reluctant to bring their acquaintance to a close.

"If I have any questions, in the future, what's the best way to contact you?" Gregory hedged, a flirtatious gleam in his eyes.

Claire was prepared. She handed over a business card. "Call or email anytime, Mr. Felt."

"Gregory," he corrected.

"Gregory," she acknowledged, then left the conference room, knowing that he was staring after her, possibilities entering his mind.

She strode down the hall, nodded to the receptionist, then hurried to the stairwell.

Her next stop was the public library, where she could use the computers anonymously and completely immerse herself into Gregory's accounts as if she were really him. She had his valid signature, his employee ID, his picture, and she could bypass any passwords.

The Chicago Public Library was humming with early evening activity. School-age kids sat at the computer banks, so Claire went to the checkout desk and requested a private conference room. Once settled, she logged on to the public library Wi-Fi and pulled up Hughes & Ross's server. Moments later, thanks to Felt's ID, she was logged in to the company address book. She did a search on *World Alliance Order*, both individual words and collectively.

Similar to her searches in Robert's emails, the contacts were benign and didn't give her anything she hadn't already tracked down. Next, she searched the company call logs. This proved to be more difficult since calls could be made outside of the office lines. She typed in searches for any international calls, then started to narrow them down. In the past three months, there had been eighty-nine calls to the UK. Claire selected the numbers and copied them into her tracking software.

The software did an automatic search on the numbers, pulling up the businesses they were registered to. She made note of the ones that looked promising. Then she opened up another browser to log into T-Mobile's website. She'd noticed Felt's phone was T-Mobile, and with his social security number she'd found in Hughes & Ross's HR records, she sent a request for a password change. Seconds later, she was logging in to Felt's T-Mobile account and looking through his records.

She did a search for calls with international prefixes, then she sent the report to one of her dummy email accounts, which she would then forward to her regular email account.

Claire started a new round of searches by typing in the

last name *Raine* with various spellings, coupled with *World Alliance Order*, and then each UK number in succession. She had dozens to go through, but she continued, keeping focused and clicking on any links that looked valid.

When she was more than halfway through the phone numbers, a link came up that contained the words *All Hails Pub*. Even if Claire didn't have a photographic memory, she would never have forgotten the name of the pub where she'd met Paul Raine.

Her pulse skyrocketed just at seeing the pub's name in the link. But the link was broken.

She stared at the broken web address and noticed the four letters: *epay*. A thought occurred to her. It seemed there had been a financial connection between the UK number, the words *World Alliance Order*, and All Hails. What if . . . Her mind raced, sorting through possibilities. What if the pub was connected? What if Paul Raine hadn't followed her into that pub? What if he'd been *waiting* for her?

An announcement came on the PA system, alerting Claire that the library would be closing in fifteen minutes. She leaned back in her chair and rotated her shoulders. She'd been sitting in one position for hours, but she might have just discovered a connection she hadn't seen before. She didn't know how long it would take her to hack into the pub's financial records, but she needed to get to London as soon as possible. Once she had a bank account number for the WAO, she'd be able to track down more and then start shutting them down. Her confidence rose, and she pushed back the fear created by the anonymous phone call. Now, she had to find a way to break into the British banking system.

She logged out of everything and erased all her history.

Then she picked her briefcase up and headed out of the library. Apparently she hadn't escaped the snow by leaving

Utah. It seemed that Chicago had been hit by a blizzard. She stepped out into the driving wind and snow. Clutching her suit jacket closed at her neck, she hurried along the sidewalk. The streetlights only made the night look more disorienting, since the glow highlighted the falling snow but didn't reach the sidewalk.

It was because of the wildly spinning snowflakes that Claire didn't see the man cross her path until she nearly collided with him. She put her hand on his arm to steady herself, then she opened her mouth to apologize for almost running into him. But no sound came out because he raised a large, meaty hand and clamped it over her mouth.

CHAPTER 11

CLAIRE BUCKED AGAINST the man's strong arms as they closed about her. She screamed, or at least tried to scream. It sounded more like a muffled cat cry. The darkness was swift to cloud her vision. Whatever the man had injected her with was fast acting. This man was too big to be either Paul or Handel, but she had no doubt he was with the WAO. They'd found her.

"Not again," she whispered before the blackness took over completely.

Her body might be drugged, but her mind slipped into a dream that was virtually her memory. And it was as if she were back at the compound.

"You work both sides?" Claire asked in her memories of Bethany, whose face peered at her through the flat-screen.

"We *control* both sides," Bethany said. "Did you ever think of what would happen to the economy if we truly had world peace?"

Claire stayed silent.

"We would self-destruct," Bethany continued with a hint of a smile. "We wouldn't need cops, lawyers, judges, or governments. We'd stop buying weapons. Our military bases would be empty, our fighter jets grounded, battleships inert. Preachers would stop preaching because everyone would already be enlightened. We would have nothing to fight for . . . and nothing to live for."

"Life would change, but—" Claire protested.

"If there is no opposition, there is no purpose or achievement," Bethany cut in.

Claire was no philosopher, but even she could see Bethany's claim was deeply flawed. Yet Claire had been in many training sessions now with Bethany, and no matter how Claire tried to get through to the woman—reach the college student she had once been—Bethany wouldn't crack.

"Consider the business world," Bethany said. "If companies made straightforward deals and there was no conflict or competition, then everyone would have plenty of money. Inflation would skyrocket, and the economy would collapse. The value of a dollar would be mere pennies."

Another wild theory, but it made Claire curious. "How are you controlling business deals?"

Bethany looked pleased. "You'll need security clearance to know the details, but just think of how a few well-placed people started that protest in Brussels. Influencing business deals isn't that much different."

Claire didn't know what to believe. If Bethany thought she was speaking sense, then someone had convinced her of it. "What do you want with me?" Claire finally asked.

"Ah, I thought you'd never ask." Bethany winked. "Like I said earlier, we're branching out, so to speak, and targeting the biomedics field now. Technology and medical advances are enabling people to live longer than ever. But the lengthy patent process for new medical equipment and devices is preventing many experimental devices from earning approval in a timely fashion. We need someone on the inside to approve patents more quickly than they can now with standard regulations."

"There's a reason for the lengthy process," Claire said. "Testing needs to be done, and some tests can take months and years to know if they are actually working."

Bethany said nothing.

A sickly heat bloomed in Claire's gut. "You want medical devices in the market that are faulty?" It would be a health hazard, to say the least.

"Think of the lawsuits, the funerals, the scientists applying for more government grants to retest products, the media that will spend hours and days reporting on the tragedies—"

"I've heard enough," Claire said, her tone rising with her temperature. "I'm sitting here strapped down to a chair, threatened by you and the WAO, and you think I would willingly agree to this plan?"

"You're a brilliant woman," Bethany said in a calm voice. "We don't expect you to do anything willingly." The woman leaned forward a little and lowered her voice. "But we'd especially like your help. Handel Raine has opened a new project with you as the lead researcher. With your help, we plan to transform the medical world as we know it. You'd be compensated very well. You'd also live."

That was when the screen went black.

A chill ran through Claire, pulling her from the past back into the present. She was no longer dreaming of the compound interrogation room but lying on something cold. Shivering, she opened her eyes, dreading what she might see.

The light was faint, and at first she couldn't tell where it was coming from. Then she realized she was outside, lying on the ground. Snow continued to fall, landing haphazardly on her skin. She was in an alley. Alone.

Claire lifted her head, trying to recall how she'd gotten in this position. Then she remembered the large man who'd stuck a needle in her side. If he was with the WAO, why had he left her here? She moved to a sitting position and gasped at the pain in her side. Her vision blurred, then refocused. She pressed her hand against the jabbing pain. Her fingers came away with blood on them. Hadn't she been injected with something? Or was she injured?

"Miss, are you all right?" a deep voice said.

"She's bleeding," a woman said.

"I'll call the police," the man continued. "I think she was attacked."

The woman gasped.

Claire blinked rapidly, trying to clear her vision and make out the two people who had entered the alley. She exhaled and tamped down the nausea pushing its way from her stomach to her throat. "I don't need the police," she said, her voice sounding weak. "I'll be fine." She checked for her purse, but it was gone. Her cell was still in her pocket. The briefcase was a few feet away, opened with papers spilling out.

Claire moved to her knees and shoved the papers back into the briefcase, then she used the wall to get to her feet.

"You should sit down," the woman said in a panicked voice. "We're calling for help."

"No," Claire said, taking a step forward and nearly biting her tongue as the pain in her side took her breath away. All she knew was that she couldn't talk to the cops. She couldn't risk them taking her fingerprints. Looking up her real name. Getting any sort of identification on her. She nearly stumbled as she took the next step. Gripping her side, she walked out of the alley.

"Ma'am," the man said. "Are you sure you don't need help?"

"I'm fine," Claire said. "I'm nearly home."

She wasn't exactly sure how she made it to the hotel, walking through the wind and snow, not feeling her frozen feet. Perhaps the cold had helped numb the pain in her side as well. When she reached her hotel room and peeled off her clothing, she found she'd been stabbed.

The man who'd attacked her hadn't been from WAO, trying to drug her and take her back to the compound. She'd been mugged. A simple, good old Chicago mugging.

If the wound wasn't throbbing with heat and pain, she might have felt relieved.

She'd stopped bleeding, but her clothing was ruined. After taking another shower, she went to the hotel gift shop and purchased a tube of superglue and a couple of ACE bandages. Back in her hotel room, she glued her skin together, then wrapped the bandages tightly around her waist. She booked a flight to London leaving the next day, and then she finally dropped into bed and fell asleep.

CHAPTER 12

THE RINGING CELL phone woke Paul before dawn. He snatched it off the bedside table and checked the caller ID. With a groan, he answered it.

"Scrap the pro-choice case," Bethany said into the phone. "We have reason to believe that Claire Vetra is returning to London."

Paul was immediately awake. "What? She's ... dead." *Dammit.* What was going on? How did Claire Vetra suddenly show up and he not know anything about it?

Bethany barked a laugh. "That's what we all thought. But our voice recognition software is never wrong."

Once a person's voice was in the system, the program could automatically link it to any incoming phone calls to any of their shadow offices. Paul knew Claire Vetra wasn't dead ... but he'd been keeping an eye on Kelly Anderson since she left the Sisterhood.

"When's she coming?" Paul said, his heart thumping. What if the WAO found out that he'd known she was alive all along?

"We don't know exactly," Bethany said. "The call was

traced to Park City, Utah. She made a phone call to the Hughes & Ross London branch."

"Dammit," Paul said for Bethany's benefit as he shoved off his blanket and rose from the bed. The woman who'd been lying next to him rolled over and blinked her brown eyes open. Paul crossed the room and went into the bathroom, shutting the door.

He kept his voice low. "I don't understand. Claire Vetra died in that explosion six years ago. Her dental records confirmed her body." For a nice sum. But the WAO didn't need to know any of that. After he'd helped her escape WAO, he'd left her fate up to the Sisterhood. They'd alerted him two years ago when she left. Claire had promised to never reveal anything about the WAO organization or its operations. It had been the price of her freedom.

Paul was suddenly thrust back into playing two sides.

Few people knew that Claire hadn't died in that fire: himself and the members of the Amazon Sisterhood.

He could live off the interest of the amount that the Sisterhood had paid him for delivering Claire to them, but he'd heard nothing from his contact there since Claire had left the organization. He'd been told she'd gone completely underground. He'd done searches from time to time but hadn't found anything.

But if she was coming to London and the WAO knew about her existence, that meant she was no longer under the protection of the Amazon Sisterhood. And she was no longer in hiding. The Sisterhood would have never let her become traceable, especially by the WAO. The Sisterhood would have never allowed her to make a phone call. They knew the security risk of voice recognition software. Claire had to be working alone.

What was she thinking?

"The voice recognition software is one hundred percent accurate," Bethany said in that steely voice of hers. "There's no doubt she's alive and apparently trying to find us. We need to stop her, Paul. There's no telling what her plans are or what she's capable of."

He went silent, but not for long. "Send me any information you have. I'm on it."

"Good," Bethany said in a light voice, although there was a hint of warning in it. "I know that you scouted her all those years ago, and we all thought she'd be a stellar addition. Not every job can turn out perfect, but don't screw this one up. The WAO is counting on you."

Paul knew Bethany was sleeping with his father. Every word he uttered would be repeated back to Handel. It wasn't like Paul had ever completely trusted Bethany anyway. He had brought Bethany in all those years ago when she'd been an eighteen-year-old intern at the Biomedic Centre. In fact, he'd approached her at the same pub where he'd met Claire. Bethany had been much more pliable than Claire, though. She'd been a wide-eyed innocent, leaving home for the first time after living under the control of her mother. Once Bethany entered the WAO system, she'd become almost the ideal candidate. Handel had been extremely pleased, and Bethany had risen in ranks faster than anyone else.

"Thank you for the call," Paul said through gritted teeth.

"You're welcome." Bethany said.

Paul imagined her smiling her annoying little smile. She was probably with his father at this moment.

"I'm sending everything to you now," she continued. "Claire better not leave London."

"She won't," Paul said, clenching his teeth to keep himself from slamming a fist into the bathroom door. When Bethany hung up, Paul braced his hands on the counter. Why couldn't she have stayed hidden, wherever she'd gone? Why couldn't she forget the WAO and move on with her life? Paul had risked everything to allow her that.

He lifted his head and stared at his image in the bathroom mirror. He'd aged over the past few years. The crow's-feet about his eyes had deepened, and his dark hair had taken on a few silvery strands. One day he'd age out of his job, and then he'd become like his father, stuck at the compound, running operations digitally.

Paul turned on the shower, and when the steam filled the small space, he stepped into the tub and closed his eyes against the hot water.

The bathroom door opened.

"You're up early, babe," Vanessa said, drawing the curtain aside and joining him.

He pulled her against him. He'd been seeing Vanessa on and off again for about a year. They never went to her place, and he always asked her to meet him at whichever hotel he was staying in.

"I have to get back to work earlier than I thought," he said against her warm, wet neck.

"You promised me two nights," she said in her pouty, sultry voice. One that Paul was well familiar with.

He liked Vanessa but had only seen her as an occasional indulgence. The last couple of times they'd been together, she'd been acting more disappointed in their short stints, which usually amounted to a single night, then several weeks apart before he called her again. He'd explained that his job was unpredictable. She hadn't seemed to mind.

But now he was actually starting to regret he couldn't have those two nights with her. He stepped out of the shower and grabbed a towel.

Vanessa protested, as he knew she would, but it was better this way. He needed all the time he could get to prepare for the re-emergence of Claire Vetra. He had to stop her from whatever she was planning.

Paul dressed quickly in the bedroom, then packed his duffel bag.

The shower turned off just as he zipped up the bag.

Vanessa opened the bathroom door, a towel wrapped around her trim figure, her dark hair dripping about her shoulders.

"When will I see you again?" she asked.

Paul could tell she was holding back tears, or maybe anger, or both. "I don't know."

Vanessa folded her arms.

"Soon, I hope," he said, stepping up to her and kissing her on the cheek. She smelled tempting, and he almost stayed. Wanted to stay.

He left without another word.

By now, he was sure that Bethany had assigned the pro-choice case to another operative. Finishing off the job would be quite easy since Paul had already laid the groundwork for it. Last month, a controversial abortion case had gone to trial, where a millionaire business owner was suing his ex-girlfriend for custody of her unborn baby. A baby she was planning on aborting.

He'd hired protesters to block her path to the abortion clinic, and when the media found out the details, they had a field day.

Paul had created several identities to send in hearsay to the news stations, and the frenzy continued. In two days, the judge would hand down her verdict, and Paul had already prodded several pro-life and pro-choice groups into demonstrating outside the courthouse. Two of his underlings would be attending the rally and tossing out a few firecrackers.

People would panic, police would Taser protestors, citizens would be arrested. All in all, it would be a good day. A clean job. Whichever operative Bethany assigned would have to keep everything choreographed and send out a few tips to the police in advance.

By the time Paul had driven the thirty minutes to his flat, Bethany had sent over four emails. Paul bolted his door, turned on the Wi-Fi scrambler, and booted up his laptop.

"Where are you, Claire?" Paul murmured. "And what are you doing?"

Paul would never know exactly how much Claire could have brought to the WAO. But he'd failed when following his father's orders when she escaped. And now the WAO wasn't about to let her run free. Not after she'd pretended to die.

He logged in to his tracking software and typed in parameters under both Claire and Kelly. None of the hits that came up matched her. Next, he browsed through the emails that Bethany had sent over. Of course the number that Claire had called from would be out of service by now.

It took only a few minutes for Paul to find out which cell provider the number had come from. Then he hacked into the back of the cell phone company's operation system. He typed in the number and found it had already been reassigned. He continued searching until at last he got a lead. Two numbers had been registered to Kelly Anderson. One number was recently canceled, and the other number was newly activated.

Paul smiled. He'd just found Claire's number.

He exited out of the cell phone company's database and pulled up the tracking software. With a phone number, all he had to do was enter it and wait. The software would pinpoint the user's location.

Minutes later, Paul felt deflated. The last known location was Chicago several hours ago. Had she ditched the second number as well? The tracking software hadn't pulled up a current location.

Unless . . . If she was flying over the Atlantic, maybe the tracking software wasn't sophisticated enough to pick up her live coordinates.

With a lighter heart, Paul opened the next email from Bethany. It was the recorded transcript of Claire's call to the London office. He listened to it. Even without the voice recognition software, Paul would have known it was her voice. Some things he never forgot. He wasn't sure if she deserved credit for courage—because she was either being extremely stupid, or she had a plan that even he couldn't guess at.

What had led her to call Hughes & Ross in the first place? What had she discovered? She couldn't have known of any connection between Hughes & Ross and the WAO. So she must have been digging.

Or hacking.

A chill skittered through him.

He clicked on a folder on his laptop, entered the password, and pulled up his meticulous records on Claire's activities for the past six years. Four years in the Amazon Sisterhood. And then she went off the grid. He started looking for any hints that she might have learned something that she could use against the WAO. Something that he'd missed, although he couldn't see how that was possible. He didn't miss things.

An hour and two coffee cups later he saw it. Perhaps it was because he was thinking outside of the box and dispelling any of his previous conceptions about Claire and how he'd trusted that she'd stay undercover. But there it was . . . in black and white.

A financial record had come up, linked to Kelly Anderson. One year ago, she'd paid $1250 in American dollars to have the caskets of her parents exhumed and relocated to another cemetery.

Why?

Paul plugged the names of Claire's parents into his search browser: Trent and Kathryn Vetra. First he went the standard way of Google and Yahoo. Links to their obituaries came up. A page on the mortuary site loaded, along with comments of condolences. A class reunion Facebook page had been started. An old LinkedIn profile. A blog with a list of donors to a cancer fundraiser. Both of her parents were on that list.

Paul entered a new search into the tracking software, but it only generated the same hits. He typed in different search words, but still nothing of significance came up. Wherever Claire put her parents was anyone's guess. What Paul wanted to know was *why*. She couldn't know about her parents' connection to the WAO. If she knew that, then she'd know that her parents' deaths were no accident.

His phone rang, and not surprisingly, it was Bethany.

"Yes?" he answered.

But it wasn't Bethany. It was his father, using Bethany's phone.

"You have twenty-four hours, Paul," Handel said in his deep, gravelly voice. "And I want to see pictures before you dump her body."

"She might be coming on vacation," Paul quipped. "People do that, you know."

"Claire Vetra is not *people*, and you know that."

Paul couldn't disagree with that.

"We thought she was dead. She's been hiding. I don't know how, but she's somehow evaded all of us," Handel said. "Bottom line, she knows too much. We've all been fools."

Paul's father hung up before he could reply. If his father found out that Paul had known about Claire's escape, that he had *aided* her, Paul knew everything would be over for him. Handel Raine hadn't shied away from getting rid of family members before, and he wouldn't now.

"Where are you, Claire?" Paul muttered. "What are you doing?"

Causing the deaths of a handful of people stained his soul, but helping Claire escape had given him a satisfaction that he'd rarely known in his life. Whether it was in defiance against his father or because it felt good to watch Claire slip through the cracks of the WAO, Paul might not ever truly know.

But he did know that he couldn't allow Claire to go free a second time. He'd regret taking her out, but she'd put herself at risk. He just hoped he'd find out why before he had to pull the trigger.

CHAPTER 13

CLAIRE WALKED OUT of Heathrow Airport only to be greeted by a cloudy day and a light drizzle. She inhaled the damp air, feeling both anxious and relieved to have made it this far.

Pushing back thoughts of turning around and flying back across the Atlantic, she continued putting one foot in front of the other and forced herself to hail a taxi. The damp air, the traffic sounds, and the accents of the people she'd passed in the airport had all combined to raise her pulse.

Seven years had passed since she'd been in London. She could do this. The nightmares would stop only if she exposed the WAO. She had to find them, and then she had to cripple them.

"Where to, ma'am?" the driver asked.

Claire was pulled out of her thoughts, and she looked at the taxi driver. His dark eyes were the same brown as Paul's. But the driver's face was rounder, his nose wider, his skin darker. Not Paul.

She gave the driver the name of her hotel.

The taxi pulled away from the curb, and when the driver honked at another car, Claire clasped her hands together tightly. They were shaking. She'd broken out in a cold sweat. Taking off her jacket, she laid it on the seat next to her. The temperature was cool at best, but she felt like she was sitting in a sauna.

"Are you all right, ma'am?" the driver asked over the alternative music playing on the radio.

Claire smoothed her hair back. "I'm fine," she said. "Tired from traveling."

"You're American?" the driver said, taking a corner a bit too sharply.

Claire grabbed onto the seat to hold herself upright. "Yes."

"California?"

At one time in her life, she might have smiled at his question. "No, I'm from . . . New York." She was from nowhere.

"Ah, New York," the driver said, and continued to talk about a cousin or someone who lived there.

But Claire wasn't listening. The sights of the London streets blurred past, and memories ticked by like a second hand on an old-fashioned clock. She couldn't let the dark overtake her. She had to stay in the present and keep her brain moving forward.

The taxi driver was still talking, and Claire concentrated on the words coming from his mouth. But she couldn't hear them because just then, the taxi slowed to a stop at a stop sign. Across the street was the All Hails Pub. The very one that Claire intended to visit.

Memories crashed into her. She still remembered everything from that night. The strobing lights of the dance floor and how the colors had glinted off Riya's hair. Gerrard's large hands pulling her into a slow dance. Paul appearing. Gerrard leaving. Then Riya disappearing. Claire remembered the way her stomach had twisted and her vision had blurred after she'd drunk the beer from Paul. How when she felt her legs give way, he'd picked her up in his arms.

She'd later found out it had all been a part of her conditioning, or rebirth. The WAO was retraining her mind to think how they thought, to believe what they believed, to become one of them.

The taxi pulled up to a curb, and the driver turned to announce they'd arrived at the hotel. Claire thanked him in a voice not much louder than a whisper, then climbed out as the driver removed her carry-on from the boot of the taxi.

She checked into her room, all the while fighting the flashes of memories bombarding her. Perhaps she'd come back too soon. Perhaps her mind wasn't strong enough to withstand the onslaught.

Claire turned on all the lights in the hotel room, including the two lamps and the bathroom light. Then she crossed to the large window and opened it to let in the cool, damp air in order to stay alert. But the coolness only reminded her of the isolation room at the WAO. Her mind was moving faster than she could stop it. She didn't want to remember the isolation room. She didn't want to return there mentally.

But the darkness had already crept to the edge of her vision, and she grasped the windowsill as the traffic sounds outside morphed into memories of the tinny clatter of the food tray being slid through a narrow opening into the isolation room twice a day.

Claire didn't know how many hours she'd been inside the dark room after being moved from where the medics had examined her. There was no sound in the new place, and the cold had long ago seeped through her clothing and numbed her skin. She reached out in front of her, but it was too dark to see even her hand in front of her face.

Heart slowly thumping, she used the wall behind her to

rise to her feet. The wall and the floor felt like concrete, yet they were smooth as if painted over with a thick, glossy paint. Claire took a step, finding the ground solid and hard. She trailed one hand along the wall as she took another step, then another. Ten steps later, she reached a corner where the wall turned. She continued to follow the next wall. This time, it was twelve steps until she reached the second corner, which turned inward.

Square. The room was a box. There was a metal door of some sort, but there was no handle. She felt along the edges and slid her fingernail into the thinnest of cracks. No light, or sound, or air seemed to be coming through the seams. Claire reached upward and found she couldn't touch whatever type of ceiling there might be. From somewhere overhead she heard the sound of a fan kick on. The air that blew down on her was warm. Blessedly warm.

For a moment, Claire stood in place, wrapping her arms about her trembling body, and let the warm air wash over her. She didn't know how long she stood there, but quite abruptly, the fan shut off, and the cold crept back in.

Claire started to move again, one careful step at a time, shuffling alongside the wall until she estimated that she'd reached her original location.

She tried to think back to how she'd ended up here—the bar, Paul . . . Had he put her into a car? Had he handed her off to someone else? Had she done something that had landed her in prison? She hoped that was it—she was in a jail cell, and in the morning, she'd be given a chance to call a lawyer. For what, she didn't know. But she'd get out. Surely she hadn't committed any real crime.

But morning didn't come, or at least no light of day dispelled the darkness in the room.

When she heard the sound of shuffling footsteps, she'd risen to her feet again and leaned against the wall.

The door didn't open, but a small opening at the bottom of the door slid up. The light that flooded through was like a flashlight being shined into her eyes. Claire squinted against the glow, and before she could take one step forward, the light was gone.

Something had been pushed through the opening. It smelled like broccoli.

She kept one hand on the wall as she moved around the perimeter of the room. When she felt she must be nearing the tray, she knelt down and inched closer until she reached it. Feeling around, she discerned a bowl, a spoon, and a plastic bottle of water. She drank half of the water first, guzzling so fast that she spilled the lukewarm liquid down her chin. She wiped at her face, then located the spoon. Picking up the bowl, she found it contained a hint of warmth. She lifted the bowl closer and smelled. It wasn't meat or pasta or any spices. She took a small bite and found that she'd been given a bowl of cooked oatmeal.

She forced herself to eat slowly. When she finished, she licked the bowl, then stayed sitting by the door. Listening.

On the second, or maybe the third day, a new sound startled Claire out of a half-sleeping state.

The wall was talking, or more specifically, a screen on the wall above her head had turned on. Claire looked up, her eyes watering at the brightness of the glowing screen. It was about three feet above her head if she'd been standing.

A man's image appeared, and for a moment, he reminded Claire of Paul, the man from the bar. But this man was older. He wore a silk button-down shirt, and his longish hair was combed back, sporting generous streaks of white. But his voice was nothing like Paul's.

"Good morning, Claire Vetra," the man said in a deep, hoarse voice.

A shudder ran through Claire at the sound. The only way she could describe his voice was as eerie, or sinister, but she wasn't in a cartoon, so that was ridiculous. She blinked her eyes, assuring herself this wasn't one of her convoluted dreams and that she really was in some sort of a cell, isolated from everything.

Perhaps this was a judge, or a lawyer, or an officer of the law?

"My name is Handel Raine, and I'm the director of the World Alliance Order," he said, a smile lifting his lips, as if he were proud of his title and whatever organization he'd just named.

Claire had never heard of it. "Where am I?" she croaked out. "What's going on?"

"All in good time," Handel Raine said, his eyebrows lifting as if he were amusing himself just by watching her. "You are now going through a purification process," he continued. "Once you've cleansed your body and mind of outside impurities, we'll move you to the next level of training."

"Training for what?" Claire asked, but the screen was fading to black. "Wait!" she shouted. "I have more questions! I need to get out of here."

But she was left alone again in blackness.

Claire snapped back to the present when someone honked below her hotel room. The trembling in her body started again. Releasing her grip on the windowsill, she walked to the small table in the corner of the room and opened a water bottle. After taking a long drink, she unzipped her carry-on and took out three blue pills. She swallowed all of them, then she crawled onto the bed and pulled half of the bedspread over her legs. She left all the lights on, afraid that if she fell asleep and awoke in the dark, she'd remember new terrors.

She shouldn't have returned to London so soon. Six years hadn't been long enough to forget. The memories were still piling into the forefront of her mind, becoming too strong for her to resist. The only way to get peace would be to numb her brain for a few hours. She only hoped that would be enough.

CHAPTER 14

"Yes, I'm trying to reach one of your patrons," Paul said. "Her name is Kelly Anderson."

"Just a moment, sir, I'll transfer you to her room."

Paul rose from the chair and desk in his small flat and crossed to the window that opened to a back alley. Not much to see there. Especially in the drizzly rain. According to his tracking software, a woman by the name of Kelly Anderson had checked in about twenty minutes ago. His software had brought up eight other Kelly Andersons staying in hotels throughout London. Two of them had proved promising. Neither had been Claire.

But this Kelly Anderson had just checked in, which matched the previous results of her cell phone number being actively located just over an hour ago. Paul had to hear the woman's voice for himself—to confirm that Claire Vetra was indeed back in London.

The phone rang four times, and then it clicked over to an automated voice messaging system. Paul hung up.

Had she gone out? The cell phone tracker hadn't moved, but she could be at a café within a block and there wouldn't be a change in the activity log.

Paul called the front desk again. "My apologies," he started out. "I've not been able to reach Kelly Anderson. I've got an emergency message for her that I don't dare leave on the answering service. Do you happen to know if she's still in the hotel? I can meet her in the lobby."

"I'm sorry, sir, we couldn't give out that type of information even if we did keep track of our guests in that manner."

"I understand," Paul said. "I'll come by your hotel then and show you my police badge."

"You're a cop?" the clerk asked, his voice changing to a more official approach.

"Yes, but I need to keep Kelly Anderson's concerns confidential, which is why I didn't introduce myself as such," Paul said.

The man paused. A good sign.

"She's American," the clerk said. "I'm sure you know that already."

Paul chuckled good-naturedly.

"I'm sure jet lag has caught up with her," the clerk said in a lowered voice.

"Of course," Paul said, knowing this was the clerk's way of telling him that Claire hadn't left the hotel. "Thank you, sir, for your help." He hung up. It was time for Paul to leave his flat and find out her next move.

He packed his briefcase carefully, adding all the essentials: his Glock, a silencer, and a backup cell phone. Paul dressed in jeans, tennis shoes, a dark jacket, and a ball cap, along with an oversize camera that would hang on a strap about his neck. He'd look like the average annoying tourist.

He took the elevator to the parking garage and started up his nondescript black sedan. The hotel was only a few kilometers away from his flat, and he drove there quickly while keeping an eye on the tracking app. Once he arrived at the hotel, he parked across the street. He set the tracking app's settings to alert him when Claire's cell phone changed location.

He reached into the glove compartment of his car and pulled out a stashed energy drink. Spending the night with Vanessa always left him tired the next day. After drinking half of it, he settled back into the seat to wait. It was déjà vu in one sense, but a lot had changed in six years. Claire Vetra was no longer an innocent college student.

The hours passed slowly, and still Paul watched. The sun made its presence known for about fifteen minutes before it was swallowed up by another bank of clouds. The sky went from a dull gray to a deep violet with the approaching evening. Streetlights switched on before the darkness could fully engulf the road.

When he saw a woman exit the hotel's front entrance, he knew immediately it was Claire Vetra, a.k.a. Kelly Anderson. She wore dark, fitted clothing. Her hair had been cut into a shoulder-length bob and bleached blonde, to nearly white. She moved quickly despite the heels that she wore. Over one shoulder was the thin strap of a purse, and her red-painted nails gripped the purse against her side as if she were afraid to let it go.

She must be packing heat.

Paul was ready. He reached for the Glock beneath his seat and slipped it neatly into the pocket lining the inside of his jacket. Then he opened the door of his sedan and climbed out, wincing at the stiffness of his joints. But he couldn't delay. Slinging the camera strap over his head so that it dangled against his chest, Paul started to walk, following Claire at a distance.

One part of him was filled with disbelief that she was here, in London, a place she'd sworn never to return. The other part of him was filled with anger. Had she lied to him from the beginning? Was she going to betray him? They both knew that she had a lot of power over Paul. She could tell his father the true events of the night of her escape, and that truth would ruin Paul. Even *he* couldn't get off the radar fast enough to avoid his father's wrath.

What are you doing here, Claire, or Kelly, or whoever you think you are now? Paul wanted to ask her. He wanted to grab her slender arm, back her into a side alley, and demand answers. But even if he did that, he knew he wouldn't be able to trust her. The fact that she was here, now, proved that.

Paul's anger only multiplied as she turned in the direction of what he suspected was her destination: the All Hails Pub.

Paul wanted to laugh, then he wanted to rant. Did she think she'd find him there after all these years? Or perhaps she'd question the bartenders, ask them if they remembered a dark-haired man who spiked the drinks of unsuspecting women seven years ago?

Paul rounded the corner only to come to a sudden stop. Claire was nowhere to be seen. Up ahead, the sign for the pub swayed gently in the wind, and to tell the truth, Paul began to feel unsettled—an unusual feeling for him.

Had Claire already gone into the pub? He increased his pace, keeping an eye out for her dark clothing. As he neared the pub, the thumping of the music spilled out onto the street. He walked inside; it had been years since he'd been here, but not much had changed. The place wasn't crowded yet, and only early drinkers were sitting at the bar. A couple of tables were filled with what were probably coworkers, hashing over office gossip.

Paul scanned the place for a woman in black. She was nowhere to be seen. Then an idea occurred to him, and he crossed through pub and opened the door marked Employees Only.

The bartender called something over to him, probably telling him not to open the door, but Paul was already through before anyone could stop him.

He was momentarily slowed by the dimness of the office space, with its messy desk and outdated computer. The place had once been a private meeting room that could be reserved for groups. Paul continued toward the door that he knew once led to the small employee parking area behind the pub.

He opened the door and stepped into the night air.

"Hello, Paul."

Claire.

He turned. No, it wasn't Claire.

It wasn't Claire, but the woman was blonde.

And she wore all black.

Her blonde hair was thick, braided, and hanging over one shoulder. If Paul were to guess, she was in her fifties, although she could pass for midthirties to the less astute observer.

She stood about ten feet away, a cigarette in her hand. The lazy smoke coming from the glowing end was a contrast to the hard thumping of his pulse. He withdrew his Glock and raised it, pointing the gun at her chest.

She didn't seem bothered that he was pointing a gun at her. Her gaze scanned his body, then refocused on his face.

Two streetlights competed above her, giving her an ethereal look. Paul guessed her to be of Scandinavian descent, if her pale skin and crystal-blue eyes were any indicators. There was no fear or apprehension in her eyes. Whoever she was, she clearly wasn't afraid of a man with a gun.

"Paul," the woman repeated, taking a step forward.

He was surprised at the tone of her voice. It was soft, questioning, as if she knew him, but he had no idea who she was.

He kept his gun aimed at her. "Not another step." The woman he'd been following couldn't be this person. Claire, or who he thought was Claire, had short hair.

The woman stopped. "They named you *Paul,* right?"

It was a question, but it seemed that she was talking more to herself than him.

"Who are you?" he asked.

"I'm sorry about the surprise," the woman said. "I know you were seeking someone different. But I needed to talk to you."

Paul stared at her. "About what?" Did this woman have something to do with Claire? Were they partners?

"No one can know about this meeting," she said.

Did this woman know about the WAO? Is that what she was referring to?

"I'll decide that when I know what you want," he said. It wasn't often he was caught off guard. First, the arrival of Claire Vetra, and now the appearance of this strange woman.

He took another step closer. Even if she dove to the ground or turned and ran, there was no way she'd escape his aim. But she looked completely unfazed, and she stared at him with an intensity that he found unnerving.

"I think we're alone back here," Paul managed. "Tell me how you know my name."

"You know Gerrard," the woman said.

Paul gave a short nod. Gerrard was the man who'd harassed Claire that night in the pub so many years ago. He'd been baiting Paul. Did this woman work for Gerrard? Was this some sort of twisted payback?

"He's been working undercover for me for the past ten years," the woman continued.

"*For* you?" Paul asked. Who was this woman? Was this the female boss Gerrard had referred to?

"When he was booted out of the Order, we lost our key insider. Until you brought in Claire." The woman smiled. She was beautiful in a classical way.

"You—you work with Claire?"

"It's a bit of a story, and this is probably not the moment to fill you in," the woman said. "Claire is back in London, as I'm sure you already know." She waved her cigarette at him, motioning at the space between them. "Thus, our meeting behind the pub."

Paul was desperate to know how this woman knew Claire, but first he had to know how she was connected with the World Alliance Order.

"If you know about the Order, and if you're apparently a free woman . . . I need answers, now." Paul took a step closer.

She didn't flinch. Just took another drag on her cigarette.

"This gun is no idle threat," Paul ground out.

She blinked as if she'd just heard him. "I don't suspect anything you do is idle, Paul. Your father and I go way back, to the very beginning of the WAO. You might say that I was at one time a significant partner."

Paul's mind spun in different directions as he tried to recall the history of the Order. Surely he would have heard of a woman who'd escaped alive. Or perhaps everyone thought she was dead, like Claire.

"You were one of the founders?"

She seemed to hesitate then. "Yes." The word was quiet, almost uncertain.

Paul narrowed his gaze. So this woman had helped

establish the Order, and then she left. What had her crimes been? After she'd left, she'd probably dyed her hair and had plastic surgery, because Handel would have never stopped looking for her.

"I've been watching you for a long time," the woman said. "And the time has come that we need to join forces and work together. I need your help, Paul. We're going to bring the Order down."

Paul could only laugh. This woman was insane. "If you think you can bring the Order down through me, you're nuts."

She didn't blink, didn't move.

"First of all, I don't take directions from *you*," Paul continued. "The WAO is rock solid. No *one* person can ever breach the organization. Not me, and not whoever you think you are. The Order has influence and connections all over the world. The operatives have sworn their lives to protect the system."

"Yes," she said. "And that's why I need to work with someone who's already on the inside. Someone who's above suspicion. Someone who Handel Raine trusts implicitly."

Paul took another step closer. He could shoot this woman now and put an end to her crazy ideas. Yet, he hesitated.

The woman only smiled.

It wasn't a nice smile.

"First," she said, lifting her cigarette to her mouth, "we need to stop Claire. I think her mind has finally cracked." Her blue eyes blinked at Paul innocently. "She has just become our greatest threat."

CHAPTER 15

CLAIRE HAD JUST ordered a beer when the woman came into the pub. *Nora.* A woman Claire had hoped never to cross paths with again.

Claire slipped off her chair to the floor and stayed hidden as Nora scanned the bar. Claire stayed crouched in her place as Nora went into the ladies' room, then came back out into the pub.

Holding her breath, Claire waited for Nora to leave. She could only be here for one reason. It was too much of a coincidence. Claire had been in London only a few hours, and already she was being followed.

The floor was unpleasantly cold and sticky, but Claire didn't move as she watched Nora's legs and dark heeled boots cross the pub once, then twice.

Claire pulled out the beanie in her jacket pocket and pulled it over her hair. With her newly dyed blonde hair, she had to remember that her hair color might capture more attention than she wanted it to.

She'd change the color tomorrow, she decided.

But she had a bigger problem right now. Nora Mickelson

was still in the pub, looking for Claire. She supposed she shouldn't be surprised that she was being tracked by the Amazon Sisterhood. They were the ones, after all, to help her escape the WAO. And Paul.

Paul was the one she needed to get to first. The Sisterhood would have to wait.

Nora's presence complicated things. A lot. Claire was surprised that the woman had come this far and hadn't sent one of her operatives. Claire supposed she deserved to be reprimanded. She'd completely disappeared, taking with her years of investment and training.

Claire moved her hand until it was resting lightly on the gun strapped just above her hip. Undoubtedly Nora was packing as well. The pub really needed to have a weapons check at the front door.

Claire watched as Nora walked around the dance floor and opened the Employees Only door. She was going into that room—the one Paul had carried Claire out of. It was like a bad nightmare on repeat.

Claire waited two minutes, then she rose from her hiding place beneath the table.

She had to get out of there before Nora came back into the pub. But Claire couldn't go out the front door or the rear door without someone noticing her. She went into the ladies' room and holed up in one of the two stalls, hoping that Nora wouldn't renew her search there. When the crowds picked up for the night, she'd find her way out of the pub.

An hour passed, then another thirty minutes.

Finally, Claire felt she could leave the stall. When she stepped back into the main room of the pub, a lot more people were inside. A few couples were dancing on the dance floor. Half of the stools at the bar were occupied, and four or five tables had groups of people sitting at them.

Claire quickly scanned the room for Nora. She wasn't in sight.

Taking a few deep breaths, Claire walked to the bar and eyed the bartender, a woman with spiked black hair and enough metal in her ears to set the TSA on edge.

"Hi," Claire said, sliding across a fifty-pound note. "Can I speak to the manager?"

The bartender eyed Claire up and down. "What's the problem?"

"I have a couple of questions about operations here," Claire said, handing over a business card that stated she was with the International Health Code department. A completely bogus company, of course.

Fortunately, the bartender was smart and said, "All righty . . . I'll be right back. Take a seat." She gave Claire a half smile, part smirk, then pushed through a door to the back kitchen.

Moments later, the bartender returned with a thin, wiry man behind her who looked like he'd had one too many hangovers. The bags under his eyes were impressive if nothing else. But most of all, Claire recognized him as the bartender who'd been working the night she'd been abducted.

"Kelly Anderson," she said, sticking out her hand to shake his. "Remember me?"

"I don't," the man said, taking her hand.

"Edward Daines, right?"

His gaze was predictably wary as he nodded. The bartender moved off to prepare a drink for a couple of people sitting at the other end of the bar.

"How long have you managed this bar, Mr. Daines?" Claire asked.

"About six years. I started bartending about nine years ago," he said, folding his tattooed arms.

Perfect. Claire pulled up an image on her phone. "I'm not really with any health organization," she said in a voice just above the drum of the music. "I need you to tell me what you know about one of your patrons." She turned the phone to face him and watched his expression.

His pupils widened, but he shook his head no.

"He used to be a regular when you started out," Claire pressed.

"I can hardly remember people coming in from weeks ago, let alone years ago," the manager said.

"You and I both know that one of a bar manager's duties is to know their patrons," she said. "Look again."

Daines leaned a bit closer but then only shook his head. "No, I'm sorry. Who is he?"

"I think you know who he is," she said in a smooth voice. "Although I'm not sure which name he used. You might also find this interesting." She flipped to the next picture she had saved on her phone. It was a mug shot of Mr. Edward Daines. "Does your parole officer know that you're still dealing?"

His mouth opened, then shut. The color leaving his face was indication enough.

"Your parole officer might be very interested in speaking to this person," Claire said, moving to the next picture of a young woman's mug shot. "I think she's coming by tonight around midnight. Correct?"

"H-How did you know?" he asked. "Who are you?"

"I'm just someone who wants information on this man," she said. "In exchange for the information, I won't make a certain phone call."

The man hesitated, but not for long. "Come into the back office. I'll see what I can find."

Claire wasn't stupid. She had enough dirt on this guy to send him back to prison for a long time. She followed him into the office. As soon as she stepped inside, she shut the door and withdrew her small pistol. She'd save her specialized dart gun for later. The desk contained an outdated computer and haphazard stacks of invoices. The trash bin in the corner overflowed with litter, and tacky posters with souped-up trucks lined the walls.

By the time Daines turned around, having grabbed his own gun from the desk drawer, she had already zeroed in on him.

"Drop your gun, sir," Claire said. "Or your pretty little bartender will have nightmares for life from finding her boss's brains all over the desk."

He lowered the gun, then dropped it so that it clattered to the floor.

Claire bent and picked it up, then slid the gun into the waistband off her pants, all the while keeping her own gun trained on him.

"Talk."

Daines's face paled even more. "He came in here a few nights a week. At first, he never said much to me, but then he, uh . . . asked where he could get a specific drug." He dragged a hand over his mouth as if he were feeling jittery just remembering it.

"That's mild compared to what must have happened next," Claire prompted.

Daines nodded, then in a significantly subdued voice he said, "He paid me to add the drug to drinks for certain people."

"People? Do you mean ladies?" Claire asked.

"Yes, *ladies*," Daines said.

"Do you know what he did with those women after he drugged them?" Claire asked, her voice rising as she closed the short distance between them and pressed the barrel of her gun against his temple.

Daines looked like he was going to be sick. "No," he whispered.

With her left hand, Claire lifted her shirt to show the deep scars that ran across her abdomen.

Daines actually flinched. Which probably saved his life.

"I should shoot you right now, Edward Daines," Claire said. "But I'm letting you live so that you can pay for your crimes in the old-fashioned way."

Daines nodded, perspiration dripping down his face.

"What Paul's number?" she asked.

Daines looked to the phone sitting at the edge of his desk.

"Pick it up and read me the number."

He did so, and Claire memorized it, then commanded, "Turn on your computer."

With shaking hands, Daines powered up the computer. Claire was trembling too. She'd never come so close to pulling the trigger on a living human. She could smell the man's fear, mixed in with the scent of old pizza, stale beer, and something worse. Had he pissed himself?

When the computer was booted up, she handed over a thumb drive. "I want all your financial records loaded onto this, starting with the day you were hired."

Daines complied, and as he did, the stench of urine grew stronger. The smell was messing with Claire's mind as memories of the isolation room came calling again. She forced her mind to stay in the present, forced her gaze to stay on the computer monitor as the files transferred. It was taking too long . . .

"Never mind," Claire said. "Give me the whole hard drive."

He looked up at her, surprised, but then quickly set to work dismantling the computer.

"It's right there," Claire said.

He popped it out.

"Set it on the table." Claire snatched it up.

"Close your eyes," she demanded.

He did, and actual tears trailed down his cheeks.

She shot twice. Once into the plaster above his head and once into the computer monitor, which sent shards of thick plastic across the room.

The buzzing of the bullets faded. "Enjoy prison," she said into the deathly silence.

As she left the office and shut the door, she thought she heard a sob.

CHAPTER 16

THE CAFÉ WAS intimate, dark, and only a block away from the pub. The blonde woman with the braid had told him her name. Paul wasn't quite sure he believed Nora was her true name, but at least it gave him a way to identify her.

Nora had ordered coffee, and Paul did the same.

"You've changed, Paul," the woman said.

"You don't know me," he said, although he was starting to doubt himself more and more.

"I told you, we've been watching you for a long time." Nora took a sip of coffee from the steaming mug in front of her. "This is nice," she added, looking around the joint.

"We're not on a social visit." Paul had pocketed his Glock out of courtesy, but it was still within easy reach, although he didn't relish the idea of causing a scene in this small café.

He noticed Nora's hands shook slightly as she brought the mug to her mouth again. So, she was nervous. That was definitely to Paul's advantage.

"I suppose I should tell you more about my organization and why I think we need to partner," she said. "Six years ago, you took a bribe from us."

It's her. Paul should have known from the moment he saw her. The blonde hair. It was a trademark of the Amazon Sisterhood. Part of their disguise and, he supposed, their appeal as well. No one expected a beautiful blonde woman to be a deadly foe.

"You're Nora *Mickelson*?"

Her smile was slight. "I am. I was sure you'd figure it out a little earlier, though."

Paul's mind reeled. Nora Mickelson was the director of the Amazon Sisterhood, an airtight organization that was best described as high-powered, high-dollared vigilantism. If you could afford to hire them to do your bidding, it would set you back a pretty penny. But it was all based on rumor. No one from the Amazon Sisterhood had actually been caught, and no deal or transaction had actually been traced.

Paul knew better than anyone because he'd tried multiple times to break into their digital fortress. Once, years ago, he'd been contacted by a woman claiming to be a member of the Amazon Sisterhood. They had a deal they wanted to make with him. Half a million dollars for Claire Vetra.

Paul had turned the woman down flat. But when he'd discovered what his father was doing to Claire, Paul had changed his mind.

"Ah, so your memory is coming back," Nora said, leaning forward. "I trust that everything with the transaction went smoothly."

"It did," Paul said, holding her gaze. "The woman who contacted me—Frances—said she'd report in later. She never did."

Nora nodded. "There was never a secure way to send you an update. And security always dictates our actions. We take only calculated risks. But I'm assuming you've been tracking Claire all along?"

"I have," Paul confirmed. "Irene let me know that she left the Sisterhood and went off the grid."

"Yes," Nora said. "Claire stayed with us for four years, but she didn't go through the healing process quite like we hoped." She eyed Paul. "I'm sure you aren't surprised to hear that."

"Not completely," he said, his neck heating up. Not many people could have mentally survived the things that his father had put Claire through. The physical side was another matter altogether.

"She was quite broken when we got her," Nora said. "It took time to convince her that we weren't the new enemy." She tapped the table. "She was like a sponge, though, learning anything and everything. Once she was fully on board, she became our most innovative team member."

When Nora paused, Paul said, "But?"

"But then she disappeared."

Paul sucked in a breath. "I knew she left, but I didn't know she disappeared on *you*." He also knew her assumed identity was Kelly Anderson.

"It's been twenty-three months since we've seen any evidence of her, until this week," Nora said. Her eyes actually looked worried, which was ironic for a woman who ran a powerful underground organization.

"What do you know about her activities this week?" Paul pressed.

Nora leaned back in her chair for a moment, staring past him, as if she were trying to decide how much to reveal. "She's on a path that could be destructive to both you and me. She's after your father, I know that, but to get to him she knows she'll have to go through you first." Now Nora leaned forward. "Paul, she knows everything about the WAO and everything about the Amazon Sisterhood. She's like a walking time bomb. Do you know what she spent years doing with us?"

Paul shook his head.

"She became our top hacker," Nora said in a low voice. "Claire manipulated the Chinese markets, she altered the British Parliament results, she channeled millions of dollars away from the top drug lord in Bolivia." She shook her head. "All of this, and she's afraid of the dark."

Paul raised his brows. "What do you mean?"

"She sleeps with the lights on, Paul," Nora said. "Why do you think she does that?"

Paul was reluctant to answer. Maybe she'd slept with the lights on as a kid and it was a habit. But he knew better. "My father put her in the isolation room as part of her psychological conditioning. No lights and no sound for weeks."

Nora's eyes hardened, and Paul didn't blame her. The Amazon Sisterhood might be made up of ruthless vigilantes, but they'd never forced anything on one of their own.

"Your father's a coward," Nora said. "Always has been."

She had referred to his father, but it might as well have been Paul. He'd long ago decided that this world was meant to be fought over. And that's what he was doing—fighting. With that came risks and casualties.

"How ... how dangerous *is* Claire?" Paul asked. "I followed her to the All Hails Pub, but then I lost her. Do you think she knew I was following her? Is she playing a game?"

"I can't answer that," Nora said. "But she's been one step ahead of me so far. I've had two of my best programmers building up security firewalls. We've had a couple of temporary breaches that fortunately we were able to block. I can only assume they came from her unless you're hacking for the WAO now."

"Not recently," Paul said. "I'm working on outside projects only."

"Bringing in Claire?"

Paul gave a brief nod.

Nora's eyes stayed hard. "And you're going to do it? Why?"

"Like you said, she's a liability." Paul shrugged. He couldn't feel sorry for Claire now, or sympathetic to Nora's plight.

"She won't survive another training session or psychological conditioning at the WAO," Nora said.

He looked away for a moment. "My father doesn't want her trained."

"Ah, you're bringing her down then."

Paul didn't respond.

Nora pushed her coffee mug away. "I want her, Paul. If only to prove to your father that he can't always get his way. She's gone off the deep end, and if we don't put a stop to whatever her plans are, we're all screwed."

"So you want her dead too?"

"No," Nora said in a hard voice. "You don't understand how valuable she's been to the Sisterhood. We need her back. Even if it takes months for her mind to heal, we'll take her back. She has the potential to be our most powerful weapon."

CHAPTER 17

CLAIRE CHECKED THE tracking on her app. It had brought her to this street, and if the number was still one of Paul's, then she should be close to him. The street contained an eclectic mix of cafés, shops, and pubs. She hovered next to a bookshop, staying away from the crowd of people near the pub about halfway down the block.

A taxi pulled away from the café across the street, capturing Claire's attention. Paul was in one of these places. She crossed the street, then passed by the café, looking in through the window. She almost stopped when she saw Nora and Paul sitting at a table on the far side of the room.

Claire had time for only a quick look before she had to keep walking.

She hadn't seen Paul for years, but he was much the same. He still had the dark, wavy hair, now flecked with streaks of silver. His eyes were hooded and black as he gazed at the woman across from him.

Claire scanned the street offerings and walked back to the Late Night Bookshop, where she took up residence inside, near the front window. She pretended to look at a book while keeping an eye on the café. Claire had a feeling that the bookshop sold a lot more than books, based on the number of young adults who came and went.

What was Paul doing with Nora? How had they found each other? When Claire had tracked his number, she'd been surprised to discover that his location was only a few kilometers away. Was it a coincidence, or had Nora and Paul been working together?

Claire had known that Paul had taken a bribe from the Amazon Sisterhood. When she'd started digging into the details of her escape from the WAO, she'd discovered the financial record, and it had only made her despise Paul more.

Was it because she thought he might be better than his father?

"Did you find something, ma'am?" the shop clerk asked. The pimply teenager barely lifted his eyes from his phone to look at her.

"Still looking," Claire confirmed. She wondered how long Paul and Nora would be inside the café and what they were talking about.

She had to get Paul alone so that she could drag the information out of him that she needed to get to his father. Then, and only then, could she get rid of Handel Raine. Until she knew the location of the WAO, Paul's death would do her no good.

But seeing Nora had changed things. The fact that Nora and Paul were now apparently talking meant Claire was outnumbered.

The streets outside were dark, and the illuminated shops gleamed like beacons. If Paul and Nora came out of the café right now, they might see her silhouetted in the bookshop window.

She had to move again. She'd made at least one important

discovery. Paul knew she was in London, but this time the mouse would trap the cat.

"Have a good night, ma'am," the clerk mumbled to Claire as she strode out of the entrance.

A couple of pubs were about a half block down the road, and the adjacent sidewalks were filled with young, boisterous people.

Taxis came and went, giving Claire an idea.

Paul would be summoning a taxi, and so could she.

Claire crossed the street toward the café, but instead of walking past it, she leaned against the wall. She'd been expecting to wait for an hour or more, but less than fifteen minutes later, Nora exited. The woman walked quickly, her heeled boots clicking on the pavement. She lifted a hand, and moments later a taxi pulled up.

When Paul came out, Claire was ready to follow. She watched him walk in the same direction as Nora, and for a moment Claire wondered if they were traveling to the same location. She dismissed the idea when she saw Paul cross the street, and as soon as he stepped into the taxi he'd hailed, she left her position and strode forward.

As she got into her own cab, she said, "Can you follow the taxi up ahead? That man left his phone at the café." She smiled as the driver looked back at her, his thick brows raised. "I'll pay you double."

The driver smiled. "Sure thing, ma'am."

He pulled away from the curb and sped after Paul's taxi.

"I don't want him to know we're following him," Claire said. "We, uh, met at the café, and he was really nice. I want to surprise him."

"Ah," the driver said, grinning, then glancing at her through the rearview mirror. He continued to follow the first taxi.

When Paul's cab stopped on a street that Claire realized was only a short way from the All Hails Pub, she watched as Paul climbed out, then strode to a parked sedan.

"Well, here's your chance," her driver said, slowing down as well.

"Not yet," Claire said, gripping the seat in front of her. "Let's follow his car now. I don't think he's realized he left his phone yet. It will be a bigger surprise when I show up if he's worried about it."

"Good plan," the driver said.

Claire knew he was just counting on the extra money he was earning; her explanation was flimsy at best.

As the taxi driver continued following Paul, Claire committed the streets they were passing to memory. She had to get the address of the compound from Paul. All of her research hadn't given her what she needed. And she planned to do whatever it took.

"Ah, he's turning into that parking area," the driver said.

"Slow down and then stop a distance away," Claire said. "I don't want him to see me quite yet."

"Should I wait for you?" he asked.

"No, but thank you." She held up her phone. "I can always call another taxi."

The driver handed her his card. "You can call me if you need to."

Claire smiled and took the card. Then she handed over the cash for the fare. She climbed out, leaving a smiling driver behind.

Paul had already disappeared into the building up ahead. It was just as well. Claire straightened her jacket and brushed her fingers along the bulge of her gun. As she entered the building she looked at the list of names on the mailbox alcove. Most of them were numbers. But Claire had no problem knocking on doors.

She hesitated in front of the elevator and decided to take the stairs. More space and light.

As she reached the second floor, the checkered red-and-black carpet reminded her of the lower hallways of the WAO compound. The soft swishing sound that her shoes made on the carpet echoed the sound of her wheelchair as it glided over the stiff fibers of the rugs lining the WAO hallways.

They'd strapped her to a wheelchair because she'd been too weak to walk and too weak to hold herself upright. She estimated that she'd been in isolation three or four weeks, and all the while, she'd barely eaten.

What little food they'd given her had been bland—usually cooked oatmeal or plain toast. Once in a while she was given banana slices. In the early days of isolation, Claire had felt hungry all the time. She'd devoured whatever was pushed through the narrow slat at the bottom of the metal door.

But then she became suspicious of what the food might contain. It seemed she was sleeping more than twelve hours a day. And when she wasn't sleeping, the flat-screen would turn on, and she'd be drilled with questions about her childhood, her education, her beliefs.

She quickly learned that when she didn't answer, the room would stay dark and no food would be delivered. When she did answer, the room would lighten and she'd receive meals. She used to stare at the black screen, in the dark, waiting for it to light up, as if it were heroin and she were addicted.

She knew her mental state had started to deteriorate when she began to cry whenever the flat-screen began glowing. She'd answer the questions with more and more detail, trying to unlock whatever information they were seeking. All the while, she could think of only one thing: Getting out of isolation. Feeling the wind. Seeing the sky. Breathing fresh air.

She told herself that she was a rat in a weird science experiment, and this would all be over soon. Or perhaps it was just some extended dream from which she'd awaken and later laugh about. Or maybe she'd been in a car accident, and she was now in a coma, hallucinating.

The day she was brought out of the isolation room, she'd had no strength to resist being carried. She couldn't have run even if she knew where to run. They'd hoisted her into a chair, pulling straps about her arms, her wrists, across her lap, over her torso, her thighs, around her ankles. As if she were some wild animal that could tear herself free. She'd gone from existing in a ten-by-ten room, alone, to having unlimited space around her but being unable to move in it.

"Claire Vetra," a man had said as he wheeled Claire down a long hallway of red carpet with black designs. "We're pleased with your progress. You have earned your way to the next training level."

The hallway had seemed endless. Brass lamps perched on cherrywood side tables, the carpet stretched forever, and the walls were interspersed with abstract black-and-white paintings. The hiss of the wheelchair wheels was the only audible thing, and it reverberated throughout her head like a whisper of warning.

Before the man wheeled her into the examination room, Claire had passed out from exhaustion.

But now she was no longer in the WAO compound, and when she completed her mission, the entire operation would be destroyed. So she put one foot in front of the other along the black-and-red carpet until she reached the first apartment door. She stopped, breathed, then knocked. No one answered, so she continued to the next door, repeating the process.

By the time she reached the third floor, she was doubting her method. Surely there was an easier way to find out which was Paul's place. The door in front of her was plain like the others, but one thing was different. She could smell something cooking from within. It smelled like stir-fry and made her stomach rumble.

After Claire had escaped the WAO compound, it had taken her digestive system months to recuperate. And still, sometimes she struggled with eating. She'd lost over thirty pounds at the WAO and was able to gain back ten of them eventually. Her rigorous exercises kept the missing twenty off, although her muscle tone should have added weight.

Claire knocked on the door, and then she heard footsteps. She moved to the side so that if the person looked through the peephole, they'd see only a portion of her hair and the side of her face. If it was Paul, Claire didn't want to give him any reason to not open the door. She slipped her specialized gun from the inside of her jacket and held it down behind her thigh so that it would be out of view as well.

The person was hesitating. And they weren't calling through the door asking her to identify herself.

"Claire," a man said, and then the door swung open.

She stared at Paul.

His body stilled, and his dark eyes locked on hers. In their black depths, Claire was reminded of the days of isolation she'd spent in a place he'd brought her to. She remembered how Paul had stood by and watched the rounds of injections she'd been given. How he said nothing when she was being questioned by his father. And how he'd been gone when his father decided to further experiment with mind control.

This Paul might be older, but he was the same man who'd first drugged her in a pub, then stolen her life away.

"Paul," Claire whispered, her voice unexpectedly hoarse. She lifted her gun with a steady hand.

Paul didn't even blink.

"Let's take this inside," she added.

CHAPTER 18

OF COURSE CLAIRE was here, in his flat, with a gun aimed at his head. Nora had warned him. Claire had been broken by the WAO but then rebuilt by the Amazon Sisterhood. Nora wanted her back, and now Paul understood why.

The woman had become a machine.

Her dark hazel eyes were 100 percent focused on him, but he had no doubt she'd already calculated the placement of his furniture, the distance to the windows, and the fact that he had a concealed weapon.

Claire used her foot to shut the door behind her, keeping her gun still pointed right at his head.

"It seems you've been expecting me, Paul," she said. "Or else you wouldn't have opened your door."

Paul lifted his hands in mock surrender. "It's been a long time, Claire. You look . . . different." Up close, he could see the dark beneath her eyes, the concave of her cheeks on a face too thin. Energy and tension emitted from her as if she were a coil ready to spring free.

"Everyone changes, I suppose, whether they want to or not," Claire said, her voice a low hum. "It's been six years, Paul. I must say, you haven't changed much."

Paul felt her gaze take in everything about him. He might not recognize the brand of the gun she carried, but he did recognize the cold determination in her eyes. He had no doubt she'd shoot.

"You broke our agreement," he said. "You promised never to return to London."

"That was before," Claire said.

"Before what?"

"Before I found out that the Sisterhood paid you a half-million dollars to fake my death for the WAO."

Paul stared into her eyes. "Does it really matter? I got you out, didn't I? And from what I've heard, you excelled at the Amazon Sisterhood. Although they aren't too happy right now. Why did you go AWOL?"

Claire blinked, but her grip remained steady on the gun. "I'm tired of being lied to." Her eyes narrowed. "I'm tired of people like you and your father who think they can treat others like puppets and ruin lives."

"Not everyone gets to walk through life smelling roses," Paul said, his temperature rising a notch. "We have to do what we need to survive."

Claire's mouth curled into a smile. "Then you'll understand me more than anyone. I know about my parents. I know how they were killed. And I know why you took me to the WAO."

Paul kept his mouth shut. He didn't know where she was going with this.

"I've just been a pawn to you," she continued. "But that ends today. You have thirty seconds to give me the location of the WAO compound."

"You know I can't do that."

"I knew you'd say that, but according to my therapist, it's quite healing for abuse victims to return to the site of their abuse." She took a step forward. "A little arson would be very healing as well."

Paul winced. He knew about the scars and burn marks on her body. Nora had told him that the Sisterhood had paid for Claire to undergo cosmetic surgery to get rid of the worst ones.

"One flame can cancel out a different flame, right?" Claire said.

"You've put me in a terrible position," Paul said, holding her gaze while he calculated how much time it would take him to withdraw his Glock versus how long it would take for her to pull the trigger of her gun. "The WAO knows you're in London. Bethany called me early this morning."

"Let me guess," Claire said. "Voice recognition software when I called Hughes & Ross?"

Paul nodded. He would probably have to disarm her first, then shoot her right after. Maybe it would be more efficient to use her own gun. He just wished he didn't have to kill her at such close range. He'd been favoring more of a sniper approach so that he wouldn't have to look into her eyes while doing it.

His nightmares were plentiful enough.

"So you understand my predicament," he said.

She seemed to waver. "What did Nora want with you? Double the money for taking me down?"

Paul released a breath. Claire was right about one thing: he was tired of the lies as well. "She wants you back."

Claire scoffed, just as Paul predicted.

"Nora has only her own interests in mind," Claire said. "She told you some story about how I'm their most brilliant protégée, and she doesn't want poor, broken Claire fighting her demons alone. Nora wants to lock me down and put me through psychoanalysis therapy. Then she'll have every single movement of mine monitored for the rest of my days. I'll be shutting down the bad guys, while I'm treated like a prisoner." Another step forward. "I'm done with people owning me. From now on, I work only for myself. And frankly, I don't care what happens to me after I finish off you and the WAO."

Paul saw the almost imperceptible movement of her finger, and just as she pulled the trigger, he dove at her feet.

They tumbled to the floor, neither of them making a sound, each straining to gain control of her gun. Paul grabbed her wrist, while her other hand clawed at his face. She missed his eyes, but he might have new scars from her surprisingly sharp nails.

Paul used his weight to pin her down and keep her arm with the gun motionless. But she slammed the palm of her hand into his throat.

He gasped for air, feeling like his throat had just collapsed. Gritting his teeth with a groan, he wrapped his free hand around her neck and started to squeeze.

She struggled beneath him, fighting like a caged animal with her petite form. But Paul was stronger by nature and trained in hand-to-hand combat, so although she put up a good fight, he was able to keep one hand crushing her wrist, keeping her from aiming the gun at him.

Her eyes bugged, and her breathing went shallow. Paul kept his eyes locked with hers as her face drained of all color. And then she jerked up and spat at him. Something hit his face, and Paul cried out as bits of what felt like fire scorched his skin. She'd spat an acid vial at him.

The burning of the acid shocked him at first, then he scrambled off Claire and ran to the kitchen sink. Turning on the water, he dunked his head under the faucet. "What did you do?" he yelled.

"It's a new defense mechanism developed in India," Claire said. "It's making inroads in the sex trade there. It's most effective if the woman has someplace to run after spraying the perpetrator."

The burning had lessened, but who knew how much damage it had caused?

"Don't worry, your face will be pretty again in a couple of weeks," Claire said. "It's more like getting hit by an airbag than anything permanent."

Paul lifted his head to stare at her with disbelief.

She had the gun in her hand again.

Heart pounding and stomach sick at what he was about to do, he acted as if he were about to reach for a towel, when in fact he withdrew his Glock.

Claire was faster.

CHAPTER 19

CLAIRE WATCHED PAUL'S fury morph into a stunned expression. Then he collapsed to the floor. "You're not dead, you idiot," she said. "You're just going to wish you were."

He stared up at her, those dark eyes full of fear and confusion, but she knew very well he couldn't move. The red burns on his face from the acid were quite harmless, second degree at the most, and spitting the acid capsule at him had proved very useful.

She stared back at him, her mind turning. If she killed him, she wondered how long it would take for Handel Raine to find out. From there, how long would it take for him to track her down? Could she find the WAO compound before he found her?

She didn't know if she could stand to see the man's face again, and if she did, she would have a hard time not shooting him immediately. She didn't want him to die oblivious to her plans for the WAO. She wanted him to be a witness to his crumbling empire.

Claire walked the rest of the way into the kitchen and stood over Paul for several long moments. Her emotions battled within her. She wanted to finish him off, but she wanted his father more. "It's your lucky day, Paul," she ground out. "When you're ready to tell me where the compound is, send it to this email." She dropped a card onto his stomach.

He only blinked. His voice wouldn't work for a few hours, and neither would his limbs.

She turned from him and examined the flat. The place was sparse to say the least, and she had a feeling Paul spent very little time here. She crossed to the table and picked up the laptop. It took only a few seconds to remove the hard drive, which she slipped into her pocket. Then she searched the single bedroom. She found a couple of SD cards and pocketed those. Then finally, she made her way back to the kitchen alcove, where Paul still lay, unmoving. She took his cell phone, which he'd left on the counter.

Without another glance at him, Claire left the flat. On her way down the stairs of the building, she started dialing Paul's most recently answered and called numbers.

When a woman answered at the first number, Claire inhaled sharply at the familiarity of the voice. "Nora," she said in a curt tone.

"Claire?" Nora said, her voice falsely warm.

Claire had once trusted that voice and allowed herself to believe that the Amazon Sisterhood had truly delivered her from the clutches of the WAO, only to become another pawn. When Claire had found out the truth about her parents, she knew she could no longer work for the Sisterhood.

"Listen to me, Claire," Nora said. "You don't have all the information. We need to work together because *you're* a target now. Handel Raine and the WAO know you're alive. But Paul has agreed to work with us, so we need you to come back to the Sisterhood safely."

Claire was past believing the woman's lies, and she hung

up the phone before she had to listen to Nora's voice any longer.

The darkness of the night created a momentary balm for Claire's rising anger.

"We'll take care of you," Nora had told her that first night when Claire had arrived in the renovated French château.

Claire had been smudged with dirt and ash, and she was thirty pounds too light. The burns and carvings on her body had been treated and reopened and treated again. The skin on her stomach and chest looked like she'd been whipped for witchcraft in the sixteenth century. The Sisterhood had placed her in an ivory-and-pale-green-colored bedroom that captured the morning light.

Claire had been set free, at last, but as she healed she realized that although there were no isolation rooms or restraining chairs or injected drugs, the walls surrounding the château and the complex security system were a new kind of prison.

She'd been told she could leave any time but would have to take on a new identity. At first Claire had balked at that idea. She'd have to start over in college with her degree since none of her credits could transfer. She'd have to settle for a minimum wage somewhere if she didn't go to school. And . . . her body had a long ways to heal.

So, Claire had stayed.

A few weeks later when she was strong enough to start exploring the Sisterhood château and ask questions, she was assigned a roommate.

Frances was tall and willowy, with naturally curly short brown hair. She wore oval glasses and was perhaps the most educated woman Claire had ever met. Barely thirty years old, Frances had earned two PhDs in finance and economics.

"First, you need to see the gardens," Frances had told Claire the day that she moved into the shared room.

Claire was no longer considered an "invalid," so she was now to become a productive part of the Sisterhood.

"I've seen the gardens," Claire had told Frances. The medical aide had practically forced Claire to walk on the garden paths twice a day to build up her stamina.

"Not where we grow vegetables and herbs," Frances said, and crossed to Claire. "Come on, get up." She stuck out her hand in that matter-of-fact way, and Claire took it, pulling herself up.

The air was moist and fragrant in the gardens with the scent of ripe oranges and peaked rose bushes.

"Everything we eat is organic," Frances said, glancing over at Claire. "It sharpens the mind and creates natural energy."

Claire could believe it. She'd started to regain her strength and with it, her mental clarity.

Frances walked her to the east side of the château. "This is where we grow the vegetables, and beneath those shade trees we grow plenty of herbs as well."

The rows of plants were well cared for, and the scent of rich earth was somehow comforting. Claire's mother used to garden in their tiny plot behind their townhouse, and the scent of the fertilized dirt sent a wave of nostalgia through her.

Claire closed her eyes and breathed in.

"Lovely, isn't it?" Frances said.

Claire opened her eyes and looked directly at Frances. "I sleep with the lights on."

"Me too." Frances's smile was soft. "You're not alone, Claire. The members of the Amazon Sisterhood all have a past that we're trying to overcome. Not that I'd wish mine on anyone, but it gives me a drive to make things right for others."

The depth in Frances's dark-gray eyes became more understandable.

"I was thirteen when Nora pulled me from the sex trade," Frances said in a straightforward tone. "It took me six months to get free of my drug addictions and another year before I stopped having nightmares that my pimp would find me." She pulled up the long, loose sleeves of her blouse. Old needle scars followed the path of her blue veins.

Claire winced.

"Once an addict, always an addict," Frances continued. "I don't shoot up heroin anymore, but I still dream of a fix. And I know that if I left this château, I'd never make it back alive. One hit would kill me now." She let her sleeves fall back, covering her arms and their ugly history.

"You've never left the châteaux?" Claire asked, incredulous. That would mean Frances had lived here for seventeen years.

"I've tried," Frances said in a contemplative voice. "Once, I prepared to go on a shopping trip with some of the other Sisters. I made it past the first gate, and I had a panic attack."

Claire gave a slow nod. "How many gates are there?" The thought of gates locking her in wasn't sitting so well in her stomach.

"There's a series of three checkpoints," Frances said in a breezy tone. Her eyes focused on Claire. "No one will stop you if you want to leave. You could walk out right now, bare feet and all."

Claire looked down at her bare feet and smiled. It was one of the things she'd discarded when she arrived at the château. Anything that felt too confining, she'd gotten rid of.

She wore loose-fitting dresses or pants and blouses now. No shoes, no socks, and she never slept beneath a blanket. She kept the lights on, the door open, and if it wasn't too cool, the window open.

"You seem happy and content," Claire told Frances.

"I still have bad days, but for the most part, I feel blessed." Frances spread her arms. "I mean, look at this place. What's not to love about it?" She started to walk along the path that weaved through a thicket of oleander bushes.

The fragrance was almost overwhelming to Claire.

Frances slowed and looked over at Claire. "Maybe someday I'll tell you my whole story. But for now, I don't want any pity. I think of all the directions my life could have taken, and honestly, I owe my existence and peace of mind to the Sisterhood."

Claire nodded. She could very well understand that. The therapist who met with her daily hadn't even asked her about the WAO compound yet. They'd only talked about her childhood, although Claire couldn't understand how that had anything to do with her abduction as a college student. Both of her parents were long gone, and she'd had no contact with any of her relatives for years.

But Claire could feel that she was becoming stronger—more sure of the stability of her mind and firmer in her body.

"Will you come to my yoga class tonight?" Frances asked.

Claire had avoided any of the activities that were done in groups. She knew many of the women participated in yoga, and there were other programs as well. Her therapist had told her when she was ready, she needed to attend the self-defense courses.

Frances moved closer, although she didn't touch Claire. No one touched Claire, and that's how she wanted it.

"I believe you're ready," Frances said in a soft tone. "Meeting the other women will be nice, and you'll become strong again through yoga. Your mind and physical endurance are intimately connected."

Claire knew that Frances was speaking the truth, but she didn't want everyone's eyes on her, wondering or knowing or speculating.

"It's very relaxing," Frances said. "The women here have all come for different reasons, not all of them as traumatic as yours, perhaps. But no one will ask you questions. You will take the lead in any conversation should you choose to speak."

Claire looked away.

"Try it this once," Frances continued, "and then you can decide from there."

Claire swallowed and darted a gaze back to the woman. "Are the lights kept on?"

"Of course," Frances said.

Claire had to remember she wasn't the only damaged person, broken woman, abuse victim . . . All words that her therapist had told her not to label herself as. She was to refer to herself as "in transition."

"I'll come," she said.

Now, as Claire reached her hotel room, she realized that she missed Frances. It didn't take her long to pack and wheel her carry-on out of the hotel room. She wouldn't check out, since having her name still listed on the hotel registry might serve well as a decoy.

Catching another taxi, Claire directed the driver to a different hotel, where she checked in under yet another name. Walking into her new hotel room, thoughts of Frances still plagued her mind. Frances had been right about so many things.

Claire turned both of the door locks, then flipped on all

the lights in the room. She pulled off her jacket and stripped down to her underwear. Later she would load Paul's SD cards to her laptop and hook up the hard drive. But first she had to find her mental center. She began the first yoga pose that Frances had taught her. Claire focused on clearing her mind. She had to refocus on her goals and not let her run-in with Paul and her sighting of Nora—a woman who'd been like a mother to her—interfere with her plans. As Claire went through the yoga positions, she thought about the last time she'd seen her friend.

Frances had been restless for days, and during the nights, she'd tossed and turned with nightmares, frequently crying in her sleep. The first night had startled Claire, but when she tried to wake Frances from her bad dream, Frances had just thrashed and nearly sent Claire to the ground.

After that, Claire left her alone while she lay awake listening to her cry in fear. In the mornings, Frances had refused to talk about her night terrors, but each day she grew more and more pale. When Claire had reported her worries to Nora, Nora had told her that Frances was the one who would need to ask for help. It was part of their empowerment program.

Claire had approached Frances on a warm afternoon, as Frances had knelt on the edge of the herb garden, pulling at tiny weeds.

"I know you're not sleeping," Claire had told Frances. "Maybe if you tell me what you're dreaming about, it will ease your mind."

Frances's hands had stilled, and she didn't move for a moment. Then she turned her head, slowly, and looked at Claire. Frances's gray eyes were red rimmed, her eyelids puffy from crying.

"You want to know my story, Claire?" Her voice was harsh, and it felt like a knife stabbing into Claire's gut.

Claire took a step back and raised her hands. "You don't have to. I just want to help—"

"Would it *help* if you knew that my own mother sold me to a pimp in Brixton?" Frances spat out.

"No," Claire started to say, but Frances continued in a tone that Claire had never heard her use.

"Would it *help* if you knew that my own uncle molested me, and when I told my mother, she told me that *I* was a slut?" Frances continued. She rose to her feet, her soiled hands clenched at her sides.

Claire took another step back. "Frances—"

"Or would it help if I told you that my mother defended her brother but got rid of me?" She pulled at her sleeve so hard that the sleeve ripped away from the shoulder seam. The scars on her arms were transparent in the dappled sun coming through the overhead branches of the trees.

She pointed to one of the scars on the inside of her elbow. "This is from my first heroin injection. Do you think I did this to myself at thirteen years old?"

Hot tears dripped down Claire's face as she shook her head.

"My uncle's 'friend' did this," she continued. "All it took was one needle, and I was addicted."

Claire wanted to reach out to Frances, but she was shaking too much.

"And every day since, I can only think of when I can get back out there ... when I can get another hit." Frances dropped to her knees on the ground and started to dig.

"Don't go," Claire had whispered. But Frances hadn't seemed to hear her.

After a few minutes, Claire had left the garden, her cheeks still wet with tears. She went to their room and sat on her bed, with her knees pulled to her chest. And she waited for Frances. She would apologize to her friend.

But Frances never did return to their shared room. She left that afternoon.

Six months later, the Sisterhood called off all searches.

"I'm doing this for you, Frances," Claire whispered to herself as she continued the yoga stretches Frances had taught her. "For you and for me. And for all those who can't fight back."

CHAPTER 20

PAUL ROLLED TO his side on the hard kitchen floor. The feeling in his body was returning in slow increments, alternating between tingling and a deep ache. His face throbbed with painful heat, and he could only concentrate on breathing as he waited for the drug to wear off.

He'd never felt so trapped and helpless in his entire life. And while one part of him realized this was similar to what he'd put WAO recruits through, the other part of him raged against Claire.

She hadn't killed him, and he wanted to know why.

She'd planned this—all of this. Her gun didn't have bullets, but darts. She'd had the acid vial inside her mouth when she knocked on his door.

In other words, she was playing with him.

When the debilitating numbness had subsided in his arms, Paul pushed himself to a sitting position. He groaned as his muscles trembled with the effort. Just that one movement and he was out of breath.

"What are you up to, Claire?" he mumbled. His tongue felt thick as if he'd just spent a couple of hours in a dentist chair. His legs were currently useless. Looking at the oven clock, he saw that he'd been on the ground for nearly two hours. He wasn't sure what he'd been drugged with, but it was powerful.

He closed his eyes and waited for the drug to wear off. Replaying her words in his head, he tried to figure out what he was missing. She'd told him she wanted the address to the compound, but he couldn't let her near there. His father would be waiting for her. She'd know that, and she wouldn't go down quietly.

It was either him. Or her.

He had to stop her. No matter what it took.

Whatever he agreed to with Nora couldn't ever happen. Claire was too much of a live wire.

Even though Paul hated to admit it, his father was right. Claire had to be taken out.

A numb warmth spread along Paul's foot, and he tried to move it. Finally, the drug was fading. He'd been on the floor for so long that the kitchen was beginning to lighten with the arrival of dawn.

Paul pulled himself to his feet and leaned heavily against the counter. His phone was gone. Of course. He remembered that she'd taken it, but his brain had seemed to be only half working at the time. With great effort, he pushed himself upright and began to walk, one slow step after another. He made it to the bathroom and flipped on the light.

He winced at his reflection in the mirror. Claire had done a number on him. His face looked like he had a wild case of hives. Pulling open the vanity drawer, he searched for a tube of ointment—anything that might help. He found an anti-itch cream that would have to do. He spread it gingerly onto his face.

The burns started feeling better already, but it would take some time to heal. Once he rinsed off his hands, he moved through the rest of the flat, looking for what else Claire might have taken. The hard drive on his laptop had been pulled out, and a thorough check of his bedroom revealed she'd taken his SD cards. She now had information on his projects—and that would be incriminating enough.

Paul sat on his bed as the morning light spread across the room. It was time to make the call. His head had started to pound, likely a side effect of the drug wearing off. He reached behind his headboard where he'd secured a backup phone in case . . . well, in case something like this happened.

Just as he was about to dial the WAO headquarters, his front door rattled like someone was trying to get inside. From his position on the bed, Paul could see across the hallway to the front entrance of his flat. The doorknob turned, and Paul watched the intruder step into his flat, then shut the door.

Paul wasn't in the mood for a robbery.

But the intruder wasn't a robber.

"Bethany," Paul said.

Her head snapped in his direction, and their gazes met across the hallway. She wore a long dark-green coat coupled with black leggings and boots. Pulled over her dark hair was a navy knit cap. Her eyes were lined with black makeup, making her look like a waifish runway model. She might be tall and lean, but she was no wilting flower.

The surprise on her face was unmistakable, although she quickly blanked her expression out. Classic Bethany.

"You're alive," she deadpanned.

Paul knew his reflexes and thought patterns were slow, but he could comprehend that something was off in the way she'd sneaked into his flat. She hadn't even knocked to see if he might answer.

"What are you doing here?" he asked in a rasp.

Her gaze flickered away for an instant, then it was fully back on him. What was she looking for? What had she been expecting?

"I've been trying to reach you for hours," she said, motioning to the mess of the room she stood in. "What happened here?"

Paul hadn't even bothered about the fallen lamp and tipped-over end table. Damaged furniture was the least of his concerns.

Bethany's eyes were darting about the room, taking in the scene, and all the while she wasn't coming closer to Paul. She was keeping her distance. To give her the advantage?

"What are you doing here, Bethany?" he asked again.

She released a short breath and focused her green gaze upon him. The steadiness of her expression told him that she was packing heat and that he'd interrupted whatever plans she'd been about to carry out.

Bethany still ignored his question. "Where is she?"

"Gone. She drugged me," Paul said. "I've been incapacitated for hours."

"What did she say?"

Paul exhaled and pushed up from the bed. The muscles in his thighs and calves burned with the effort. He knew that Bethany would report everything back to his father. And while Paul knew that telling them Claire was here to destroy the compound was pretty important information, he couldn't say the words. He told himself he wasn't protecting Claire in any way, but he also didn't like Bethany breaking into his flat.

"She's a wild card," Paul said. "She ranted and then shot me with a dart. I believe her mind's cracked."

Finally, Bethany took a couple of steps toward the hallway. She was still a good twenty feet from him, standing closer to the front door than to his bedroom.

"She's unpredictable, is all I can say," Paul said.

"She was here, in your flat, and *she* drugged *you*?" Bethany said, her mouth pulling into a thin line. He didn't miss the slight narrowing of her eyes. "You're going soft, Paul."

This was an ironic statement coming from her. *He'd* brought Bethany into the WAO years ago; she owed him for her success. "She spat acid in my face," Paul explained. He wouldn't be surprised if Bethany had a listening device on her, allowing his father to hear every word. "Tell my father that his orders will be fulfilled."

Her smile was faint, knowing. "He will be told, but he won't appreciate the delay."

Paul shuffled into the front room so that he was standing only a few feet away from Bethany. She held her ground, as she should. He remembered her as a scared but resourceful teenager. Her resourcefulness won out. And now, her green eyes didn't waver.

"Next time, Paul, don't let her get away," she said, as if he needed to be told.

Paul merely held her gaze until she turned away and strode to the door. Whatever she planned to do in his flat had been foiled by his presence.

The thought gave him no comfort.

He scanned the damage in the room. He'd put it to rights later, but his muscles and joints were still aching as if he'd run a marathon. Stepping into the bathroom, he grabbed a few aspirin and popped them into his mouth.

He knew he needed to pack, to get out of the flat for a while until he could regroup and figure out what Claire really wanted with him and why she hadn't killed him after she'd incapacitated him.

But his body wasn't cooperating, and his headache had only grown worse. He forced his feet forward and entered his bedroom. Pulling out a backpack from his closet, he put in a change of clothing and a few toiletry items. Then from underneath his bed he pulled out a metal case. Unlocking it with a combination, he opened it to reveal the disassembled parts of a sniper rifle.

He transferred the parts to a portable case, then slipped it into the backpack.

When he rose to his feet, his head screamed in pain, and he nearly blacked out. Paul turned toward the bed just as blackness overtook him, and the bed broke his fall.

CHAPTER 21

THE DART THAT Claire had shot Paul with had more than one benefit. Not only did it incapacitate, but it also left a small metal bead inside the victim. One that could be used as a tracking device.

Claire had finished her yoga stint, showered, and slept for a couple of hours while the hard drive she'd stolen from Paul uploaded to her secure server. When she awakened, she uploaded Paul's location to the tracking app on her phone. He was a slow starter that morning, and Claire decided it must be the effects of the drug.

She watched the tracker as Paul moved about the city. He seemed to be stopping in several locations. The app detailed each spot, and it looked like they were pubs and cafés. Claire straightened. The pattern to his movements might seem random, but Claire knew it wasn't.

For starters, all of the places were open late. She googled several of the names and found media write-ups on them as popular hangouts. Which meant these locations would naturally attract young women ... Claire exhaled. Paul was covering his tracks. He was destroying evidence of past misdeeds.

She turned her attention to the hard drive files that she'd copied. What would Paul keep on his computer? The files were saved by numbers—dates?—and acronyms.

She opened the first one and read through a contract between Hughes & Ross and a Chinese investment firm. Hughes & Ross had a contract to provide advice on which shares to sell on a specific date: August 24, 2016.

Frowning, Claire pulled up another Google search. On August 24, the DOW had plunged more than 1,000 points, finally closing at 588 below the previous day's close. She continued to read the linked articles, learning that on the same day Apple had reported strong growth in China for the months of July and August.

Investors started buying Apple shares, and the stock market's plunge softened.

Claire opened the next file. Another contract between Hughes & Ross and a different Chinese investment firm. Same terms. Same date. She clicked on file after file until she'd looked at over thirty agreements.

The WAO had staged the stock market dive.

Her heart rate increased as she found a group of files starting with *APL* followed by a series of numbers. The first file she opened confirmed her suspicion. The WAO had been behind the Apple announcement. Not only had the WAO crashed millions of dollars in sales that day, they'd also controlled the rise back up.

Astounding.

Claire wasn't going to wait for an address from Paul. It seemed he was focused on running around in a panic and gathering up any evidence he'd left behind.

Instead, Claire looked up the FBI database. She'd found a way to hack into it months ago and had been tracking several FBI agents. She needed an agent who didn't have dirt on his or her hands and who had enough seniority to be respected by the bureau as well as enough acumen to follow through on a lead.

She pulled up her top three candidates and reviewed each of their credentials again. Her attention was caught by Loren Hales. The agent had testified in high-profile US national cases, and the media recognized her as an expert.

Claire copied the email address into the secure email database she'd built, then she sent out a dummy email, asking for a confidential address to which Claire could send leads.

She didn't expect an answer for a while, so she was surprised to see the email reply come in only seconds later.

Emails are never confidential, it read.

Claire smiled. She'd definitely found the right agent to tag.

She started to type:

My name is Summer Harper, although you won't ever find me under that name. I've uncovered a conspiracy ring that controls the DOW numbers on the US stock market. I'd like to send you the contractual evidence, but I cannot be linked to the information.

The reply came:

Summer, you might want to contact your local law enforcement. I don't handle conspiracy theories from anonymous people.

Claire nodded. That was fair.

Look up August 24, 2016.

Minutes passed.

What's your claim?

Claire typed: *I need an email address. I have dozens of documents, but after you see only one, you'll know what you're looking at.*

Another minute passed. Agent Hales sent over another email address.

Claire smiled and attached the first file, then hit Send.

She checked Paul's tracker as she waited. He was no longer at a pub or café, but now at a library. It seemed Paul needed to get online, and without his phone or hard drive, the library had been his choice. This both pleased and troubled Claire. Pleased her because she'd made things difficult and troubled her because he didn't seem to have a home base other than his flat. She was hoping he'd make his way to the WAO compound so she could follow him there.

Agent Hales emailed back.

We need to talk, Summer.

Success. Claire sent her a Skype number that linked to her cell phone. When her phone rang, she answered. "Summer here."

Agent Hales said, "Why did you contact me?"

Claire proceeded to tell the agent her method of deduction, then said, "Bottom line, you've proven trustworthy."

"Next question," Hales said, not sounding too flattered. "Where did you get this contract?"

"I can't tell you that yet," Claire said. "I'm sending over the rest of the files, and you can start a quiet investigation. You don't want any part of this case exposed too soon."

"Too soon for what?" the agent asked.

"The people who are behind these conspiracies will bury themselves deeper if they find out they're being investigated," Claire said. "Right now, they're only watching me."

The agent seemed to consider this for a moment. "How are you connected?" she asked.

"I can't share that information now."

Agent Hales paused. "All right. I'll play your game. But I'm going to want more answers soon. Should I contact you at this number?"

"Send an email, and I'll let you know how you can contact me," Claire said, her heart soaring. The agent took her seriously. And even if she wasn't, looking into the contract would surely bring up more questions and leads.

"Summer," Agent Hales said, "I need to ask you something else."

Claire waited.

"Are you safe?"

Claire exhaled as her hand absently touched her stomach. "I haven't been safe for years, perhaps not for my entire life."

CHAPTER 22

PAUL WANTED TO slam his fist into the library desk, but then the librarian would call security. Instead, he slowly released his breath. The library's internet service was extremely slow. Not only had he been forced to purchase a new laptop that morning, he was still waiting to access the online server where he'd saved a mirror image of his old hard drive. He had to make sure that it was still intact. And then he had to get that hard drive out of Claire's hands and delete any backups she'd created.

His mind churned.

Why had he opened the door? And why hadn't he shot her as soon as he saw her? He wanted answers, but he hadn't gotten any. He'd taken the wrong risk. Closing the laptop, he slipped it into his backpack and left the library. He wasn't ready to put down roots in a hotel room, but he didn't have a choice now.

He pushed through the glass doors and stepped into the afternoon light. The shadows had lengthened, slipping into evening. When he reached the bottom of the stairs, he turned north. He walked perhaps half a block when he had the sense he was being watched.

Slowing, he checked his phone and turned so that he could glance behind him, as if he were watching for traffic.

No one caught his interest, but the feeling persisted.

Paul continued down the rest of the block, then turned the next corner, taking a right. He stopped and leaned against the brick wall of a bakery. Then he waited.

Two minutes later, a woman wearing a khaki jacket and black boots turned the corner. Her dark hair was in a short pixie cut. She wore little makeup. Paul didn't recognize her, and she didn't look at him and continued walking.

Paul waited another couple of minutes, watching the woman. She walked to the next corner, then turned and disappeared from sight.

Paul straightened from his slouch against the wall. Just as he turned and started walking the opposite way, a bullet volleyed past him, tearing the edge of his sleeve. Paul froze for an instant, staring in disbelief at his torn sleeve. Red bloomed around the tear. He'd been hit.

Then the adrenaline caught up to his mind, and he started to run, sprinting for the next corner. As he moved around it, he took one glace back to confirm that the woman who'd just tried to shoot him was indeed the dark-haired one in the khaki jacket.

She was running too. Straight for him.

Paul grunted, increasing his speed. There were pedestrians, cars, motorcycles . . . nowhere to take cover and shoot back. Besides, he couldn't turn a London street into a battle zone. He didn't look back again, but his pounding heart and the raised hairs on the back of his neck told him she was still chasing him.

At a slight break in the traffic, he left the sidewalk and barreled into the road. Honks burst around him, but Paul kept his focus on avoiding the cars that were going too fast to stop in time.

Someone yelled at him for being an idiot. A woman cursed him out. Still, Paul ran.

He made it to the other side of the street and ran another dozen meters until he cut into an alley. He scanned for a door, a Dumpster, or anything to take cover. When he spotted a metal utility ladder leading to the roof, he started to climb, hoping he could get out of sight before the woman arrived.

Moments later, he'd scrambled onto the roof and lay flat on the cement. From his position on his stomach, he assembled the sniper rifle. Then he looked at his arm. The blood had slowed, and he felt only a sting, like he'd gotten road rash. So the bullet hadn't gone in. He peered over the edge, aimed his rifle, and waited.

He didn't have long to wait. She ran past the alley, and Paul stilled. His breathing had calmed, but his heart rate was in overdrive. She should have stopped and checked out the alley.

Amateur.

And then she was back, slowly walking down the alley. She looked into the doorways, one at a time, all the while keeping an eye on the end of the alley that opened onto another street.

Paul guessed the woman to be in her midtwenties and not too experienced, or she would have spotted his sniper rifle aimed right at her head. So, who had sent her? His father? Nora? He assumed she was a dispensable assassin, because if she missed once—which she had—they must know that he wouldn't let her go free.

She walked with one hand in her pocket—where her gun most likely was. He tracked her movements, the tilt of her head, the tenseness in her shoulders. One sound from him and she'd be trigger-happy.

"Don't move," he hissed.

She stopped.

"Hold your hands up," he continued.

She moved her hands out to her side, lifting them away from her body. And then she tilted her head up and met his gaze.

"Tell me who sent you," Paul ground out. "Or this bullet goes through your heart."

She blinked but didn't say a word.

Paul waited. But what was she waiting for?

And then he knew. She was stalling. She had backup.

Paul looked to the front of the alley just as a young man arrived. He wore a ball cap, a dark nondescript jacket, and appeared to be in his thirties. The way he held himself erect told Paul this was no amateur. Paul shifted his target from the woman to the man. The man didn't take the time to check doorways. One glance at his partner, and he looked up to see Paul.

Was this who'd shot Paul? Perhaps the woman had been a decoy, and she wasn't the assassin. But the man was already reaching for his gun. As soon as Paul saw the metal glint, he pulled the trigger, then rolled away from the edge of the roof.

Shots ricocheted along the roof's edge, but Paul didn't stick around to take in the damage. He scrambled to his feet and ran headlong across the rooftop, then leaped up onto a higher roof and continued moving. He scanned the rooftops, estimating how far he could get before the woman decided to climb up on the roof too. If he was lucky, she'd attend to her partner. But Paul never trusted luck.

The evening sun had set, and shadows had deepened. The cooler air felt good against his perspiring body. He found another metal utility ladder that he could climb down. As he started down the ladder, he noticed his hands were shaking, and the wound on his arm had decided to act up.

He needed to clean the gash and probably get it stitched up.

Once on the ground again, he rejoined the main street and spotted a coffee shop. He strode to the small shop, and as he entered, the smells of baked goods and coffee sent his stomach roiling. He was perspiring again. Quickly locating the restroom, he hurried inside and locked the door. He set down his backpack and gingerly peeled off his jacket.

Now that his arm was exposed to the air, it started to sting again. He stripped off his shirt and turned on the sink faucet. He used his other hand to cup water, then he let it trickle over the wound. The blood had crusted around the wound, but the introduction of the warm water made the blood separate and drain down the sink, coloring the porcelain a dull pink.

Paul grabbed a handful of paper towels and pressed it against his arm. Suddenly, he felt light-headed, and he sat on the floor just before his vision darkened. He leaned forward and rested his head on his knees, willing the feeling to pass. After a few moments, he lifted his head, then he pulled out his phone from his pocket. He called a number that he had memorized.

His father answered on the third ring.

"What's is going on?" Paul asked.

Handel Raine chuckled. "I told Bethany they were too amateurish for you."

Paul blinked slowly and stared at the bathroom stall in front of him. Had it all come to this? His life spent working for his father, and now, because Claire had deceived all of them, his father was after him?

He didn't want to ask why; he didn't want to know why.

Hanging up on Handel, Paul pulled out the business card that Claire had dropped onto his stomach while he'd been prostrate on the floor. He might be giving Claire a different type of death sentence, but that wasn't his concern anymore.

Nothing Paul could do would reinstate his father's loyalty to him. One ordered hit was proof enough. He pulled up his email on his phone and sent the address of the WAO to her encrypted account.

CHAPTER 23

CLAIRE HUNG UP with FBI Agent Hales and sent over a ZIP file of contracts that would at the very least indict the WAO. It wouldn't be enough, Claire knew. She could never do enough until the WAO was completely gone.

Which meant it was time to move again. She couldn't stay in one hotel room for too long, even with her fake ID. Surely Paul and Nora knew her different IDs, or they wouldn't have been able to track her down.

She rolled her carry-on out of the room and down the carpeted hall. Bypassing the elevator, she took the stairs. In front of the hotel, she boarded the first bus that came along. She didn't care about the direction it was going. Eventually she'd reroute herself once Agent Hales got back to her.

It took less than thirty minutes before her phone rang.

"What do you think?" she answered without preamble.

"I think you've hit a gold mine, Summer," Hales said, sounding like she was trying to hold back her excitement.

The words felt like a delicious bit of triumph washing over her. Claire plugged her other ear so that she could hear better over the hum of the city bus.

"From everything I've found, this web goes extremely deep," Hales said. "Some of the information may be impenetrable. I've sent one lead to my most trusted adviser in the UK. He said that he couldn't crack through it."

"I can crack through whatever you need me to," Claire said in a quiet voice.

Hales paused. "You're a hacker?"

Claire didn't answer.

Hales released a breath. "I need to ask this again, Summer. Are you in a safe place?"

Claire looked around her, at the people on the bus, at the line of shops passing by as they traveled. "I'm as safe as I can be."

"We can find you a safe house," Hales said. "You don't have to stay on the run."

"No," Claire said, her hushed voice rising. "It would involve too many people. I prefer to work with only a single contact—you."

"All right." Hales cleared her throat. "I want you to check in with me every twenty-four hours. Once I have enough evidence to officially open the case, I'll be terming it *Summer Day*. Can you remember that?"

"Of course," Claire said.

"You must disassociate yourself completely from anyone with the WAO," Hales continued. "Once we get everything in order, we'll start to move in, and that can take weeks or even months to infiltrate the first level of the organization, especially because I'm involving international agencies. If we can't come up with a plant, we'll have to bribe from the inside." Now Hales sounded like she was smiling. "Six months from now, we might have our first arrests."

Six months . . . Too long. Claire was already in London. She was already on the path. Paul and Nora knew she was here. Handel Raine knew she was alive.

She closed her eyes against the hot tears forming. Breaking down in public wasn't an option. "I'll call you in twenty-four hours," she said in a quiet voice, then hung up the phone.

She might not be alive in twenty-four hours. The bus slowed as it approached a stop. Here was as good a place to get off as any. Claire rose from her seat and exited the rear entrance. Just as she stepped onto the sidewalk, her phone buzzed with an incoming email. She knew it was to her private account. When she saw the sender addy, she guessed it was from Paul.

Her heart rate quickened as she opened the email.

Paul had sent her an address.

Claire stared at the location. Redcar was a coastal town in North Yorkshire. She looked around the street she'd arrived on, located a coffee shop, and hurried inside. She ordered coffee and found an empty table.

She copied the address into a maps app and pulled up the area. Zooming in, she saw that it was the location of an old power plant. Next she googled the power plant and found that it was still in operation.

Had Paul sent her a decoy address? Did he think she was idiot enough to go to the location and find him waiting for her?

Claire sipped at her too-hot coffee, thinking. Maybe Paul had just sent her a random link to see if she'd reply so he could track her location.

If truth be told, it hadn't taken him nearly as long to send her the address as she thought it might. In fact, she was surprised he'd send an address at all. What were the chances of it being the correct one?

Another sip of the coffee scalded her tongue, but she barely noticed because another thought came into her head. *If* this address was the location of the WAO compound, then that meant the compound was underground. This made sense, because in all her months there, Claire had never seen a window or a bit of sunlight.

She'd been nearly unconscious when Paul stole her from the isolation room and took her from the compound. And she'd been drugged when she'd arrived there. She'd never seen the place from the outside, above ground or underground. It was entirely possible that the compound was completely underground—under the power plant?

Claire stared at the Google images on her phone of the power plant.

If this was the location of the compound . . . then she had another question. Why had Paul finally decided to give it to her? Was he setting up an ambush? Or had something else happened? Had the drug dart she'd shot at him had worse effects than predicted? Or was he now a target of his father's for failing to defeat her?

Despite all the questions she had, she knew she had to go to Redcar. She had to see the power plant for herself, to know if it was the location for the WAO compound. She might be walking into a trap, but she at least hoped to take down Handel Raine with her. His son, Paul, would be second-best prize.

It was getting late in the morning, and the bus route she pulled up on her phone would be complicated. So she decided to take a taxi, even though it would give her less anonymity. She'd travel to the adjacent town to get a hotel room and plan from there.

When the taxi pulled up to the coffee shop, Claire climbed in, grateful to be finally moving forward, yet her agitation had begun. Night had fallen, and the lights of the city zoomed past as the taxi drove.

"Can you change the music?" Claire asked.

The driver grunted and changed the radio from some teenage pop song to a classical music station. Claire froze. It wasn't possible.

A Bach song crept throughout the taxi, settling into the upholstery and filling the air with its mournful notes.

Handel had loved Bach. Or so it seemed that night when he came to "punish" her for Paul's actions.

"No," she whispered to herself as she grasped her carry-on next to her on the seat. She hadn't let the driver put her suitcase in the trunk. And now she clutched it like a lifeline.

"My son seems to have developed a soft spot for you," Handel had said in a low voice when he entered her room at the compound.

As usual, she'd been strapped into bed that night. Not with the same restraints used on the chair she sat in during the day, because only her wrists were bound, in addition to a single strap fitted across her waist. She was able to move her legs, which helped her sleep better compared to her nights spent in the isolation room.

She'd almost fallen asleep when she heard the footsteps echoing down the hallway. It was after eleven p.m., an unusual time for a medic visit. When the door had swung open, Claire decided that she should have expected a visit from Handel . . . she just hadn't expected it at night in her private bedroom. Every time she'd seen him in person, it had been in one of the medic rooms or testing rooms.

The faint glow of the light bead that rimmed the ceiling cast most of his face into shadow.

Her voice stuck, and she knew she wouldn't have said a word if she'd been able to. She kept her gaze on Handel and watched as he turned and locked the door. It was always locked behind whichever aide left her room last, but now he was locking himself in . . . with her.

Claire's throat tightened, and she suddenly felt desperate for a drink of water.

Handel didn't seem to be bothered by her eyes, which were filled with fear at the sight of a roll of duct tape he carried with him.

"Bethany tells me that your testing scores are only average," Handel said. "That you're deliberately compromising your testing so we think you're not as intelligent as we know you are." He tilted his head, his dark eyes searching hers.

Beneath his gaze, Claire's skin warmed until perspiration pricked under her arms and behind her neck.

"We have all your transcripts, Claire Vetra," Handel continued in his smooth voice. "We've read your essays from Columbia University. We know your mind—your *vast* mind. And your memory."

He stepped closer to the bed, and instinctively Claire shifted her legs to the far side, away from him.

He didn't seem to be bothered by her cowering movements. "Tonight I'm going to give you something to always remember. Something that will motivate you to per-form to your best ability on all our testing processes. You're a unique study for us, Claire. Your parents both have photo-graphic memories, and so do you. Does this mean it's genetic? Directly from the parent to child? Or does it some-times skip generations? Is it carried by the mother's DNA or the father's? Or are you a special case?"

Handel set the duct tape on the bedside table, then he reached into his pocket and pulled out a smartphone. At first, Claire flinched, thinking it might be some new torture device. But he simply put it on the bedside table and turned on a classical music piece.

Claire's parents had loved classical music, but listening to it here, in this bare room with Handel, didn't give her the warm memory of her parents. It caused bumps to rise on her arms.

Above her, Handel said, "So you see why your testing is very, very important to us. Recording your brain patterns is essential since we're trying to duplicate your intelligence. Just think of a world in which we could create and sell a new drug that would raise IQs. Yes, the drugs we are giving you are experimental, but we are only administering them under controlled conditions. We can't know if they are doing what they're supposed to do if you don't participate to your fullest ability. Tonight, I hope to encourage your participation."

Handel turned from the bedside table and walked toward the end of her bed. Before she could understand his purpose, his hand snaked out and grabbed her ankle.

Claire gasped as he strapped her ankle down.

She knew she couldn't get away. Even if she hadn't been strapped down, she had no weapons, and she had very little strength or stamina. Her minimal diet ensured that she'd become a weak prisoner. But she still twisted as hard as she could when he grabbed her other ankle. He was much stronger, and it took minimal effort for him to completely strap her down.

She lurched up, off the bed, but only went a few inches before she was tugged back down by the straps.

"You're a live wire, Claire," Handel said in a purr. "I don't mind, though."

He stood by her head now and slowly lifted his hand; Claire could only stare at the perspiration that had formed on his upper lip. When he touched her cheek, she snapped her head to the side and tried to bite him.

He jerked his hand away, avoiding her teeth, and then he backhanded her.

The sound echoed in the bare room long before the blood rushed to her face and stung hot. A metallic taste reached her tongue, and she knew her mouth was bleeding.

Handel was swift to rip off a piece of duct tape and press it over her mouth.

Claire inhaled sharply through her nose as her chest tightened and her vision blurred. Her erratic heartbeat, and the moisture breaking out all across her skin, told her that a panic attack was coming on. But there wasn't a thing she could do about it. She clenched her jaw tight and closed her eyes. It was as if her body were taking control—shutting her down for what Handel would do next.

So Claire didn't watch as Handel unbuckled his belt and removed his pants. She didn't watch as he reached for the smartphone and turned up the volume of the classical music. She didn't watch as his hand touched her bleeding lip, then trailed down her neck, over her T-shirt and breasts, and to the waistband of her pajama bottoms.

She only squeezed her eyes shut more tightly as he tugged off her bottoms, then climbed onto the bed. And then she tried not to breathe in his scent of cinnamon and antiseptic.

The taxi driver honked, jarring Claire out of her nauseated stupor.

She was shaking, and she was about to throw up. "Pull over!" she called out. "I'm going to be sick!"

The driver swerved the taxi to the left and stopped at the curb.

Claire practically tumbled out of the car. She knelt on the sidewalk and vomited as her stomach tried to helplessly expel the memory of Handel violating her again and again.

CHAPTER 24

PAUL HADN'T BEEN to the WAO compound in Redcar for months. When he worked his jobs, he was away for weeks and months at a time. And since the disappearance of Claire, he'd been reassigned to oversee the political projects division, which he'd run out of his London flat.

The sun was still an hour away from rising, so the dusky sky spread a purple-gray behind the glow of the power plant towers. The towers were a blight on the seascape beyond the plant, while at the same time creating a powerful image of modern technology. But the true modern technology lay beneath.

Paul parked the car he'd rented two streets away. Then he locked his backpack in the trunk. He pulled up the hood on his sweatshirt. Anyone seeing him would think he was a jogger out for an early run. A jogger with a bullet wound in his arm. But he hoped he moved reasonably well and convincingly.

He circled the block, keeping an eye out for any vehicles near the power plant. The shift would change over at 7:00 a.m., so he still had a good hour before the workers would be arriving or leaving.

Picking up his pace, he ran along the opposite side of the road from the plant. The chain-link fence, topped with barbed wire meant to keep out rowdy teenagers, was still in place. The south side gates would open by remote for the power plant workers. The north side gates only opened for the WAO employees.

This was the gate that Paul was most interested in. If he activated it with his WAO chip, then his identity would be logged in to the system. His father would know that he'd returned. He already knew Paul was still alive, so that wouldn't be any surprise.

But Paul wouldn't open the gate today; he was saving that for later when his plan was set up.

For now, he needed to know when his father would be inside the compound. It was time for his father to pay for his crimes. When Handel had ordered the hit on Paul's life, that had made it personal. And it was time to settle it between the two of them.

Paul slowed his jog and bent over, as if he were out of breath. He took a couple of steps toward the chain link next to the gate and reached his hands out. Feigning a calf stretch by grasping the fence, Paul slipped on a pair of sunglasses, then he watched the surveillance cameras situated above the door that led to the stairs that descended into the underground compound. The cameras moved slowly, thoroughly scanning the half-dozen meters in front of the door. When the cameras swung wide, Paul slipped out an infrared camera from his sweatshirt pocket and clipped it onto the chain link. The infrared camera would be spotted eventually, but Paul hoped that until then, he'd get plenty of data. The infrared camera would also pick up and record him stretching against the fence. But again, Paul hoped he wouldn't be recognized at first.

He stretched his other calf, taking his time, and then he pushed off the fence and rotated his shoulders. Looking both ways, he crossed the street again, jogging slowly and not looking back.

Once back in his rental car, he drove to the nearest hotel and checked in. His hotel room was small, but Paul wasn't interested in luxury. He set up his laptop on the small, round table, and logged in to the surveillance software, then connected to the infrared camera and started to record. He didn't expect much activity until 7:00 am, when any compound employees needing to relocate would use the momentum and distraction of the power plant workers' shift change as a cover.

He ordered room service, which was sparse, consisting of a couple of eggs and coffee.

The clock switched to seven, and already activity had picked up at the power plant. Nothing much was happening yet on the camera he'd placed, although he was sure the south gate was plenty busy. And then a man emerged into sight. He must have come out of the WAO door. Paul knew the double locks well; they could only be accessed by an actual key, and then on the other side of the heavy steel door was another door that could only be opened by an electronic key. These keys were registered to individual WAO team members and could never be swapped.

The man strode to the gate and typed a code into the keypad on the side of the gate. He stood back as it rolled open, then he continued through. It was Raymond, one of the doctors. Even though he wore a nondescript jacket and a ball cap, the man's broad shoulders and height were a giveaway. Gone were the reading glasses he wore inside the compound.

Soon Raymond was out of sight of what the camera had picked up. Paul wrote down the minutes from the camera recording so that he could go back to the exact time that Raymond had been in view. The next person to exit the compound was a woman.

Paul leaned forward in his chair as he watched Bethany hurry out. She kept her gaze lowered and the hood of her jacket pulled closely about her face. Her skin appeared washed-out, and she held her lips pursed together. Her hand trembled as she reached for the keypad on the gate and typed in the code.

Something had her rattled. More than usual. Perhaps it was an assassination attempt gone wrong?

When she was out of the camera's view, Paul again wrote down the time of her exit.

Then he waited some more, watching the camera's footage as the morning sun lightened the buildings at the power plant, turning them from a mottled gray to a warm ivory. It would be unusual for a WAO employee to leave too long after a shift change, but Paul wasn't going to discount anything.

An hour later, he kept the camera recording as he pulled up the previous footage and paused each frame, one at a time, looking for anything that stood out. He hadn't seen Raymond in a few months, but Raymond had known about the conflict Paul had with his father over Claire. Raymond had been the one to cover for him that night Paul had decked his father.

"You've gone too far," Raymond had told Paul, grabbing him by the arm and pulling him down the corridor away from Claire's room.

Paul's hip and knee were both throbbing from the impact of diving to the floor when his father had aimed a gun at him. The first rule inside the compound was no guns. There was too much risk that a newer member might rebel and retaliate.

Paul shook off Raymond's grasp. "*He's* gone too far."

Raymond said nothing, just continued to walk with Paul. Behind them, a couple of medics had scurried into the room to check on Handel and Claire. Handel had locked the door when he went in to check on Claire.

Everyone had heard Claire's scream, and then Handel had come flying out of the room, his face bright red.

"You should get back there," Paul spat out. "You're the doctor."

Raymond gripped Paul's shoulder and stopped him in the middle of the corridor. They were far enough away from everyone else that there was no risk of being overheard. "Listen to me. I don't like this new line of research either, but for now my hands are tied. Your father's my boss. He has more dirt on me than anyone, and if I lose this job, there's nowhere for me to go."

Paul folded his arms and stared into the man's dark-brown eyes. "He's been torturing her, you know. There are burn marks on her upper arms, and who knows how many drugs he's injected into her in order to monitor brain activity." He shook his head in disgust. "Oh, I guess you'd know how many drugs she'd been given . . . you're the *doctor.*" He spun away and hurried down the corridor.

"Just wait," Raymond hissed, running after him.

Paul stopped at the base of the stairs that led to the upper level of the compound where the employees were housed and fed—well away from the experimenting going on in this lower level.

"This research is groundbreaking," Raymond said. "Before I was a doctor, I was a scientist, so I'm not messing around here. If a drug can be found that will enhance brain activity and enable people to reach higher levels of intellect, we'll all become millionaires."

Paul held up his hand; he didn't need to hear this rhetoric.

But Raymond continued, "Think of how the world will change. The quality of life will be better. We might even be able to figure out how to live on Mars." He pointed down the corridor. "That woman has the perfect genetic makeup for our tests. If we can get her to cooperate, and you to back off, medical advances will go through the roof. Just think of what a team of scientists using their full brain capacity could do to advance the cure for cancer."

At one time, Paul might have been drawn in. But he'd been watching Claire for years. He knew what her parents had contributed to the WAO, what they'd given up when they escaped, and what risks they'd taken by having a child. They just hadn't stayed hidden well enough. When the WAO was focused on its primary mission of keeping the world in checks and balances, that Paul could support. But this new project in the biomedics field of brain study and enhancement? They weren't using white lab rats, but humans. And the WAO had made Claire their first human test subject.

How many others would Handel require Paul to bring in? The other women he'd brought in had agreed to work with the WAO once they were reconditioned and trained on the objectives. But the level of testing had never been as extreme as what Handel was using on Claire.

Paul had a feeling it was more for revenge against her parents for escaping the WAO and hiding out for years. There were other ways to test brain function and capability without putting drug after drug into Claire and submitting her to continued psychoanalysis.

Raymond's eyes had pleaded with Paul to understand—to not fight against his father. But that day, at the base of the stairs in the compound, Paul had lost respect for Raymond. The doctor had gone too far by supporting and enabling Handel.

"I need to get out of here for a while," Paul had told Raymond. "I need to think about this new direction and decide what I'm going to do."

Raymond had given a short nod, as if he agreed with Paul, although they both knew that there was no way out of the WAO. "I think that's best. What do you want me to tell your father?"

"If he asks, tell him I'm starting on Project 312."

Paul needed his father to think he was still on board with everything, despite their altercation. He didn't know what action he'd take concerning Claire, but right now his hands were tied.

Now, as Paul watched Raymond and Bethany on the recorded camera feed, Paul's hand had been forced. His father had made the fatal error of pitting an assassin against him. Paul replayed Raymond's footage again, studying the new wrinkle on his brow, the grim set of his mouth, the slight hunch of his shoulders. Raymond was weighed down by something.

Bethany's footage shouldn't have surprised Paul, but it did. She looked nervous. Her gaze darted behind her more than once, and she checked her phone three times before unlocking the gate. He knew that Raymond and Bethany both parked in different parking lots spread throughout Redcar, and rarely in the same place twice. Their permanent residences were unknown to him, mostly because he'd never bothered to find them. They both spent most of their time inside the compound. But it seemed that this morning, they were both leaving. At the same time.

Paul chewed on his lower lip. Were they leaving at the same time because they were going to meet privately somewhere?

His heart rate jumped. He couldn't know for sure, but something told him that Raymond and Bethany were involved in something that Handel didn't know about. But what?

Paul could never trust Bethany, that he knew, unless he'd been wrong about her for years. As far as he knew, she was his father's puppet and his intimate in everything.

And Raymond . . . He was a yes-man, but if Paul told the truth, Raymond had never done him a disservice. He'd helped diffuse the situation between father and son, which later enabled Paul to get Claire out of the WAO before it was too late.

Perhaps it *had* been too late for Claire after all. Despite what Nora had told him, all indicators about Claire now showed that she'd never pieced back together her shattered heart. Even the strongest and most intellectual mind would have trouble surviving the grief Handel had put Claire through.

Paul's life as he knew it was coming to an end. He could no longer operate under his father. Their ideals had grown apart. A few months ago, or even a few days ago, Paul might have done almost anything to keep the WAO above board and away from any infiltration.

But now, he knew the rotting base of the WAO was about to crumble. And he was going to help Claire. The problem was, she'd never trust him. So he had to help her without her knowing it.

Paul rose from his chair and pulled on his jacket, then grabbed the backpack with his sniper rifle. It was time to get answers—the real answers about his father's intentions for him. He was going after Raymond and Bethany. And if they were together, even better.

CHAPTER 25

"ARE YOU GOING to be all right?" the taxi driver asked Claire.

She nodded, her body still trembling, but at least there was nothing else to vomit. The driver eyed her doubtfully as he stood on the sidewalk holding the car door open for her as she climbed out.

He'd driven her the rest of the way to Redcar after all, probably because he felt sorry for her.

She dug out some cash from her bag and handed it over.

The driver took it and said, "Do you want help with your bag?" He glanced over at the hotel Claire had directed him to.

She exhaled and said, "It's just the one bag, so I'll be fine. Thank you."

The driver climbed back into the taxi and drove away while Claire made her way into the hotel entrance. Human kindness hadn't always been a part of her world, so she appreciated it when it happened.

Once she got into her room, Claire drew the drapes shut and turned on all the lights. She looked out the window, where she had a corner view of the power plant. Searching her memory, she couldn't come up with anything that looked familiar about what she saw.

If she walked around it, would she remember anything? She still wasn't entirely sure if Paul had sent her on a dummy chase. But she did know that she couldn't go to the power plant now, not yet . . .

She turned on the shower to the hottest temperature she could stand. The water reddened her skin, and she stayed beneath the spray until the temperature tapered off.

She twisted a towel around her head and wrapped herself up in the hotel robe. Her resistance had completely gone, so she took one of the few sleeping pills she carried with her. It would only give her three or four hours of sleep, but her body had exhausted itself from her PTSD episode.

She lay down on the bed, pulled a pillow against her stomach to press against the emptiness, and stared at the ceiling. *Please, sleep, come. Hurry.*

Even though Claire closed her eyes, sleep was slow in coming. The medication wasn't quick enough to shut out her looping memories of the morning she'd awakened ill in the compound. She'd vomited all over herself because she was strapped to her bed as usual. She hadn't seen Handel for a several weeks after he'd assaulted her, and she'd been more than happy with that, although she feared his return each night when she went to bed. Nothing would stop him from revisiting her any time he chose to.

The medics knew what had happened because they found her the next morning with her legs tied to the bed, her sheets stained. She wondered if Paul knew, and if he did, if he'd confront his father.

Claire's illness didn't abate, and the medics seemed concerned, but Bethany still demanded that she continue the rigors of testing.

So Claire spent her days taking tests, being shot up with different drugs, taking more tests, going through brain scans, and being fed a minimal diet. She continued to feel lethargic and nauseated most of the time, until she finally knew.

Her menstrual cycles had been light since her arrival at the compound, but now they had stopped altogether. When Dr. Raymond came into her room one evening, he said, "Bethany tells me you've complained of headaches today."

Claire had lied to Bethany so that the doctor would visit. "I need a pregnancy test."

Raymond stared at her, then blinked and looked down. His dark skin had reddened. "Are . . . are you sure?"

He wasn't going to pretend he didn't know she'd been raped, was he?

"The test will confirm it," Claire said in a cold voice.

Raymond left the room, and moments later he returned with a needle to withdraw blood. Again he left, and Claire stared at the ceiling while he was gone. All the signs were there. But would life be so cruel to her? It was bad enough that she was living in this hell.

When Raymond stepped into the room, Claire knew by the look on his face before he uttered a word.

She kept the tears back as he said, "You tested positive." His eyes seemed to look right through her. "This may change some things for the next few months." He hesitated. "What's the date of your last menses?"

Claire just turned her head away. He knew. He was the doctor. Nothing went on physically that he and the other medics didn't know about.

He left her alone then, and the tears came hot and fast.

She wanted to purge the being growing inside of her. She hated everything about the man who'd done this to her, and now she had to continue to pay the price. She finally fell asleep, exhausted from sobbing.

The days passed, and she started to think of the child as hers, and hers alone. The child was innocent, and if her child was to have any chance at all, Claire had to escape.

The day soon came that Handel walked into her room, his face spread into a smile.

Claire was alone, strapped in her chair as she finished the last test of the day. The new drug they'd given her that morning had made her dizzy, but nothing more. They hadn't given her strong drugs since the pregnancy test.

She looked up when her door opened. Everything inside of her froze when she saw the man who entered.

"Dr. Raymond has told me of your condition," Handel said, stepping into the room and closing the door behind him.

Claire gripped the edge of the desk. He knew. And they were alone again. She was still too weak to fight him off, but that didn't mean she wouldn't try.

"Dr. Raymond has advised that *all* drug testing should stop until you deliver the child," he said, his eyes scanning her thin form, then settling on the swell of her stomach that was obvious through her stretchy T-shirt.

Claire felt like a horde of spiders had just crawled across her skin.

Handel shook his head good-naturedly. "Who would have thought? I suppose you needed the extra reminder." He flashed his perfectly white teeth in a smile and stepped closer, close enough that she could smell cinnamon and antiseptic.

She wanted to throw up.

His hand rested on her shoulder, warm and heavy.

"Bethany tells me that you've been working very hard," Handel said. "We've gathered a good amount of data, and we hope to launch the new drug in a few months. Although now we'll be pushing back that timeline, of course." He exhaled, and the hairs on her neck stood up.

His hand tightened on her shoulder. "But if I hear you've reverted to your old stubbornness, then I'm happy to refresh your memory of our last encounter."

She felt his hot breath against her neck, so she squeezed her eyes shut. If he moved one inch closer, she'd jerk her head back and crack his skull.

But Handel lifted his hand and stepped away. She didn't hear his departing words before he left the room because blood was roaring in her ears, drowning out all sound. Her head fell forward, and she focused on breathing in and out until her hands were steady enough to continue the test.

When Claire woke up in the Redcar hotel room, it took a few seconds for her to orient herself and to realize she'd been crying as she'd slept. She sat up, still hugging the pillow to her hollow stomach where she'd once carried her child. The generation before and after her were both gone. She was all that was left now.

Claire climbed off the bed and crossed to the window. The late afternoon sun was mottled by passing clouds, and the wind whipped the trees planted in increments along the sidewalk. It was time to walk to the power plant, to find out if she could remember anything.

She drew on her jacket, pulled up the hood, and pocketed her gun. Outside the hotel, she walked briskly, passing a few people but not making eye contact. When she reached the power plant, it was obvious that the place was well secured. There were two main gates and one smaller one, but both were shut and appeared to be locked.

Steam billowed from one of the towers, and the lights were on in a long single-story building. A row of about a half-dozen cars and trucks were parked inside the plant's lot, separated from the street by a chain-link fence.

Claire walked at a slow pace, checking her phone often, pretending to be texting but actually snapping up close photos. She also kept an eye on the structure of the fence, the multiple gates, and most interestingly, the security cameras, which were focused on the gates, a couple of the entrances to the building, another entrance to a tower, and at the corners of the fence.

For a power plant, they sure hadn't skimped on security.

She slowed her step. A very small infrared camera had been clipped onto the chain-link fence by the north gate. It looked like a temporary fix for something, and it seemed to be focused on the entrance to the tower.

Claire studied the camera while pretending to check her phone. Someone else was watching the tower door. She lifted her phone and used her tracking app to sync to the device. Then she saved the frequency so that she could tap into the video feed from her laptop.

Satisfied that she'd made some headway, she hurried back to her hotel.

Now wasn't the time to wallow in her abuse and torture at the compound or dwell on the greatest loss of her life. She needed to find out why that camera was there and what it meant.

CHAPTER 26

PAUL SLUNG HIS backpack containing his sniper rifle over his shoulder when he saw Claire's face suddenly appear in front of the camera recording on his laptop. He froze, wondering if he'd just had some weird sort of vision. But she was still there, and she was examining the camera. Oh. She'd just synced her phone to it.

Sliding the backpack from his shoulder, he took a seat in front of the laptop. He shouldn't have been surprised at how quickly she'd located the power plant and his camera. Claire's face looked too thin, too pale, and the dark circles beneath her hazel eyes were pronounced. In short, she looked like she was barely the woman she used to be ... the woman Paul had brought to the WAO.

He didn't feel guilty for his part; no, it had been his job for too many years. But his father's actions had been reprehensible, almost from the beginning.

Through Raymond, Paul found out that his father had been obsessed with Claire's mother, Kathryn, one of their top operatives. Raymond had thought the obsession would pass, but as the months went on, Handel stayed interested in her.

Eventually, Raymond discovered Kathryn was in a relationship with one of the other doctors, Trent Vetra. And the two had secretly married.

When Handel discovered the truth, he relocated Trent to another division. Paul assumed that's when Kathryn and Trent started to plan their escape. It had been the first time in the history of the WAO that anyone had left without repercussions. Those would come ten years later.

Paul hadn't known about the hunt for Kathryn and Trent until he joined the WAO after school. By then, it had gone on for ten years. The pair had been clever and had gone underground completely. But Handel hadn't given up, and the day when that first lead came in, Paul had been in a board meeting with his father.

Handel had turned around his laptop with a triumphant smile. "Our imaging software just picked up a match to Trent Vetra."

Paul peered at the file that had been located. He knew the name, of course, but his father had always insisted on being the project lead on the case. It seemed that a local newspaper distributed in a New York suburb had run a piece about a music festival.

Handel's finger moved across the screen. "And look at that, right behind him is Kathryn and a little girl. Surely that's their daughter." His gaze locked with Paul's.

"This is your number one project now," he said. "Find out everything about them."

Paul had wanted to argue, but not in front of the other board members. The pair had left the WAO in a clean break, at least as far as he knew. They hadn't ever exposed any intel, and it seemed they wanted to raise a family and live a normal life.

Handel noticed Paul's hesitation. "You know our policies. Do you need a reminder?"

"Of course not," Paul said. "I was just strategizing."

"You're excused from this meeting."

As Paul walked out of the conference room, he knew that Trent Vetra and his wife, Kathryn, were as good as sitting ducks. Paul would do his job, and he'd do it well. Within weeks, he'd have a complete profile on the young family, and his father would have his revenge. Handel never extended mercy.

That, Paul knew well. It was why his birth mother had gone to an early grave.

Paul knew he could never atone to Claire for his part in locating her parents and then subsequently bringing her to the WAO, but he could at least give her what she wanted now. He could become the first step in dismantling his father's empire.

Pulling up the email address she'd given him, he sent a message.

I saw you on camera. Let's talk.

The reply came quickly.

I'll see you dead first.

Well then. Paul leaned back in his chair. Sooner or later, Claire would make her attempt to break into the compound, and Paul would be there to help her.

He picked up the backpack again. He'd be able to access the video footage from his phone, but he left the laptop recording the feed. Once he was back in his car, he tried a new strategy and called the man he probably should have contacted long before now.

"Raymond here," the doctor answered on the second ring.

"We need to meet."

"Paul?" Raymond exhaled, and Paul didn't know if the doctor was relieved or frustrated.

"Surprised to hear from me?" Paul asked. "Kind of like speaking from the grave?"

Raymond was silent for a moment. "Just tell me where and when."

"Thirty minutes," Paul said, even though he wasn't sure where Raymond was right now. "The parking lot behind the bank. Look for a black car."

Raymond didn't hesitate this time. "All right."

Paul was early, and Raymond was a few minutes late. The man strode from around the bank, spotted Paul's car, and climbed in the passenger side. He extended his hands, supposedly to prove that he was unarmed. Paul didn't believe it for a minute, but he couldn't waste any more time.

Paul had had very few interactions with Raymond since Claire's disappearance. Paul had worked offsite from the compound and only came in for essential meetings. Raymond's dark hair was now streaked with plenty of gray, and he'd grown a short goatee.

"Who are the people my father sent after me?" Paul asked.

Raymond glanced at Paul with his dark eyes, then looked forward, through the windshield. "Richard Oakey and Sylvia Wright."

"And Claire's sudden and surprising appearance gives my father warrant to go after me?" Paul tried to keep the emotion out of his voice but knew he'd failed.

Raymond went very still. "I think we both knew it would come to this eventually."

Paul nodded. The doctor was probably right. The day that his father ordered him to profile a set of parents with a young daughter had been the beginning of the end. "You work for my father, so why are you here?"

The doctor turned his head to look Paul fully in the eye. "You work for your father too."

"Fair enough," Paul said. "But that doesn't tell me if I can trust you."

Raymond reached inside his pocket, and Paul wondered if he was about to be faced with the barrel of a gun. Instead, Raymond pulled out his cell phone. He brought up a picture and turned the phone so that Paul could see it.

He'd known Raymond was married and assumed he might have a kid or two, but Raymond had never spoken of his family. The picture was at a park, and Raymond had a little girl on his shoulders, smiling down at him. Next to him, a tall, lithe woman was laughing.

"Olivia left me," Raymond said. "She took our daughter and said she didn't want our child growing up with a mobster for a father." His voice dropped. "I couldn't explain what my job is to my own wife. All she saw were the cash-only payments. The gun I had to carry. The security system I insisted be in our home. The days I was out of communication."

Paul swallowed against the tightness in his throat. "I'm sorry."

Raymond only nodded.

"My father hired an assassin to kill me," Paul said. "What would you do?"

Raymond pocketed his cell phone. "I can't tell you what to do, but I'm making plans to get out." His gaze locked with Paul's.

Raymond would have to change his identity and go undercover for the rest of his life—or Handel's life.

Paul knew exactly what Raymond was telling him, was agreeing with. Raymond wanted out too.

"Bethany is gone for several hours," Raymond continued. "Your father is locked down in his suite monitoring your search alert."

"And?"

"And . . . I can get you inside that suite."

Paul exhaled. "That's all I need to know."

Raymond reached for the car door handle.

"Wait," Paul said. "I won't be alone."

Raymond's gaze snapped back to Paul's. "Claire?"

"Yes."

"I don't really see her working with anyone," Raymond said in a careful voice.

"We're not working together, officially," Paul said. "My father isn't the only one who's out to get me. But I owe her this."

Raymond's brows shot up. "You've changed, Paul. What brought this on?'

If Paul could define it, he would. Perhaps the deepest part of him knew that it was due to his one mistake—the several days he'd spent tracking down where Handel had sent Claire's child. He had found only one email in which an anonymous sender had sent Handel a picture of a young boy playing soccer. The boy's back was to the camera, but Paul had no doubt it had been sent to Handel for a reason. The boy was Claire and Handel's son. Paul couldn't forget the picture of the kid. Playing soccer was such an ordinary part of a kid's life but so foreign and distant to Paul's experience as a child.

Here was a young child who didn't know his mother. He didn't know how hard his mother had fought to survive and for him to survive.

Handel didn't know that Paul knew that the child was alive and seemingly healthy. It might be the one way that Paul could get Claire to trust him.

CHAPTER 27

CLAIRE COULDN'T SLEEP. The video feed on her laptop showed no comings or goings from the tower door, but all indications pointed to this compound being the right place. If Paul had placed the infrared camera, did that mean he'd been watching for her? Or had the camera been placed by someone else?

Regardless, the lead was solid enough that Claire had to get the address to someone, even if that someone wouldn't be able to help her in time.

Before trying to sleep she'd set into motion a tracking search on the financial information she'd taken from the pub. She hoped the account numbers would have matched up by now, but the software was still churning away.

Claire dialed Agent Hales's number. Hers would show as unlisted on the agent's caller ID. "Summer?" Hales answered.

"Thanks for picking up," Claire said. "I have an address to give you, and if you don't hear from me in a couple of days, then you can search for my body there."

"What's going on?" Hales's voice held alarm, although it was calmly schooled.

"I think I've found the WAO headquarters," Claire said. "The only way to confirm is to go inside."

"Hold on," Hales said. "We talked about this. We can protect you at a safe house—there's no need for you to hunt down these locations. You need to let due process happen. If you go in, not only are you risking your life, it gives them time to cover up and relocate before we can finish preparing our case against them."

Claire was listening, and in a better world it might make sense. But she was sitting in an unsecured hotel room, vulnerable from all sides. Claire knew that she might not get out of this city alive. Paul had seen her. He might be closing in on her at that moment, and right behind him would be Handel, or Bethany, or any of the others who would think nothing of taking her life. If she died too soon, all her efforts would be in vain.

"Here's the address," Claire started, then recited the address. "I'm only going to say it once more, and then I'm hanging up. This phone line will no longer be active. I'll contact you through email next time." If there was a next time.

Agent Hales went silent as Claire gave her the address.

Claire hung up just as she promised. She removed the SIM card from her phone and melted it with a lighter, then left the puddled plastic in the ashtray.

But before she made her way into the compound or Paul broke down her hotel room door, she planned to send as much information as she could on Handel, Paul, Bethany, and Raymond to Agent Hales. She hoped that if she died inside the compound, the information she'd gotten to Agent Hales would be a strong start.

But two hours later, the few unencrypted files she could transfer showed little about the personalities behind the organization.

Claire next pulled up an imaging software that she'd messed around with before. She typed in specifics of Handel's description, then adjusted the parameters, creating a sketch such as a police sketch artist might do. The image was rough, but there was at least a likeness.

She continued to work on images of Bethany, Paul, and Raymond. Then she emailed all of them over to Agent Hales.

Her tears started to fall then, and Claire angrily brushed them away. What was wrong with her? Coming back to London had screwed with her emotions like a hot knife twisting in her gut. Her flashbacks had been under control for a long time, but now she felt a heaviness settle over her.

She took out the final SIM card she'd brought and slipped it into her phone, then went through her apps and reactivated everything. She caught sight of the date, and her breathing almost stopped.

It was her child's birthday. Six years before, she'd given birth on this day.

"It's a boy," Dr. Raymond had said in the quietest of voices when the other medics were busy cleaning up the room.

Claire had been in labor all through the night, and in the early morning hours, she'd finally delivered. Her body had been exhausted, but elation swept through her when she completed the final push and heard the cry of her child.

She'd tried to sit up to see her baby, but the medic standing next to her placed a strong hand on her shoulder. "There's still a lot of cleanup and stitching," she'd said.

Claire had looked into the expressionless eyes of the nurse, wondering how anyone could voluntarily work in the WAO.

But Claire's happiness wouldn't erode just yet. "Is he healthy?" she asked Dr. Raymond. "When can I hold him?"

Raymond's eyes locked with hers, and in his gaze she saw the answer.

"No," Claire started. "He can't take away my baby!" She started to scream just as the medic gave her an injection.

The baby's cries matched her own, but Claire's world faded to dark.

When she awoke next, hours had passed. She'd been cleaned up and moved back to her bedroom. She was, once again, strapped to the bed, something that she'd hadn't been subjected to in the last trimester of her pregnancy.

She'd closed her eyes against the sterile room, unable to stop her bitter tears from falling.

Her stomach was empty, hollow, as if she hadn't eaten for days, but she knew she couldn't eat a thing. The child she'd bonded with, although in utero, was gone. Ironically, it was her arms that ached the most, as if she'd held the child's weight in her arms. But she'd never held the little boy. *My little boy.*

She'd wanted to curl on her side and breathe her last breath. Three days passed, and no one bothered her except to bring food that she barely touched and to escort her to the bathroom. At one point, she took a shower. On the fourth day, she was strapped to her chair and set back to work, new drugs being pumped into her system.

The next morning, she refused to get out of bed. Her milk had come in despite whatever medication they'd given her, and her breasts throbbed with each movement. There was nothing they could do to her anymore. She had nothing to live for. Her child was gone. Her parents. Her freedom.

The medics dragged her out of bed and strapped her to the chair, then pushed her in front of her computer monitor.

Bethany's face appeared on the screen, and she didn't look happy.

Claire simply closed her eyes and blocked out the threats from Bethany.

An hour later, Handel strode into the room. His face was flushed with anger, and his eyes bulged. "You little whore," he'd said, grabbing her hair and snapping her head back.

Claire spit in his face.

He'd slapped her then, but Claire welcomed the pain. It felt good to hurt.

That was when Paul had interfered, and Handel had tried to shoot his own son.

Paul's whispered words of "Be patient, I'm going to get you out of here," had little effect. She didn't trust Paul either.

When Claire refused to cooperate the following day, she'd been moved to isolation.

She didn't know how long she was in isolation, but it couldn't have been more than a couple of days, because her hunger strike didn't kill her.

"I'm going to put a bag over your head," Paul's voice spoke in her ear.

At first, Claire thought it was a dream, but then her body shifted. Someone was picking her up. The darkness of the isolation room morphed into a gray. And that's when she realized she was being carried somewhere, and light was filtering through the bag over her head.

"Don't make a sound," Paul said. "You'll be in a safe place soon."

Claire couldn't have spoken or yelled out if she'd wanted to. Her voice was completely hoarse. And she literally had no strength to try to get away from Paul. Where he was taking her, she couldn't guess. But she did guess that she'd just become a pawn in some sick game between father and son.

Paul set her down on a sort of cushion, and Claire realized it was the back seat of a car.

"If you can stay still and not make a sound, then I won't be forced to drug you," Paul said, his voice hovering somewhere over her sightless eyes.

The temperature had changed. It was warm, and the air was moist and fragrant. Gone was the antiseptic smell, replaced by fresh air and the scent of flowering bushes of some type.

Claire nestled into the cushion, not caring if she survived whatever trip Paul was taking her on. Perhaps she was dreaming after all. Or perhaps this was an alternate reality of life after death. How depressing that would be.

The journey seemed to last a lifetime, although Claire had no idea how long they drove.

Voices moved around her when she was next conscious.

"She's malnourished," a woman said, her tone sharp. "Why would your father do this to a recruit?"

Paul's answer was indistinguishable.

Her arm was lifted and an IV inserted into her vein. Within moments, Claire's body started to react to the fluid.

She didn't want to revive. She didn't want to be healed and remember her losses.

The bag was removed from her head, and a warm yellow light flooded Claire's senses.

"Can you hear me, Claire?" the woman said. "Can you open your eyes?"

Almost against her will, as if her body had its own mind, Claire's eyes opened slowly. The lighting was soft, muted, and the woman looking down at her had copper-colored hair and hazel eyes.

Claire was most aware of the smells. A faint floral—lilac and rosemary.

"Hello, Claire," the woman said, her mouth lifting into an approving smile. "I'm Irene. Welcome back to life. You'll never have to worry about Handel Raine again."

First of all, Claire didn't believe this woman. Secondly, where was she now, and where was Paul?

She turned her head to take in the rest of the room. The place looked more like a living room than a hospital room, but the machinery told Claire that she was in some sort of clinic. Two windows scaled the other side of the room, and for the first time in a year, she saw the blue-gray sky.

Her body started to tremble. It was too much. She wanted to be back in the isolation room where she could waste away and forget that she'd ever lived.

"My God, they used you as a pin cushion," the woman continued, her mouth thinning into a stern line.

Claire realized then that her filthy clothing had been removed and she lay naked beneath a striped sheet. Irene touched the top of her shoulder, and Claire flinched.

"It's all right," the woman said in a soothing tone. "I just want to look at your arm."

Claire held still, not really caring what might happen to her next.

Irene paused. "Can I examine you?"

Claire lifted her shoulder in a shrug.

Over the next while, Irene examined Claire, not exactly keeping her comments to herself. When she finished, Irene said, "We're going to take care of you, Claire. You'll feel stronger than ever, and one day, you'll be able to see justice served. Poetic justice. If there's one thing we do here at the Amazon Sisterhood, it's correcting injustices."

Claire moved her lips. She wasn't sure exactly what she had wanted to say, but no words would come out.

Irene gave her a small smile. "You must be patient."

Irene's words now echoed in Claire's mind. She had been patient, for years. She'd healed and recovered with the Amazon Sisterhood. But she'd never forgotten. Everything she learned at their château, she'd remembered and stored away so that she could bring down the WAO once and for all. When she found out that the Amazon Sisterhood had no intention of taking down Handel Raine for his crimes against her, Claire had known her time with the Sisterhood was limited.

Claire straightened as a movement on the video feed on her laptop caught her attention. Someone was going through the gate at the power plant. A man was walking, quickly, toward the tower door.

It wasn't anyone that Claire recognized, but she watched as the person opened the door to the tower by tapping in a code, then entered the building.

Claire glanced at the top of the screen. It was three thirty in the morning.

She stayed hypervigilant for the next couple of hours, watching the screen and not allowing her mind to fade into more memories. At seven a.m. she was finally rewarded for her patience.

She caught a glimpse of the man who'd been in her nightmares for seven years.

Handel Raine stepped out of the tower and closed the door behind him. In the faint morning light, combined with the infrared strength of the video recording, Claire could see that he'd aged.

His dark eyes were the same, but his square face had filled out so that it was more rounded now. His clothing fit snugly, as if he'd recently gained weight, and his torso was definitely heavier. Handel's hair had thinned to partial balding. She couldn't help but look at his hands—the hands that she remembered too well. Long fingers that had hurt her.

Claire didn't breathe as she watched the man she hated walk toward the camera, oblivious that he was being recorded and that Claire, and most likely Paul, were watching him.

As Handel neared the camera, he veered off to the side, so the last image Claire saw of him was his profile. Her stomach tightened and felt like it was slowly turning inside out. When Handel passed through the gate and completely disappeared from view, Claire ran to the bathroom and heaved into the toilet.

She rinsed out her mouth with the sink water and closed her eyes for several moments. Why was Paul watching the entrance of the compound? Didn't he have full access? Couldn't he meet with his father whenever he wanted to? Or were father and son pitted against each other?

Now that there was no doubt the power plant was the location of the WAO compound, it was time to put the second phase of her plan into action.

CHAPTER 28

CLAIRE'S MIND REELED as she took her place in front of her laptop. Handel Raine had just left the compound. For a moment she worried that he'd been tipped off to her presence. Maybe he was coming to find her. Maybe Paul had set this all up to bring Claire to Redcar. The minutes passed, and no one came to her hotel room. If Handel was hunting her down, he wasn't in any hurry.

Or maybe Handel had found out what she sent over to Agent Hales, and he was leaving the compound to go incognito somewhere. Well, if that were the case, then Claire would continue in her pursuit. She knew the location of the compound now, but most of the damage she'd planned she'd be doing right from her laptop.

She took a sip of the lukewarm coffee that had sat on the table all night to steady her nerves. Then she rose again and crossed to the window. Gazing across the gray street, she wished she had a better view of the power plant. But from her position, she could see only one corner, and it wasn't where Handel Raine had exited. Was he already in a car? Walking to a parking lot? Had he seen the camera after all?

Claire paced the room for several moments, thinking. Every sound from outside and inside the hotel made her flinch. She expected that at any moment Paul or his father would be busting down the hotel room door. Even with her habit of changing cell phones, Paul had nearly found her that first time.

She picked up the mug of coffee and washed it down the drain in the bathroom sink. Then she filled up the mug with water and drank long and deep.

She was still shaking. She didn't want to take any medication that might cloud her mind or make her sleepy. She hadn't slept all night, but now wasn't the time to give in to her exhaustion.

Her email pinged, and she pulled up another communication from Paul. Unbelievable.

My father has left the compound, he said. *I'm going in to wait for his return. I can get you inside.*

Claire stared at the words. Then she let her fingers hover over the keyboard for a few moments. *What makes you think I want to return to the compound?*

Closure, Paul replied.

Claire grimaced. He was right. That's why she was here. Whether or not she lived to breathe another day, she wanted Handel to pay once and for all for his crimes.

I don't need to be inside the compound to get closure, she wrote back. She could watch the implosion from her laptop. At least in the beginning. She knew she'd never fully heal with Handel still alive. She logged out of the email so that she couldn't see the alerts of any more incoming messages.

She accessed her private server and pulled down the articles she'd written over the past year detailing everything she knew about the WAO, both from living inside the compound and from her hacking while with the Amazon Sisterhood.

She had cobbled together profiles of the main players, including Handel, Bethany, Paul, and Dr. Raymond, among others. Now, she edited each article, adding the address of the compound and the fact that it was accessible through the tower door.

Claire didn't need to go through that door and down the steep flight of stairs she knew was there in order to confirm the compound's existence. Handel Raine's presence told her everything she needed to know.

After creating the exposé, she copied over her collection of email addresses of journalists from around the world, then sent a blast. Two hundred and fifty journalists would get her article about how the WAO manipulated riots and demonstrations, manipulated the rise and fall of the stock market, and pushed through approvals for untested medical equipment. Even if only half of the journalists opened their emails and only 10 percent of that number actually followed through and did some of their own investigation, it was enough to get the buzz going.

Elation rushed through her, and for a moment, she couldn't believe she'd actually gotten to this point after years of preparation.

She checked her tracking software and found that it had come up with four hits—four bank accounts that were linked between Hughes & Ross and the WAO. Claire smiled as she hacked into each account, then set up wire transfer requests of twenty-five dollars each to funnel into hundreds of charity organizations. It would take an investigator years to track down all the donations.

At this time tomorrow, Handel Raine would wake up to a different world.

She emailed Agent Hales the four account numbers with a message that Hales might want to see where the WAO's laundered money was held, and the information that Claire had laundered it again.

Hales's reply was almost immediate. *Call me. You will dig yourself in so deep that not even I can help you.*

Claire deleted the message, then hacked into the second account that the software had produced. It was a small bank in Germany. Claire started the wire transfer process, copying and pasting in the account numbers the money would be sent to.

Sooner or later, the account owner would be called by the bank about the unusual activity, but the typical bank fraud department wouldn't catch on right away. And by the time it did, millions of dollars would already be distributed, and it would take an entire team to investigate each transfer.

By the time Claire hacked into the third account discovered by the tracking software, she was fighting off a stabbing headache. She knew she needed to eat, to sleep, and to let her eyes rest. But with the power plant across the street and who knew how long until either Handel or Paul discovered her location, she couldn't take any sort of break.

Rubbing her temples with one hand, Claire continued to cut and paste account numbers with her other hand. The stabs of pain in her head intensified, and Claire knew she was in danger of giving in to a migraine. The signs were all there. She'd had them regularly at the Amazon Sisterhood château when she'd first arrived.

Irene had found Claire crying, sitting curled up on the window seat of the clinic the morning after she'd arrived.

"Let's get you back to bed," Irene had said, grasping her arm.

Claire instinctively recoiled from the woman's touch, but when she looked into Irene's hazel eyes, she forced herself to relax. "It's just a headache," she said. "I've been in bed long enough."

"You're shaking, honey," Irene continued, squatting in front of Claire so that they were at eye level. "It's not just a headache. You might be having a migraine, or perhaps withdrawals. Although Paul said that in isolation you hadn't been given any drugs for several days."

Claire clamped her hands over her ears. "Don't say his name."

Irene went silent, although she remained where she was, crouched in front of Claire.

"I—I'll be fine," Claire finally said, wiping the tears that had fallen onto her cheeks.

"All right," Irene said. "I'll bring in your lunch, and then you might try to take a nap."

Claire nodded, but when Irene returned with a plate of fresh greens, sliced oranges, and a vinaigrette dressing, Claire didn't touch the food. Her head pain had sharpened, and she could barely move.

Irene returned to see that she hadn't eaten.

"I can get you some pain medication," Irene said, settling on the floor next to Claire.

"No medication," Claire said. Although the bright light of the room exasperated her migraine, she didn't want the lights off. The dark would be worse. Claire didn't want to take anything, not even for pain that was making her cry.

Irene took Claire's hand in hers. This time Claire didn't pull away.

"When your body heals, we can work on the rest," Irene said. "You can tell me anything you want. Or we can just sit together and not worry about talking."

Claire nodded at this. Not talking sounded good.

It was more than a week before she would leave the clinic, and when she did, she found the gardens surrounding the château were like little corners of paradise. Irene spent a lot of time with her, and Claire wasn't exactly sure at first if she was a doctor, a therapist, or just an employee of the Amazon Sisterhood.

"Can I leave?" Claire asked her one day while they sat in her assigned bedroom together. Her body had healed, but she couldn't stop her hands from shaking whenever she thought of the WAO compound.

"Do you want to leave?" Irene said.

"I don't want to be here, but I don't know where else to go," Claire said, looking down at her hands. "I feel like an empty shell. I don't think I could manage Columbia University—if they'd even take me back. My scholarship has expired. And what do I tell them? I lived in captivity for a year and was treated like a lab rat, but I'd still be a good addition to their biomedics program?"

Irene waited several moments to answer, as if she were selecting her words carefully. "You've been through a lot, and you've changed from who you used to be. But we could use your talents here, at the Sisterhood. We have work teams that you might be interested in joining."

"Who are on these teams?" Claire asked.

"Other women who are in need of our aide," Irene said in a quiet voice. "We rescue women from sex trafficking, the slave trade, and other abusive situations. We run recovery homes for addicts and homeless women who need to get back on their feet. We help women who need a second, or third, or fourth chance."

Claire nodded at this. "You're a group of Mother Teresa's?"

Irene smiled. "She's definitely someone we all look up to.

But our purposes are quite different from those of Mother Teresa."

Claire was interested. In fact, it was the first time she'd felt true hope since her child had been taken away. "Is this one of those ancient orders that have been kept secret since the Amazons?" she asked.

"You might say that the Amazons are the *inspiration*," Irene said. "But we don't date quite as far back as Herodotus in the fifth century BC. Only to the nineties, I'm afraid."

"What happened then?" Claire asked.

"Our director, Nora Mickelson, is a former archaeologist," Irene continued. "She was on a joint US-Russian archaeology team when they excavated a two-thousand-year-old burial site. They discovered graves belonging to warrior women who'd been buried with their weapons."

"Where was this?" Claire asked.

"Outside of Pokrovka, near the Kazakhstan border."

"Isn't that a long way from Greece, the famed home of the Amazon women?"

"It is quite a distance, but perhaps this group was a branch or found inspiration from the legends," Irene said.

"So, one grave, and Nora was on a new mission?"

Irene gave a small laugh. "It wasn't all that easy. Nora had been through a lot of things herself before she got out of a bad situation. The field of archaeology helped her put her own past behind her while she explored the past of other civilizations, but she still wanted to do something more. She knew many women who had come through severe trials, and some of them needed help and support, while others wanted to band together to make life better. She was inspired by the women who were buried with their weapons. Some of them were found with things like arrowheads embedded in their skeletons."

"And still women have to fight for their rights in the modern world," Claire said, looking down at her hands. Hands that had been useless when it came to keeping her child. "What was Nora trying to escape?"

"She was married before," Irene said. "And she blames her ex-husband for her son's death."

Claire snapped her head up and stared at Irene. Her words echoed through the deepest part of her heart.

"Yes," Irene said, looking away. "Nora recruited only women who could invest their full time into building the Amazon Sisterhood. It's more than a job or career—it's a lifestyle."

Claire nodded. "What if I want to leave?"

"You can walk out right now," Irene said. "But first, we'd offer you a place on the outside to stay and get back on your feet. We offer benefits such as education scholarships, rent-free apartments for the first year, and entry-level jobs with our affiliates."

Claire went silent. The Amazon Sisterhood didn't run on charity. Someone was funding all of those offers. "Where does the money come from?"

"Ah," Irene said. "I'm not privy to all the business and financial details, but I do know that Nora had quite a bit from her divorce settlement—or so I've heard. Also, the Sisterhood has ways of recuperating money that's, uh, been lost in other ways. The Sisterhood has a team that spends all their time on funneling money before it can be used in criminal activities."

Claire was surprised at this. Perhaps the Sisterhood wasn't as benevolent as Irene was making it out to be.

"We know about your photographic memory, Claire," Irene said.

Claire stiffened. Her eidetic memory had turned her into a lab rat for the WAO.

"You, of course, are welcome to join the team that

interests you the most," Irene continued. "But we'd like to try you in our computer forensics division."

It wasn't what Claire was expecting her to say. "What exactly is computer forensics?" She could write a college research paper and throw together an accounting spreadsheet for a simple budget, but beyond that she didn't count herself as a computer expert.

"The layman's term is hacking," Irene said. "But here at the Amazon Sisterhood, it's much more sophisticated than sitting in a cubicle and typing in code."

Hacking—as in breaking into company security systems to mine information. The small hope that had begun to grow within her now blossomed into a series of ideas. If she learned computer forensics, then she might finally have a weapon against Handel Raine.

CHAPTER 29

AFTER RAYMOND LEFT, Paul watched the camera feed from his phone. When his father exited the power plant, Paul knew that the countdown had begun. He started his car and drove quickly to the area, just in time to see his father's car pull out up the street. His father was driving, which surprised Paul, but then again it might be something new he did. Paul hadn't been to the compound for several months, so protocols might have changed.

When Handel turned toward the coastline, Paul frowned. He'd expected his father to drive into one of the bigger cities. His father continued driving up the coast for nearly an hour and then turned into a neighborhood.

As far as Paul knew, his father didn't have a residence in this area. The place was too suburban anyway. Neighbors would know one another's business, which would never do for Handel.

Paul stopped a couple of hundred meters away from where Handel pulled up next to a small house. His father sat in the car for several moments, as if debating whether to get out.

Across the street from where his father had stopped, a woman came out of a house, holding the hand of a boy of about six or seven. The boy was crying, and the woman seemed to be scolding him. Then a man came out of the house and called to the woman and the crying boy, holding up an object.

The boy's face transformed, and he let go of his mother's hand and ran toward the man. The kid snatched up the toy and then wrapped his arms around the man's legs. The man grinned and patted the boy's head.

Then the mother ushered the boy into the car in the driveway, and moments later, she reversed and pulled out. She turned down the street and drove right past Handel. Then right past Paul. Without looking at either car.

Paul wasn't so interested in the blonde woman and her faint brows and pursed lips. It was the boy who'd captured all his attention. His brown hair was thick and wavy, and his hazel eyes were wide set, curious. Paul had seen this child before—at least the back of this child in a soccer uniform. And the child looked like his mother—not the woman who was driving him down the street, but the woman who'd given birth to him.

Claire.

The boy was here. Living less than an hour away from the compound. All of this time . . . Had his father been making regular trips out here to this neighborhood and spying on the boy in person?

Paul's attention shifted again as his father's car moved, pulling away from the curb and continuing up the neighborhood street until it turned out of sight.

Paul sat in his car, waiting. For what, he didn't know. He didn't know what to think. Was Handel checking up on his son? Was there an emotional connection? Or was Handel up to something else, knowing that Claire was back in London? Was he about to use the innocent child as some sort of bait?

What was the adoptive family? Were they employed by the WAO? Or were they completely oblivious to where their child truly came from?

Paul's phone buzzed, and he looked down at the incoming call. He recognized Nora's number. How had she tracked down his new number? He shouldn't be surprised.

He hesitated for only a second, then he answered, knowing that as soon as he did, Nora could pinpoint his location.

"You've gone off the grid, Paul," Nora said without preamble.

"What do you know about my father?" Paul said. "In all our talks about Claire, I realize now that I'm missing something big. How long have you known Handel Raine?"

Nora was quiet.

"Nora?"

"Can you meet?"

Paul didn't like this one bit, but he had to know. His father was acting erratically—more erratically than usual—and Nora's continued interest in Claire was unnerving. Why would the woman want Claire back?

"Claire came to my apartment," Paul said.

"She did?" Although Nora asked the question, she didn't sound surprised. Her voice lowered. "Did you tell her about me? Did you talk her into working with us?"

"You and I aren't working together," Paul said.

Nora exhaled. "I know about the hit man your father sent after you."

Paul didn't question how she would know that. It seemed she knew quite a lot about the WAO; and if so, how was *she* still alive?

When he didn't say anything else, Nora pressed, "I'm

assuming you're near the compound. Meet me in the parking lot behind your hotel."

Paul didn't question how she knew anything anymore. "I can be there in an hour." He sat in the car for several more minutes, processing things in his mind, before starting the engine.

This could very well be a setup, either by his father or by Claire.

He couldn't trust anyone. Not that he ever had.

Paul started the car and made a U-turn on the street, heading away from the house of the little boy and whatever secrets were stored there.

The drive back to his hotel seemed to stretch out for hours, although it wasn't actually more than an hour. Just before pulling off the street into the side road leading around the hotel, Paul picked up his Glock, holding it with his right hand while steering with his left.

The parking lot had only a handful of cars parked there and no sign of Nora. Paul parked in the farthest stall from the hotel, backing into it so that he could have a full view of the lot.

A car door opened on a dark-blue sedan.

The woman who stepped out wore all black. She started walking toward Paul's car, her hands lifted about waist-high as if showing that she was unarmed.

Her blonde hair was thick, braided, and hanging over one shoulder, and she looked as if she were intent on one thing only—reaching Paul.

He popped open the driver's door and climbed out of the car. He stayed behind the open door while making it clear he carried a gun. Nora didn't flinch at the sight; she merely continued to walk toward him.

Her gaze took in the location of the car and the position

of his body behind the car door, then finally she focused on his face.

There was no fear or apprehension in her eyes; in fact, she looked determined. That could only mean that she was equally armed and wouldn't hesitate to draw her weapon, wherever she kept it.

"Paul," Nora said in a soft voice. The way she spoke his name startled something inside of him. It was almost familiar—not familiar like he'd met with her in the café a couple of days before, or familiar because they'd spoken on the phone. But familiar in a deeper way, as if he knew her before he'd met her behind the All Hails Pub.

He kept his gun aimed at her as he warily watched her. When she was about three meters away, he said, "Not another step. We can talk at this distance."

She gave a half smile as she came to a stop. "Is a gun really necessary?"

"Isn't it?" Paul said. "Why do you know so much about Handel Raine?"

Her eyes shifted, but he sensed she was going to be honest with him.

"That's not an easy question to answer," Nora said. "And I don't know how much time we have before stopping Claire from doing something that will get her killed by Handel."

"She's already doing it," Paul said. "I told you she came to my apartment. She shot me with a drugged dart that incapacitated me for hours. She didn't kill me, yet, because she wanted the location of the compound."

"Did you give it to her?"

"I did."

"Ah." Nora looked away, and for a moment her blue eyes seemed to waver. Paul caught the smallest glimpse of a woman who had a vulnerable side.

"So, it's already begun."

"I know Claire's close by, watching the compound," Paul said. "I saw her there." He shook his head at himself. "I don't know why I'm telling you this. Unless you want to be another target of my father's, you should stay clear. Keep running the Amazon Sisterhood—if you really want to cripple my father, that's the best way to do it."

"I'm already a target of your father's," Nora said.

Of course she was. Any organization that thwarted any of Handel's plans was a target.

Nora was still looking away when she said, "I remember when I found out they named you *Paul.*"

He blinked. What did she mean? Did she know his parents? "How long have you known my father?"

She looked at him again, her blue eyes watery. "No one can know about this meeting, Paul." And there it was again. Her voice softened when she said his name.

He lowered his gun. Something twisted in his gut, telling him he wasn't going to like what he was about to hear. He shut the car door and pocketed his gun. Then he took a couple of steps closer. A strange instinct within made him want to offer her comfort. Which was absurd.

He was close enough now to read her eyes, to see that they were searching his, as if she had questions and only he had the answers. Yet he was far enough away that he still had the advantage over her with his gun accessible.

"No one will know about our conversation," Paul ground out. "My father and I are no longer on any sort of speaking terms."

"I understand completely," Nora said. "But I'm hoping you've realized that you need a partner. You need me."

"First of all, like I told you before, I don't take directions from you," Paul said. "The WAO is rock solid to any outsiders. No *one* person can ever breach the organization. Not even an organization such as the Amazon Sisterhood. Not me, and not whoever you think you are. The WAO has influence and connections all over the world and supports scientific advancements that you can't even guess."

"Oh, I can guess," the woman said, her mouth twitching into a smile that sent a shiver down Paul's back. "In fact, Paul . . ." The way she said *Paul* was significantly less soft than before. "I told you before that I was one of the founders, but that wasn't exactly correct. I was married to Handel," she said. "I—I married him when I was already pregnant and led him to believe that the baby was his. And that baby was you."

Paul stared at her. "You're saying that my father is really my stepfather?"

"Yes, and I've never told him the truth. After I learned who he really was in our marriage, I was too afraid to because of what he might to do me—and you. We had a son together, Seth, who Handel starved to death in order to punish me." Her voice gave off the slightest tremble, then was dead calm again.

She exhaled slowly. "Once Handel discarded me, leaving me for dead, he married another woman for a short time. He told you that woman was your mother. But you are *my* son."

Paul's breathing went shallow as his mind spun with the impossibilities of what she was saying. If this woman was telling the truth, she was his mother, and Handel wasn't his biological father. No, it couldn't be true. He remembered his mother, not this woman. "You're not my mother. My mother was Lucille, and she died when I was seven."

Nora stepped forward, once, then again, but Paul didn't bother to pull out the gun again. She was standing close enough that she could possibly gain an advantage over him in his shocked state.

"I *am* your mother, Paul."

Paul couldn't move, and he wasn't sure if he was

breathing. He could laugh at her, he could shoot her and put her crazy mind out of its confusion. But her words penetrated deeper than his logical mind. He scanned her face, searched her eyes, tried to comprehend. She might have had cosmetic surgery, she might have dyed her hair, but her eyes . . . He knew those eyes from before their meeting at the pub and café. He'd looked into her eyes before. As a child.

No, he wanted to shout. *My father, or whoever he was, couldn't possibly have deceived me about my own mother.*

But Handel had. Paul's birth mother was standing right in front of him, just as real as the paved parking lot he stood in or the breeze that kicked up, stirring his clothing against him.

"How . . . Why?" He was at a loss for words. He didn't even know which question to ask first. His mind was trying to recall childhood memories from when he'd been told his mother was very sick. He'd been allowed to visit her one last time. Lucille Raine had been in bed, her eyes closed, her deep brown hair a halo about her head. Paul had grabbed the thin, pale hand and cried because his mommy wouldn't open her eyes and speak to him.

He remembered his father's firm hand on his shoulder, steering him out of his mother's room. But that wasn't the memory of Nora. Paul searched deeper still—to a time that he remembered when Lucille wasn't in the picture. It seemed that Lucille had always been there, although he'd mostly been raised by various tutors. His mind moved back to a time when he was a young boy of four and his brother had a terrible accident.

There had been a wake at a cemetery. It had been windy, and Paul had not only missed his brother, but had missed someone else even more. A woman with blue eyes. A woman that he'd questioned his father about after Seth's funeral. Handel had told him that she was the cause of his brother's accident and was a bad tutor. *Tutor.* His father had told him they could never speak of her again and that to remember her was to forget Seth.

The woman who Paul had been told was his tutor and was responsible for Seth's accident was this woman standing before him. Once that memory had surfaced, other memories, long forgotten, began to fill his mind. Sitting on the floor, doing a puzzle together. Reading a book together while nestled on her lap. Putting stickers on a chore chart. His thoughts jumbled, and his knees almost buckled. The warmth drained from his body, and he felt like a cold, empty shell. His reality had just flipped upside down.

Nora continued to watch him, her eyes moist with tears. But she said nothing. It was as if she were waiting for the truth to solidify in his mind.

Paul ran a hand over his face as if he could dispel the flood of memories piling one on top of another. He finally spoke, his voice a cracked thing. "When I came out of the pub, did you know who I was?"

"Of course," she said in a soft voice. "I almost told you then, but I wasn't sure if you'd betray me to Handel."

Paul nodded, still trying to process his altered reality. "Handel told me that you caused my brother's death."

"I've no doubt he's told you many lies," Nora said, keeping her gaze steady on his. "I've told plenty myself, but it's time to stop the lies. Are you ready to hear the truth?"

"We should talk in the car." He stepped toward the car and opened the driver's door. Nora followed and slid into the passenger seat.

Paul pulled his door closed, and the sounds of the night

muted. There was only his breathing and that of Nora—his mother—next to him.

"Start from the beginning," he said, staring straight ahead, wondering how many shocks his mind could take in such a short period of time.

It took Nora only a moment before she started talking.

CHAPTER 30

DARKNESS SURROUNDED THE car where Paul sat with Nora, but the words coming from her mouth were illuminating.

"I met Handel during my senior year at Oxford," she said. "I was studying history and was fascinated with archaeology. Handel was working on a master's in theology. He had some interesting ideas." She paused and folded her hands in her lap. If Paul didn't know better, he would have thought she was telling him a sweet story about her courtship. But anything to do with his stepfather would be far from sweet.

"Handel used to rent out the lecture hall after hours and talk philosophy," she said. "He was a bit of a legend on campus. And I'll admit, I was fascinated. There was plenty of hero worship among the female students. He'd published a pamphlet, and the women would have him sign their copies, then hold study groups where they'd memorize portions of the essays."

"Sounds like a cult," Paul said.

Nora gave a soft laugh that wasn't kind. "That's a fairly accurate description. You might say I fell under his spell. When he noticed me, above all of those adoring females, I was smitten. But then I went to a party and drank too much. I messed up and found out a few weeks later that I was pregnant. I was humiliated that I had been so stupid, and I missed two lectures in a row. Handel noticed. He stopped me on campus one day and asked after me."

She exhaled. "I saw a way out of my miserable predicament. I had done something stupid, and with Handel's interest in me, I wanted to see if I could fix my mistake." She shook her head. "I know you don't want to hear how you came into this world, but knowledge can be empowering."

Paul didn't answer. His emotions were all over the place.

"We went to dinner, and our relationship took off from there. It intensified quickly, which went right along with my plans. I wasn't in the best frame of mind. I was an emotional wreck from finding out about the pregnancy, I'd recently lost my stepfather, and my mother had her alcohol and her friends, and I guess I was floundering. I was afraid that I was becoming my mother."

Paul blew out a breath. "Did you ever find out who my father was?"

Nora shook her head. "I didn't even know half the people at the party. I don't remember much, for better or for worse. But when I told Handel I was pregnant, he stayed by my side. Of course, he thought the baby was his. I was impressed with his nobility. Handel was always one to fight for a cause, and during my early months of pregnancy, I was his new cause. I soon learned that his causes are also obsessions, and everything had to be centered around him and his ideology."

Paul nodded. "It wasn't until I was in my twenties that I started to realize the world didn't run according to Handel's philosophies."

"Yes," Nora said. "I spent many nights listening to his lectures, then going back to his flat and talking into the early morning hours. He wanted to make a difference in the world. *Really* make a difference. Not just pander to some ideology or wish." She glanced at Paul before continuing. "Have you heard about People's Protection Units made up of those who quit their jobs, leave families and loved ones, and join up with the Kurdish militia in Pakistan? They don't go through the British army or any formal training—they just go over to fight for what they believe in. They want to make a difference now, and without restrictions and rules or rankings. Handel was an early pioneer of such sentiments."

"How did he go from a student of theology to building a secret empire?" Paul asked.

"If there's one thing Handel is, it's persuasive," Nora said. "He could charm the right people, and soon, not only was he putting his ideals into action, but he had me running the operations." She shrugged. "It wasn't my dream job, of course. I would have rather gone on a dig to Egypt, but instead of exploring history, I was now creating it with Handel. Or so I thought. We married, and I graduated. After he finished his thesis, he wanted to move us away from the Oxford scene. He said that everything we did now had to be confidential. Marriage was his institution of control."

"Where did the money come from?" Paul didn't want to interrupt her too much, but questions were racing through his mind.

"He had an inheritance," Nora said in a subdued voice. "At least that's what he told me. After a few months of marriage, I'd been witness to his volatile temper, so I learned to pick my battles. I was also preoccupied with morning sickness and didn't question everything about the movement that Handel was starting as much as I should have. He came up with the name *World Alliance Order* on his own."

She fell quiet for a moment.

When she did speak, her words surprised Paul. "When you've had a child with someone and you see them act the part of a loving father, it strengthens those bonds between man and woman, for better or for worse. Even when . . . even when the child wasn't really his."

"Did you love him?"

"It was more of an obsession in the beginning," Nora confessed. "I now know it wasn't a healthy love. He was so hyperfocused on raising money for one project or another that it was easier just to let him do his thing.

The older Handel wasn't much different than the younger Handel.

"When I became pregnant with Seth, things really started to fall apart in our marriage," she said. "Handel hired Lucille to help around our house and with managing you since I was sick once again with the pregnancy." She paused. Her next words were tremulous. "The signs were plain, but I was too sick to fight against Handel about his obvious affair with Lucille."

"That's why I remember her from the beginning," Paul said.

"Yes, she was ever present," Nora said. "Seth was born, and once I recovered, I contacted a solicitor about a divorce. Handel was furious when he found out. He ordered Lucille to basically kidnap Seth. I had no idea where she'd taken him. Weeks went by, and I lived in abject fear and terror. When it became clear that I was once again at his beck and call, he brought Seth back into the home, but Lucille had full responsibility over him. And you were to be taken care of by Lucille as well. I knew I couldn't fight Handel. I had to find a different way out."

Nora wiped at her eyes and sniffled, the first real emotion that Paul had seen from her.

"He turned our home into a fortress—a literal prison—a precursor to the compound, I guess." A tremor ran through her body. "I had been cut off from the world, and my little space inside that home had become my new reality. It's amazing what the human body and mind will do to endure and ultimately survive. But I plotted and planned an escape. Two days before my escape that would include both of my sons, Handel discovered my plan."

Her voice hitched. "That was the last time I saw your brother. When Handel told me that Seth had died, I couldn't believe it. I mean my mind wouldn't accept the fact, even though my heart had become empty." She brushed away a tear. "It was on the threat of your death that I finally knew if I stayed, you'd meet the same terrible fate. Something about the combination of Handel and me was toxic. No one could push him into a rage like I could. Even if I never spoke to him again in that house, he'd find a reason to use you against me." She hiccupped back a sob.

Paul only felt numb. His father was the epitome of all the evil in the world, and Paul himself had been his accomplice in many things. Something deep inside him relaxed now that he knew that Handel wasn't his biological father. Maybe, just maybe, Paul could break out of the cycle.

"So you escaped and left me behind?" Paul said, the bitterness in his voice surprising him. He understood Nora's plight but was still having trouble comprehending the reper-cussions.

"I did it to save your life," Nora said. "And mine. I honestly didn't know why Handel had chosen to spare you yet starve Seth. I hid for months and months, working odd jobs, moving often. About that time, the internet was becoming widespread, and I used to sneak into university computer labs and try to find any information on your stepfather, or you. But true to form, he'd hired the best of the best, and there was no trail leading to the WAO. I thought he maybe changed the name."

Paul thought of what his mother was going through and what he was going through back home. He'd been sent to a boarding school after Lucille's death when he was ten and never returned to his childhood home again. His father would visit him sporadically, but there had never been any affection between them. So many years had been lost, and it was hard to fathom the passage of time.

"About three years after I left, and without finding any way to trace you, I was hired on to an archaeological dig," Nora said. "There I met contacts and spent a couple of years traveling the world and living out of a tent. It was cathartic, and eventually many of the wounds from my marriage became memories of the past." She brought a hand to her chest. "Losing my sons still hurt every day on those digs, but I was living again."

While his real mother was out in the desert, digging up bones, Paul was in boarding school doing mathematics and wondering when he'd see his father again. He was a lonely kid and didn't mix well with the other boys. His teachers seemed to target Paul and were harder and more demanding on his schoolwork. Paul hadn't thought about it much at the time, but looking back, he wondered if his father had made threats or coerced the headmaster to keep Paul in residence during all holidays.

When Paul completed the boarding school academy, he'd jumped at the chance to work for his father. He'd felt flattered that his father might finally spend time with him. It wasn't long before Paul dispelled that flattery. His father continued to be distant, and he treated Paul like he should be grateful for even breathing.

But Paul had been determined to prove himself. He had needed to win the approval of the only parent he knew.

"When did you find out about me?" Paul asked.

"It was when I tracked your name to a boarding school," Nora said. "You were twelve at the time. That was also the same time my archaeological group discovered burial mounds containing the remains of female warriors, believed to have descended from the Amazon women." She turned in her seat to look at Paul more fully. "Excavating those warrior women and their weapons really changed me. It made me realize that sometimes a woman does need a weapon, and that women from the beginning of time have had to fight for their rights."

He met her gaze in the darkness broken up by the streetlamps in the parking lot. "That's when you decided to fight?"

"Yes," Nora said in a whisper. "I decided I had become strong enough, and I determined to find my son. Another woman in my group had been through an abusive relationship too, and we talked long hours into the night. I discovered that she was a bit of a computer whiz, and she taught me some tricks on the internet and how to get in a few back doors."

Paul raised his eyebrows. "She was a computer hacker?"

"Not at the time," Nora said. "But Genevieve now runs the computer security division of the Sisterhood."

"So, you found me, and then what?" Paul asked.

"I went to the boarding school and I caught a glimpse of you when your group came out of the school and loaded onto a bus—for a field trip or something," Nora said. "It broke me. I returned to my hotel and cried for hours. I had gone backward on all the strength that I thought I'd gained being separated from your stepfather. First, I had a son who was still living and breathing, but I had missed so, so much. And second, the trauma of my marriage and my other son's death reared up with full force."

She wiped her eyes again, and Paul had to look away.

"Genevieve found me in that hotel room," Nora said. "She told me that the time would come to be reunited with my son again, but first I had to become strong on my own. We talked about the warrior skeletons we'd excavated and what their lives had been like. What they'd fought for. How they hadn't given up. One skeleton had a dagger embedded into her ribcage. She hadn't died without a fight."

"Thus the name of your organization," Paul said.

"Yes," Nora said, her voice growing stronger. "So Genevieve and I got busy. I focused on learning all that Genevieve knew, and I found ways to infiltrate the projects that your stepfather was working on. It became my new obsession—and sanity."

She reached out and touched his arm. Paul didn't move; he couldn't move. Her touch wasn't familiar but still reached a closed-off portion of his heart. A heart he hadn't been sure he even had anymore.

"I kept track of you from a distance," Nora said. "I always told myself if something were to happen to you, I'd go after Handel. But then I realized I didn't know you at all and that you could be just like him. I couldn't quite let myself believe it, but I prepared for the possibility."

Paul released a breath. "You aren't too far off the mark."

"No, Paul," she said. "You are not like your stepfather. You've been his puppet and have done things that are considered criminal in the free world. Despite that, you're good at the core."

He shook his head. "I've killed people," he said. "I've swindled companies out of millions of dollars. I've created chaos and bloodshed in order to complete the WAO's mission." He looked Nora in the eye. "I was never forced to join the WAO. You might say I was misdirected and misguided, but I still had a choice in the beginning."

"You were emotionally neglected and abused," Nora said in a trembling voice.

Paul couldn't look at her anymore, or his own throat would tighten. "Despite Handel's manipulation, I am my own man. Until he put a hit on me, I was ready to end Claire once and for all at his request. Even I could see the necessity for it." He paused. "And you must know that between Handel and me, only one of us can exist now."

The silence stretched between them. "I understand," Nora said at last.

Whether she did or not, it no longer mattered. If Paul happened to survive above and beyond his stepfather, he'd be turning his back on everything he knew. He'd go into exile and live off his savings.

Nora's phone buzzed. She took it out of her pocket and looked at the screen. "Sorry," she murmured, then stepped out of the car.

Through the closed door, Paul heard her say, "Are you sure? Can you email that to me?"

She hung up and stood still for several moments. Paul was expecting her to walk away, but instead, she opened the passenger door again. She sat down and scrolled through her phone. Then she turned the screen toward Paul.

It was an online newspaper article, and just the title told Paul that Claire had been at work.

"Investigation Opens on Multi-Million-Dollar Holding Corporation Accused of Insider Trading."

Paul scanned the first paragraph. There in black and white was the name "World Alliance Order," as well as the names of Handel Raine, Paul Raine, and Bethany Jenkins as the major private owners of the company. "When Handel sees this, he'll go underground."

"Exactly," Nora said.

"Should we let the cat hide from the mouse?" he asked, even though he knew Nora's answer.

"No," she said, her gaze steady on his. "I'm going into that compound. Handel and I have unfinished business."

"You won't come out alive," Paul said, feeling a rush of desperation moving through him. He'd just met his mother after so many years of lies. Would he be forced to say goodbye to her now? To live through her death as she had lived through his brother's?

"Genevieve will carry on the Amazon Sisterhood if it comes down to that," Nora said, pocketing her phone. "I may only have a few minutes' advantage over Handel." She placed a hand on his arm again, and this time Paul didn't stiffen. The warm pressure on his arm gave him a new feeling, one of protectiveness—a feeling he'd never felt in as long as he could remember. "I don't want to involve you in this, Paul. This is between me and the man who destroyed my life."

"He destroyed mine too," Paul said, his throat tightening. "And that's why I'm not going to let you go in there alone. He'll have to take me out before he gets to you."

CHAPTER 31

CLAIRE HAD LOCATED the compound, yet now she was hesitating. She knew it was dangerous to delay any action—no matter her decision. If she knew Handel, or Paul, they were using every available method to track her down. If she was to leave England safely and return to her Park City seclusion, the time to act was now.

Her profiles were completed and sent to Agent Hales.

Once back in Park City, she could watch things crumble for Handel Raine, Paul, Bethany, Dr. Raymond, and the entire WAO organization.

Her life would change. She would be safe. She might even get a dog.

Decision made, Claire packed her carry-on and zipped it closed, then she unplugged the laptop and was about to put it into hibernate mode when the gates started moving at the power plant. The infrared camera picked up the movement of a man walking toward the tower door.

Handel. He was returning. It was late—after eleven. Which meant that he'd been gone more than fifteen hours. Claire stood motionless in her hotel room, watching the video feed of the man as he strode across the short distance until he reached the door. The door opened from within as if someone were waiting for him. Handel entered, and the door shut behind him.

Claire exhaled. That was the last time she'd ever see the man, on video or otherwise, until he was arrested. Or killed.

She reached for the mouse, only to hesitate again.

The gates were opening again, and another man appeared. This man was broader shouldered but thinner in his torso. He walked slowly, as if he were in no hurry.

Paul.

Claire stared. He was going into the compound, after his father. And something in her gut, or in Paul's grim expression and determined stance, told her that it wasn't for a friendly father-son chat. Then Paul stopped before reaching the tower door. He turned toward the gate and held up a piece of paper for about fifteen seconds. Claire squinted at the writing. It was too small on the video feed. Then Paul tucked the paper inside his pocket and disappeared in the door.

Claire reversed the recording and zoomed in.

Paul had written a series of numbers across the top of the paper, then an address below. Why had he shown it to the camera?

Then she knew. *Me. He wants to show me.*

Claire quickly memorized the number sequence and the address, then pulled up her maps browser. The address was in a neighborhood up the coast. And no matter how much Claire zoomed in on the satellite feed, she saw only a row of houses, lawns, a few cars parked in driveways, a couple of flower beds. A typical neighborhood. Was it Paul's hideout? Handel's?

And if it was someone's hideout, why had he given out the address in such a manner?

She typed the numbers into a variety of searches, but nothing of interest or significance came up.

Claire exhaled, her mind piecing together Paul's actions over the last twenty-four hours. Was he giving Claire some sort of lead or clue because he didn't expect to leave the compound alive? Why would he want to help her? Had he really turned against his father?

Claire looked at her packed carry-on sitting on the bed, then back to the laptop. Her decision had been a long time in coming, she realized, and was probably the root of why she'd really returned to London. And why she'd refused the safe house offer from Agent Hales.

Had Claire truly believed that she'd ever return to Park City, living out the years in peace, maybe having a normal relationship with a man, getting a dog, going to the library . . .

No, whispered through her mind.

The scars on her body would never let her life be normal.

She slipped the laptop into her carry-on, then picked up her specialized dart gun.

Claire crossed to the hotel room door and opened it. She walked quickly down the corridor and took the stairwell to the main floor. She exited out of the coded entrance, emerging into the rear parking lot. It didn't take long to reach the street, and she only waited for a couple of cars to pass before she crossed it. She set off into a light jog through the deepening night.

The power plant was lit up on the south side, but the north side was heavily shadowed. Claire was out of breath by the time she reached the north gate. She paused by the camera, then wrapped her fingers around the bars of the gate and started to climb. It was straight up, but her adrenaline made the climb easy. She crested the top and dropped into a crouch on the other side.

Her breath stalled as a car drove along the road, but it continued past the power plant. Claire strode to the tower with the inset door, already not happy with how her hands were shaking.

When she reached the tower door, she scanned the code reader. It might lock her out if she typed in the wrong code, and she could only guess where to start. But then she realized that she did know where to start. She slowly pressed each number that Paul had written at the top of his paper, then waited.

Half a second later, the door unlatched, and Claire exhaled.

Paul had given her the code to get into the compound.

What sort of game was he playing?

Was she walking into a trap?

Whatever it was, this time Claire was armed, and she wouldn't go down easily.

As she pulled the door open, the dry, musty air flowed through her senses, and her stomach tightened. The smell was the same as she remembered, and memories tumbled and spun through her mind. She stepped into the dim space at the top of a stairwell and forced herself to pull the door shut behind her. Her breathing had grown erratic, and she concentrated on slowing down her breaths. Her legs felt shaky, and she reached for the wall to brace herself.

She couldn't let panic overtake her now. "Move to the stairs," she told herself in a whisper. "One step, then another." Her legs obeyed, and she stepped down the first step, gripping the metal railing tightly while holding her gun with her other hand. The last time she'd descended into this place, she'd been unconscious.

Focusing on counting to distract her mind as she went, she reached the lower floor at twenty-six steps.

She'd arrived on a landing of sorts and was facing three different doors.

Claire tried the same code on the first door, but it didn't open. The second door unlatched, so she pulled it open. The corridor that extended from the second door smelled of antiseptic. Claire's stomach roiled, and she nearly doubled over. More deliberate breaths, and she started to move. She knew the layout of the compound, and now that she was inside this hallway, she knew that she'd soon arrive at more doors, more stairs.

The place was like a maze deep in the earth, a full level beneath civilization. Lit with fluorescent lights, the corridor seemed to buzz with energy.

She hurried now, not knowing where Paul went but guessing it was to his father's quarters. She'd never been inside of them but had known they were on the second lower level on the east side. The passageways and multiple doors might confuse some people, but Claire had never forgotten one detail.

She pulled open the door that would lead to the stairwell to the second floor. Someone was coming up the stairs. She released the door handle quietly and backed away from the opening. If someone found her now, she wouldn't get very far. But then the sound of the footsteps suddenly stopped and retreated.

Exhaling, Claire waited a few moments. Then she opened the door again. She started down the stairs, keeping absolutely silent as she moved. The footsteps were back, and Claire froze.

The person was coming up the stairs in a rush. "Don't move," a woman's voice said before Claire could reverse her direction.

Bethany. Claire would know her voice anywhere.

Bethany's dark hair came into view, followed by her gun, which was pointed up at Claire.

"You didn't think we'd be watching our surveillance?" Bethany said.

Claire said nothing, just moved her finger to the trigger of her specialized dart gun.

"Go ahead and shoot," Bethany continued, her voice a sneer. "You've got all eyes on you, Claire Vetra."

Claire extended her arm toward Bethany, who was holding her own weapon equally steady. Neither woman backed down.

"Then everyone at the WAO will be my witness," Claire said, looking into the green eyes of the woman who'd supported Handel Raine every step of the way. She pulled the trigger on the dart gun an instant before Bethany squeezed the trigger on her gun.

Claire flattened herself against the stairs as a bullet struck the wall where she'd just been standing. Bethany lost her footing on the stairs and tumbled down several until her body stopped.

Claire lifted her head and stared down at the woman. Bethany wasn't moving. The dart was poking out the center of her neck, exactly where Claire had aimed. Bethany would be out for a while, and Claire would need all the time she could get.

She climbed to her feet and reloaded the dart gun. Then she looked up and scanned the sloping ceiling of the stairwell. Was Handel watching her this minute? Her gaze caught the embedded lens of a surveillance camera, and just as Claire raised a hand to acknowledge whoever was watching, the lights switched off in the stairwell. The blackness was sudden and deep.

Claire grasped for the railing to orient herself. She didn't move, didn't breathe. She listened. Below her, Bethany's breathing was shallow but regular. The darkness brought on new sounds. One sound was like a rush of air, as if there were a heating vent running somewhere, although Claire felt nothing.

Her heartbeat seemed to pick up pace as she held still and listened.

Claire hated the dark, but it could also be her friend. She just had to concentrate on light.

When she'd insisted the lights stay on in her bedroom at the Amazon Sisterhood château, no one had questioned her. In fact, the room where she went her first day to start learning computer forensics had massive windows and plenty of light even though it was a rainy day outside.

"This is Genevieve," Irene had said when a short, petite woman approached, sporting the curliest hair Claire had ever seen.

Genevieve appeared to be about fifty, and her thick curly hair was clipped back from her round, gently lined face. "I've heard a lot of great things about you," Genevieve said, extending her hand. "Welcome to my team."

Claire had shaken the woman's hand and was surprised at the strength behind Genevieve's grip. "I thought I was just here to look around."

Genevieve had an easy smile. "One thing might lead to another. Come." She led Claire away from Irene, and they walked past the various desks scattered throughout the room. There wasn't a particular order to the desks, but two screens were up on the wall, and one of them was showing the logs of the US stock market.

"What's going on?" Claire asked.

Genevieve waved to a couple of the nearby women sitting at computers at their desks. "They're searching for an insider trading breach. With the end of the financial quarters next week, it's the most risky time."

Claire watched the numbers scrolling down the screen,

then looked over at one of the computer monitors. "How can they know for sure if there's insider trading going on?"

"Come over, and I'll show you," she said.

"I don't want to bother anyone."

"You won't be." Genevieve pulled up an extra chair to a computer console, and after a series of log-ins, she opened a screen similar to the one a woman sitting close by was looking at.

"Here we are," Genevieve said. "See this medical equipment company? It went public three years ago, and revenue has been rising about five to eight percent per quarter. The company just announced yesterday that they're expecting to report a fifteen percent increase."

Claire raised her brows. "Did they release a new product?"

"They say they're releasing cutting-edge research," Genevieve said. "And they're only sharing the information in advance with top clients. Thus, they have millions of dollars in preorders."

"What do you think the research is?"

Genevieve's smile was broad. "Liz, tell Claire what you discovered."

The woman sitting at the next desk paused in her work and looked over. Her freckled face was makeup-free. "It's a new brain-stimulant drug. They've contacted their top clients in an exclusive correspondence that I was able to hack into. They claim that with enough investments, they should be able to roll out this new drug in twenty-four months. Initial investors are being promised a two hundred percent return."

Claire felt as if the room had started a slow spin. She rested her hand on her stomach as if that would help her push back the desire to throw up. "A brain stimulant?"

Liz nodded. "Yes, the medical research company has

already cited successful rounds of results in preliminary testing."

Of course they had.

"Show me the information you found," Claire said, rising and walking over to Liz.

For the next hour, Liz walked her through the process of how she located the confidential correspondence by using a software program to enter the back of the medical company's secure server.

When Liz showed Claire the report, she stared at the research that was cited. A chill crept over her skin as she read through it. There in front of her were the same processes and tests she'd been subjected to—all in the documentation.

Her face heated, followed by the rest of her body. It was like she was back in the WAO testing room, having drugs funneled into her bloodstream and being forced to answer questions while her brain activity was being monitored.

Claire tried to focus on the breathing techniques that Irene had taught her, then she turned to Genevieve, who was sitting nearby. "I'd like to join your team and learn everything you can teach me."

Claire could still remember the thrill of those early weeks as she learned to hack into the security levels of company servers.

Her four years at the Amazon Sisterhood had taught her that impossible things were possible.

So now she waited for her eyesight to adjust to the darkness of the stairwell inside the compound. No alarms had sounded when the lights had gone off, so Claire knew it was a quiet alert. She'd be found soon enough.

She began to move down the stairs, carefully, so as to not make a sound. Bethany's body was still crumpled on the stairs.

Claire paused when she reached Bethany's side. But there was no movement from the woman, and Claire stepped over her.

She was nearly to the door at the bottom of the stairs when it shoved open.

The light poured in behind two men. They rushed at her, and Claire fired the dart gun, but she hadn't taken time to aim, and the shot went wild. She turned to scramble away, but they had the advantage of surprise.

One of the men wrenched the dart gun away from her, and the other grabbed both of her arms, wrenching them behind her back.

"Handel Raine's waiting for you," one of them said.

She looked up into his face but didn't recognize his blue eyes or pale features. He was just one of Handel's thugs.

"Tell him I've been waiting to see him again," Claire ground out. Adrenaline hummed through her, and she knew that even if the next few minutes were to be her last, she was ready to accept her fate. She twisted hard away from the men and swung out her foot to catch one of them behind the knees. The man's legs buckled, but the second man was quick to steady his partner.

"Raine said you might give us trouble," the second man said, hoisting her up by the arm and practically dragging her into the corridor. "Unfortunately we can't shoot you. Yet."

Claire scoffed although tears were burning in her eyes. Each man was gripping one of her arms, and the bruises would certainly run deep. "Shooting me would be too easy," she said. "I'm sure Handel has something much more torturous in mind."

Neither of the men responded, and Claire noticed they were heading for a door that must lead to Handel's private quarters.

The door at the end of the corridor was a massive steel thing. Two cameras were trained on Claire, and as they neared the door, it slowly slid open.

CHAPTER 32

PAUL TUGGED AGAINST the straps that bound him to the chair. Everything had gone horribly wrong.

Claire was being brought by two guards at that moment to Handel's quarters. Now Paul was chastising himself for giving her the code. Neither he nor Nora would make it out of this place alive, and by giving Claire an easy way inside the compound, he'd just endangered her as well.

If Paul had been on his own, he wouldn't have gone directly to his stepfather's quarters but would have found a way to draw his stepfather out of his rooms—out of his comfort zone—away from his guards. But Nora had insisted on going ahead of him. She wanted to confront Handel alone. She told him to give her half an hour, but an hour had passed and nothing. No communication.

Fearing Nora was dead, Paul headed into the compound. First, he'd flashed the code number and address to the infrared camera, hoping that Claire would see it, then he'd stepped inside.

But things couldn't have gone more wrong. The guards had been waiting for him, and even though he'd gotten one shot off, he'd been Tasered, then dragged to his stepfather's suite. The look on Handel's face had made Paul feel ill, but the look on Nora's face made him feel like he might split in half.

"Strap him down," Handel had said.

Paul knew it was futile to resist, but he still tried even though his muscles were barely coming back to life after the Taser. He was slammed into a chair by a couple of bodyguards and strapped to it—just like what Claire had endured for so many months.

Nora watched with a calm expression, but Paul could read the alarm in her blue eyes—blue eyes that he couldn't believe he'd forgotten.

When he was strapped securely, the two bodyguards stepped back and took up their places by the door. A third bodyguard stood near the counter that separated the living space from a kitchenette.

"I didn't think you'd take so long," Handel spat out, coming to stand in front of Paul. "When your mother arrived, it dawned on me that I should have expected you two to find each other eventually." He shook his head in mock dismay. "It's my mistake that I didn't see this coming. Shame on me. But shame on both of you."

"So you admit she's my mother?" Paul said.

Handel's dark brows lifted. "Of course she is. You were such a stupid and gullible boy. It was almost cruel to deceive you like that." He turned sharply away and faced Nora. "We created a useless piece of junk. My only regret is that Lucille wasn't able to bear children. We would have created a solid empire."

Nora's eyes narrowed. "It's time I confessed something."

"What now?" Handel ground out.

In that instant, Paul knew what his mother was going to tell Handel.

"Paul's not your son."

Handel didn't move for a moment as he stared at Nora. Then, slowly, his neck turned red. "What did you say?"

Her voice didn't waver when she spoke again. "I said Paul is not your son."

Handel blinked, then he turned his head to look at Paul.

For a moment, Paul thought he saw sorrow and grief in Handel's gaze, but that quickly hardened into something unreadable.

"Did you know about this?" Handel said through gritted teeth.

"Not until recently." It was a relief in a way; even if he didn't make it out of the compound alive, he felt a new hope. If Handel's blood didn't run through his veins, then perhaps redemption was possible.

"You were always a piece of work," Handel said after a charged moment.

The insult didn't bother him. He glanced at Nora, who was watching him intently, as if she were trying to tell him something without speaking. He looked back at Handel. "Did my *mother* tell you the good news?"

Handel's hands curled into fists. "She has told me about the online article—which we are working to eliminate right now before more pop up. We know we can't stop the deluge completely, but for now we're making strides to slow it down. And that's why I'm glad we're having this nice little *family* meeting."

Paul felt like his stomach had flipped upside down. Until now, he hadn't realized how much he had come to hate everything about this man: the raspy tones of Handel's voice, the spittle that collected at the sides of his mouth, the way he clenched and unclenched his right fist when he made threats.

"*You*, dear *son*, or whoever you are, will be our fall guy,"

Handel said in a triumphant voice. "Bethany is already removing any trace of my involvement at the WAO and replacing everything with your name. And Nora . . ." His eyes flickered to her, then back to Paul. "She's coming with me to ensure that you act your part."

"I'm not acting any part for you," Paul said. "And now that I know you're not my biological father, I have no connection to you at all. I'd rather die than do anything for you again."

Handel chuckled, but it was higher than his normal pitch. "I'm the only father in your life, Paul. That is, as long as you might live. And, believe me, you'll get your death wish, eventually." He gave an exaggerated wink. "I'm now pleased that you weren't killed yesterday. You're so much more useful to me alive right now. But trust me, I have no problem pulling this trigger."

His stepfather withdrew a gun and strode to Paul's side. Handel pressed the barrel against Paul's temple. Nora released a small gasp, but she didn't move. Neither did Paul; it wasn't the first time Handel had pulled a gun on him.

"Is this what you wanted our lives to come down to, dear *wife*?" Handel said.

Nora finally shifted and stepped forward. The three bodyguards in the room pulled out their guns.

Handel raised his other hand. "Easy, Nora." He nodded to three bodyguards stationed about the room. "You're surrounded by men who are more than happy to do my bidding. You'll only send Paul to a quick death if you give me any trouble."

Nora took another step forward, and Paul had to admire the woman for it. "Put the gun down, Handel," she said in a calm voice. "This is between you and me. Not Paul."

"Do you know what I think, Nora?" Handel said with a sneer. "I think you've been tainting him for a long time. I wouldn't be surprised if you had something to do with Claire's pretend death and now her return to wreak havoc on the WAO."

Before Nora could answer, the flat-screen on the wall flickered. Bethany's face appeared. Her usually pale complexion was mottled with red as if she'd been exercising. "Sir," she started. Her gaze cut to Nora and Paul briefly, but then her attention was right back on Handel. "Claire Vetra has entered the compound through the tower door."

Handel's face drained of color. "Alert the guards, and have them bring her here," he ground out. "We're just getting started."

"If it's all right with you, sir, I'm going to bring her in myself," Bethany announced.

Handel shook his head. "No, she's—"

The image had already shrunk on the screen, then disappeared completely.

"Get her back on the live feed," Handel ordered one of his guards.

The guard crossed to the flat-screen and pulled up Bethany's work space, but it was empty.

"Show us cameras eight and nine," Handel demanded.

Paul watched the video feed of Bethany hurrying along a corridor, carrying a gun. He wished he could reach through the screen and stop her.

"Radio Mike and Barry for backup," Handel continued. "And show us the north stairwell cameras."

Another series of images popped up, and Paul stiffened as he saw Claire come into view. She was moving down the stairwell slowly. He almost smiled to himself when he recognized her dart gun. She'd come ready.

Then Claire stopped, and Bethany appeared in the video. It was over in seconds when Claire fired at Bethany. Bethany crumpled on the ground, and Claire pocketed her dart gun.

Handel was glued to the screen, his breathing erratic. "Cut the lights," he rasped, his voice strained.

Nora inched toward Paul and slid something under his wrist. It felt cold and thin and hard. Then she moved back into place, all without Handel noticing her as he and the guards were riveted to the screen.

Paul lifted his hand as much as he could and saw that she'd slipped him a razor blade. It would be enough to cut the bands.

"Bethany!" Handel shouted at the flat-screen. She didn't move.

Paul knew she wasn't dead, but he wasn't about to tell his stepfather yet. The distraction was working in Paul's favor, and he used the razor blade to nick the one band he could reach.

He gave a slight nod to Nora, and she lifted her chin slightly.

"Claire used a dart gun, Handel," Nora said.

He spun toward her and stared. "Are you sure?"

"I know my weapons. Always have," she said.

Handel released a breath, and then he looked back at the screen. Claire had made her way down the stairs in the dark, stepping over Bethany's body, but then the guards pounced on her. The video feed swapped from one camera to the next, following their path to Handel's quarters. Claire was on her way.

Next, Handel zeroed in on Paul. "You have a choice to make, Paul," his stepfather said. "Claire, or your mother."

Paul stared at his stepfather. "What are you talking about?"

"Only one can live, for now, and the other I'll keep as hostage to ensure that you do as I say."

Claire would be here in moments, Paul knew. He glanced at Nora, who was now looking at Handel. Paul had nicked the strap enough that he could burst through it with the right effort, then free the other strap. But even with Claire on her way, they were outnumbered. Three bodyguards, Handel, and the approaching guards who had Claire—they would have the distinct advantage.

And then Nora slid her gaze, ever so briefly, to the fire extinguisher on the far wall. Paul understood. He didn't know the details, but he had a hunch that something was about to burn.

CHAPTER 33

CLAIRE SHOULDN'T HAVE been surprised at the sight that greeted her in Handel's domain. But her breath caught nonetheless. Paul was strapped to a chair in the center of what looked to be a rather plush living room. The sight of the chair caused a shiver to run through Claire, but that wasn't the only flashback playing out.

Handel Raine held a gun and was pointing it at the door Claire had come through.

And on the other side of Paul, a woman with her back to the door was a familiar figure. *Nora.*

Claire's mind reeled. She'd expected Paul—but *Nora?*

Why was she here? How could she afford to be in the presence of a man Nora herself had said was a longtime enemy?

Nora spun to face the doors as they slid open. Her blue eyes locked with Claire's. Claire expected to see desperation, perhaps fear, in the woman's gaze, but Claire saw none of those things.

Instead, she saw grief.

Claire hadn't been in the same room with Handel since

the day he'd tried to shoot Paul, and it looked like not much had changed. She was still wary of Paul's actions. Had Handel really turned on his son? Or was this all a ploy to bring her back to the compound?

The doors slid shut behind Claire, and the men who'd brought her stayed right by her side, their grips still firm on her arms.

Handel's expression stretched into a smile as he scanned Claire. "You look surprisingly well," he said.

A shiver raced through her at the sound of his voice and the memories it brought to her of whispered words, threats, and rantings about his grand plans.

Just seeing him made her feel as if her heart were no longer connected to her mind. This man had stolen everything from her—her identity, her life, her child, her hope.

"Too bad you had to hurt Bethany," Handel said. "I would have extended some mercy toward you, but now it's too late. We're waiting for Paul to tell us what his choice will be." He looked right at Paul. "Which woman?"

Paul shook his head.

Handel raised the gun higher and swung it toward Nora.

Nora didn't move, but she spoke in a low voice, "I told you, I'm willing to do a trade."

"You've already brought what I wanted," Handel said, nodding toward Claire. "What more could you possibly offer me?"

Claire felt sick. Had Paul and Nora lured her here in order to turn her over to Handel?

"Yes," said Nora. "You have everything in place now. Let Paul live. He can stay and help clean this up. I'll take Claire with me. We'll disappear, and you'll never see either of us again."

Claire stared at the woman she once trusted. She'd give

up Paul, who she was apparently working with, to his monster of a father? Claire looked at each of her bodyguards. If she could just get to the hidden knife in her shoe, she might have a chance. She tried to wrench away from the men, but neither of them budged.

Claire looked at Paul and found that he was looking directly at her. The expression on his face was confused, as if he wasn't sure what Nora's intentions were either. Paul lifted his chin and slanted his eyes to a spot on her left. Without moving her head, Claire glanced over to see a fire extinguisher mounted on the wall. It was in a strange location, she thought. Why did Paul want her to notice it?

What was he trying to tell her? She hated him almost as much as she hated his father. What did Paul expect her to do with a fire extinguisher?

Nora was still begging for Handel to stand down, so Claire took another look at the fire extinguisher. It was then she noticed something was different about it. Instead of a lever on the side, it was a pin, like one might see on a grenade.

Was it . . .?

Nora stepped toward Paul, but her gaze was still on Handel. "This is not the right way to end this," she said. "Paul is not the bargaining chip here—Claire is. She alone can reverse all the damage that's happening right now. Give us a chance to reverse the effects."

Claire snapped her attention to Nora. What did she know already?

"Please," Nora said, gentling her voice in a way that Claire hadn't ever heard. "You've been free to run the WAO without me . . . Paul is all I have left."

Claire's mouth dropped open. Were Nora and Paul—?

"Stop, Nora," Paul said in a low voice. "My stepfather

won't shoot me. Not when he needs a fall guy." His gaze met Claire's.

Stepfather? Handel was Paul's stepfather? Her mind raced with the new information. That meant her son wasn't Paul's brother. They didn't share the same blood. Even if she didn't make it out of this compound alive, she at least knew that Paul was not related to Handel.

"You're right, Paul," Handel said, but his tone of voice was far from comforting. "Don't you think we should catch Claire up to speed? She'll find out soon enough." He focused on Claire and said, "Nora is Paul's mother."

Claire felt her body grow cold. She had been set up. It seemed she'd arrived in the middle of a domestic dispute. That they were family—albeit a twisted, dysfunctional family. They would unite against her. Nora was Paul's mother, and Handel was his disgusting stepfather.

"Paul just found out too," Nora said in a quiet voice, looking at Claire. "I've had some work done, necessary work, so that I couldn't be identified." She tucked some of her hair behind her ear. "I colored my hair, changed everything I could think of, and when I started the Amazon Sisterhood, my main goal was to find my son and stop the monster I used to be married to."

"Actually," Handel said. "We're still married, honey."

Claire felt light-headed all of a sudden, and if the guards hadn't been holding her up, she might have collapsed. Was Nora really Paul's mother? The woman's profile did remind her of Paul . . . But if she'd been married to Handel, did that mean Nora had been part of the WAO? Or was *still* a part of it?

Handel chuckled at Claire's reaction. "Welcome to the family, Claire." He took a few steps toward her, his gun now aimed at *her* forehead. "Unfortunately, too much time has passed, and I can't trust you—even though you would be useful if you ever could obey orders. But we've given you enough chances to prove yourself."

"Stop it, Handel," Nora pressed. "Listen to me. You know that I have as much to lose as you do. Let me take Claire. You and Paul can work out your plan to go into hiding. This will all blow over in a few months when all evidence has been erased."

Handel kept his gun pointed at Claire but shifted his gaze to Nora. "You always were a compelling actress." His eyes darted from Nora to Claire, then back again to Nora. "You gave up *your* son, walked out on me, and have spent the last decades trying to tear down everything that we built together."

"You're the one who started dismantling our lives first," Nora said in a cold voice. "Your affairs, your drinking binges, your need for absolute control . . ." Her voice finally broke. "You killed an innocent child."

"That was an *accident*," Handel cut in, his face growing red.

Paul's gaze was locked on to Claire. He gave the slightest tilt of his head toward his wrists. Claire looked at the way he was strapped to the chair—a chair similar to the one she'd spent plenty of time in. The strap on his left hand wasn't secured—even she could see that.

He'd be able to get out of the chair and help her . . . help her do what?

As Handel and Nora continued to argue, something in Claire's memory turned, and she remembered being told by Dr. Raymond that throughout the compound were canisters of tear gas in case the police ever invaded the place. The employees and testing subjects were to put on the stored gas masks and activate the canisters. Every room had a cupboard with gas masks.

Claire scanned the room. Beyond the living room and its couches and single coffee table was an island counter separating the space from the kitchen. The kitchen was all-white, and a row of cupboards sat above the stove, oven, and sink. But there was also a row of cupboards beneath the island counter. In one of those cupboards, Claire guessed there would be gas masks.

Paul's gaze was intense on hers, and she gave the slightest of nods. There was no way that she could wrest free of the two men who were holding her unless there was some major distraction. But for now, she needed to be the distraction for Paul to reach the canister.

"Trade Nora for me," Claire said. "I'll recall the emails that I sent out. I created a software to do it automatically, and I can use the same software to send out a report stating that the original email was a false report." Claire would do no such thing. The damage was already done, and time would push her agenda forward.

Handel seemed to consider her offer. "No," he said at last. "This is Paul's decision. Only one of you can live. I need to teach my son consequences."

Claire tugged on the bodyguards' grips. "Please," she begged, making herself sound desperate. At least she had Handel's full attention. Out of the corner of her eye, she could see Paul working on something with his hand. He was cutting the rest of his band. Claire lunged forward, not making it very far.

Handel sneered. "You're hysterical. I guess we'll just have to drug you again. Unless Paul gives me permission to choose you as the next WAO sacrifice."

Claire twisted hard against her captors, crying out as if she were in complete distress.

"Fortunately, I have something right here in my kitchen that I think you'll enjoy." When Handel turned, Paul burst from the chair.

Paul sprinted across the room and broke the case encloseing the fire extinguisher. Then he pulled the pin from the side.

"No," Handel said, lunging after his son.

The closest bodyguard grabbed the canister and tried to put the pin back in, but the tear gas was shooting from the canister like a full-powered fire hydrant.

Handel fell back, sputtering and coughing. Paul pulled the collar of his shirt over his nose and mouth with one hand, and with the other hand, he drove a fist into the bodyguard's nose. The man screamed and sank to his knees, holding his face, then he fell to the floor, gasping for breath in the cloud of tear gas.

The air was already burning Claire's mouth and throat with its sweetly sick taste, and she tried not to inhale too deeply. The men holding onto her decided to save themselves. One of them stumbled to the door and typed in the code to unlock and open it. The tear gas spread quickly, and Claire found her gag reflexes coming on strong. Her eyes burned and teared, and she knew she was about to pass out.

She vaguely realized that Nora had made her way into the kitchen instead of leaving Handel's quarters. Handel beat her there, and he shoved her out of the way as he opened a cupboard and grabbed a gas mask. He pulled it on, and Nora pushed him. Handel staggered on his feet, but he was obviously gaining his strength back by breathing clean oxygen.

Claire was free, but her body was failing. She covered her mouth and nose with her hand and inhaled the tiniest bit. The tear gas made her throat feel like she'd swallowed a bottle of drain cleaner.

"Get down!" someone shouted, and Claire realized it was Paul.

Above the panic of guards escaping the room and Nora screaming at Handel, Claire heard the sound of a gun go off.

She dove to the floor, finding the air clearer but still tainted. Her eyes were watering so much that her vision was blurry. She blinked rapidly, but her eyes only hurt more. And then she saw one of the guards lying prostrate on the ground several feet away. She tugged the top of her shirt over her mouth, trying not to breathe in too deeply as she crawled toward the guard and pulled his gun out of his grip. The man was still breathing but unconscious.

Another bullet sounded above her again. Someone was shooting at her.

Claire turned to see Handel crouched behind the chair Paul had been strapped to, his gun pointed at Paul, who was tugging on a gas mask that Nora had just handed him.

Nora turned, saw where Handel was aiming, and started to run right at him.

Handel's arm didn't waver as Nora threw herself at him. Just before she crashed into him, Handel pulled the trigger.

Paul dove to the ground, but his body hit hard, and his head snapped against the floor. Then, with horror, Claire saw the blood bloom on his neck. He'd been hit.

"No," Claire yelled. She crawled to Paul, her eyes burning and her lungs gasping for air as she held her shirt over her mouth. Paul's eyes were open, but he was staring straight up at the ceiling, unmoving.

The blood was soaking his collar and the rug beneath him. Claire tugged up the side of his shirt and pressed it over the wound. "Paul, can you hear me?"

He blinked, slowly, then his lips moved.

"Hang on," Claire said. Blood had seeped through the

fabric and onto her hands. She didn't want to remove the pressure, but she had to get him oxygen. "I'll get you a gas mask."

"Don't ..." Paul said in a voice that was fading fast. "Don't forget the address." He sputtered, and blood bubbled from his mouth. Claire stared at him in shock.

"Your child—" he started, then another shot rang out.

Claire turned to see that Handel and Nora were on the ground, grappling for Handel's gun. She didn't know who had shot the gun. Two gas masks were on the floor, forgotten for the moment in the struggle. She had to get the gas mask. She had to drag Paul out of here and get him help. She had to save Nora from Handel.

She turned back to Paul. His eyes were closed, and he wasn't moving.

"Paul?" Claire whispered.

He didn't answer.

"No," she said. "Don't die on me." Her lungs felt like they were on fire, and she blinked against the stinging in her eyes. She had to get clean air or she wouldn't be able to save anyone, least of all herself. She had to kill Handel and get the gas mask.

The sound of a gun clattering on the floor caught her attention. With strength that Claire didn't know she had, she scrambled forward, nearly toppling over the pair, and reached the gun before Handel could retrieve it. On her hands and knees, her hands covered with Paul's blood, she took aim at Handel. His eyes widened only a fraction before she pulled the trigger.

Someone screamed, and Claire didn't know if it was herself or Nora.

Handel slumped against the floor. Claire had shot him dead center in the forehead.

She turned to Nora, but the woman had collapsed. Claire

reached for the gas mask and tugged it on. She inhaled, once, then twice. Then she turned to Nora and tugged the second gas mask over the woman's head. Nora wasn't moving, and Claire didn't know if the woman was alive, but she couldn't see any signs of major bleeding.

Somewhere in the corridor beyond the open door, an alarm went off, and beyond the tear gas, Claire smelled smoke.

She had to get out of there. She'd get Nora out, then come back for Paul.

But her body was shutting down, and she had to hurry. Claire grasped Nora's ankles and dragged the woman toward the door. The going was slow, and painful, and every muscle ached in Claire's body as she pulled Nora's weight. She passed a couple of the bodyguards lying on the floor. She didn't stop to check if they were breathing.

Claire made it to the corridor, and she collapsed next to Nora, trying to breathe and willing her strength to return. The air wasn't much clearer there. Smoke had taken the tear gas's place.

Claire lifted her head to peer through bleary eyes down the corridor. Gray smoke moved slowly toward her. She groaned as she forced herself to rise and crawl back toward the room. She had to beat the smoke, had to get Paul out of that room before it was too late for them all. She could only hope that Paul was still alive.

Only five feet to go. Four feet. Three.

A new alarm screamed out, and the door slid shut. Claire reached out as if she could stop the massive metal door from sliding, but it pushed past her, brushing against her fingertips. Now Claire was separated from Paul. There was no way to get the door open. Even if she knew the keycode, she didn't have the strength to reach the pad.

Claire collapsed on the hard floor and let her head fall

back. She couldn't fight any longer. Paul would bleed out and die if he wasn't already dead. Handel was dead. It was over. All of it.

She turned her head slightly so that she could see Nora. The woman was barely breathing, but Claire had no more strength to help either of them. She expelled her last full breath just as a dark figure emerged out of the smoke, coming right toward her.

CHAPTER 34

CLAIRE ROUTINELY STAYED past everyone's departure time in the computer lab at the Amazon Sisterhood. She liked working alone in the absolute silence. Despite the months of therapy with Irene, the yoga exercises with Frances, and the walks in the garden with Nora, being by herself had been the most healing of all. That, and learning her way around computer hacking.

Claire kept all the lights on in the massive room. The high windows captured the glittering night sky filled with stars, but there could never be too much light. Now, Claire crossed to one of the lower windows and cracked it open. Frogs croaked in the garden below the window, and Claire found it soothing to be only a few steps away from nature. She inhaled the faint breeze that stirred through the window.

Tonight she'd be testing the software she'd created during her off-hours. Sleep was not a priority when she had found something worthwhile to work on for herself. Thanks to Genevieve, Claire had become expert in the art of hacking, and it had given her an idea: to create a software program that was undetectable by any computer security system. The program only existed in an internet cloud. Claire could access it anywhere, anytime, and everything inside the cloud would be completely protected.

She returned to her computer desk and logged in to the cloud. Even with Genevieve's sharp eye, she'd never discovered Claire's project. Claire could hack into the back doors of corporations without leaving a trace or any sort of trail for another security programmer to discover.

Claire affectionately called it the Ghost. But the more she thought about it and developed the software, the more accurate the title was. Claire was a ghost of her former self, so as she used the software it was like only a part of herself was involved.

The Ghost cloud opened on the monitor, and Claire started to run a series of searches. Sometimes she let Ghost run the searches overnight, but tonight she couldn't wait for the data to come back in the morning. With all the components in the software now completed, she was ready to begin the first project.

She typed in the names of her parents. Trent and Kathryn Vetra.

On the left side of the screen, a list of links started to load, and as new links popped up, other ones disappeared. The software was not only tagging links, but it was also filtering them. The filtered links that were also considered solid sources started to fill a new list on the right side.

Claire watched in fascination as links appeared and disappeared. At the bottom of the screen, text was simultaneously compiled. The most relevant information was being pieced together so Claire felt like she was reading a Wikipedia document.

Kathryn was born in Bristol, England.

Trent was born in Maple Grove, Minnesota.

Social security numbers, driver's license numbers, bank account numbers, tax filings, and insurance payments all downloaded.

Claire had just created a speed pass to identity theft.

She skipped over the account numbers for now and skimmed the summaries of her parents' early lives: the names of teachers, schools, local foods they most likely ate, buying habits . . . She slowed when the grade school report cards came in. Perfect scores for her mother, and then her grades took a dip during her first year at a boarding school. Her father's grades were average, mostly Bs.

An article about her father at the age of twelve filtered through, announcing his win at the state science fair competition. Claire read the article slowly. The science fair project was based on the mutations of DNA that are transferred from mother to child.

Her father's grades continued to be average, but he earned a perfect score on the SAT and other college entrance exams and was offered multiple scholarships.

Her mother rallied in the second year of boarding school, and then right before graduation, she dropped out. The school had issued an incomplete transcript, and there was a six-month gap of information before the links started to compile again.

Trent Vetra had traveled to England as part of a research group that was testing DNA origins. The scientific report that downloaded stated that the DNA testing was being done on people with unusually high IQs. An email chain between her parents started up. Her parents had met when her father was in London. Her mother took the IQ test and scored extremely high, and her father included her as an entry in the DNA collection.

Claire tapped her fingers on the desk as she read. Her mother had been a dropout, but her intellect was off the charts.

Her father had earned average grades, but he'd been a science prodigy.

The software seemed to slow down, and the links were coming less frequently, most of them deleting after a few seconds. Claire watched the summarized report at the bottom of the screen stall.

And then the program seemed to wake up again. Link upon link poured in. But they were different in nature. Series of texts and emails between her father and . . . Nora. He'd worked with Nora? He was in daily communication with her.

Her mother started working for the WAO.

Three months later, Claire's father started working at the WAO.

What was the connection and relationship between the three of them?

And then Claire's heart nearly stopped.

Her parents had left the WAO, and there were many private memos throughout the organization about trying to locate them.

Nora had gone quiet, but her father hadn't. He was still communicating with Handel Raine.

And the communication had been about *her*.

Her father had been updating Handel on Claire's progress. There was nothing from her mother. Nothing from Nora.

Until . . . An email exchange downloaded. Her father and Nora discussed the possibility of running tests on Claire when she turned twelve. The tests would advance his scientific theory of DNA upgrading if two people with extremely high IQs mated.

Mated, like animals in a science study.

Claire read through the emails again, growing more and more bothered as she read.

Was Nora secretly tied in with the WAO? Was she in a relationship with her father?

Had her own mother been duped?

The next links that came up were of her parents' horrific crash. Their obituaries. A small article in the local paper about the tragic loss to the community and how their young ten-year-old daughter would be sent to a relative's home to live.

Claire closed down the software. She rose from the desk, her breathing erratic. She paced the computer lab for several moments. Then she went to her bedroom, which had felt empty ever since the day Frances had left. Claire took one of her antianxiety pills to stop the shaking in her hands. Then she strode down the hallway, up the stairs to the next level, and knocked on the door to Nora's living quarters.

Nora always kept an open-door policy, and anyone at the Sisterhood could approach her any time. She might not have meant two a.m., but Claire needed answers now.

Nora opened the door a few moments later, in the motion of tying on a black silk robe.

At the risk of exposing her after-hours activities, Claire said, "I've got some questions to ask about the relationship between you and my father."

Nora opened her mouth, then shut it again. Then she pulled the door wider and motioned Claire inside the suite. Claire had caught only a glimpse of Nora's rooms once before, but stepping inside, she felt like she was entering a museum.

The Turkish rugs on the floor were soft and exquisite. A huge painting hung on one wall, illuminated by its own gallery light. Claire couldn't place it, but she was sure it was an original painted by a master. On the antique-looking tables scattered throughout the parlor were squat statues, elegant figurines, marble pieces, and jeweled boxes that looked like something out of a treasure hunt movie.

Claire had the sense that she was surrounded by priceless artifacts.

"Sit down," Nora said. "I'll bring some tea."

Claire sat on a silk-covered ottoman and waited while Nora poured steaming water out of a pot that was kept on a burner. Had Nora been awake too? Or did she always have hot water ready?

When she finally sat across from Claire, Nora took a sip of her steaming brew, then said, "What do you want to know?"

"What was my father to you?" Claire asked, focusing on Nora's mannerisms.

Nora wrapped her fingers around her teacup as if seeking warmth. "We were working together to stop Handel Raine. At least I thought so."

Claire narrowed her eyes. "What do you mean?"

"We had a plan, and your mother was part of it, of course," Nora continued. "Your mother started working at the WAO, becoming a trustworthy employee, learning the system and the passwords."

Nora paused, looking down at her tea. "Your father and I . . ." She looked back up at Claire. "I was in love with him, but he was never fully accessible. I mean, we had a relationship, but your mother sufficiently distracted him from me."

"He was in love with my mother?" This gave Claire hope at least.

"He was," Nora said. "He promised to still help me with Handel—to help me get my vengeance, no matter how long it took. But, your mother, she wasn't a fool. She talked him into completely breaking ties with me after they escaped the WAO together. They lived in hiding, although with the advancements in technology and the internet, that had become impossible."

"You tracked them," Claire stated. It wasn't a question.

"Of course," Nora said. "Your parents not only had information about the WAO that they were hiding from me, but they knew about my connection, and they could identify members of the Sisterhood."

"I saw the emails between you and my father," Claire said, throwing it out there. She was surprised when Nora didn't ask her how she found them.

"He emailed me privately, of course," Nora said. "He didn't want his dear wife to know. But he'd been continuing in his DNA research since you were born, and he wanted to run some tests. So he sent me DNA . . . from you."

Claire swallowed against the dryness in her throat. She suspected as much, but hearing it in person from Nora made her feel disgusted with her father. "So my father was using me as a lab rat?"

Nora gave a half shrug. "That's one way to put it, but at the very core, your father was a brilliant scientist. He'd given up his unlimited funding and support from the WAO, and he'd cut off things with me. This didn't mean his ideas died. If anything, he became more obsessive because it was the forbidden fruit now that he'd created a suburban life with your mother."

Claire stared at the woman. "Did my mother find out?"

"Yes, and she was furious," Nora said. "I think she was more upset that your father and I were communicating than she was with your father sending out your DNA samples for testing and research. He knew the top researchers were at the

WAO, but he didn't want to use them for obvious reasons. So he came to me." She looked away. "Your mother turned out to be my worst nightmare. She sent me a long, rambling email, threatening all sorts of things. Exposing me. Exposing the WAO—which I wouldn't have minded. Your father was the most brilliant man I knew, at least in most ways. He was the one scientist who could make significant advances in DNA research. Your mother wanted to bury her head in the sand and play mommy."

"Was it *you*, then?" Claire asked. "Who told Handel Raine that my parents hadn't completely disappeared?"

Nora's gaze cut back to Claire, and Claire knew.

She set down her teacup with shaking hands. She couldn't be in this room anymore, and she couldn't look at this woman. Claire rose to her feet so that Nora had to look up at her. "How did you do it?"

"My hackers have always been better than Handel's," Nora said in a quiet voice. "I had one of them forward a link to an article that showed a picture of your mother at a farmer's market in the town they were living in."

Claire didn't react for a moment. Her stomach hardened into a small knot, and she felt like she was going to pass out and throw up at the same time. She turned and crossed the room to the door, needing to get away from the sight of Nora.

"I never expected Handel to kill them," Nora said, her voice reaching across the space to Claire.

Claire stopped but didn't turn around.

"When I found out they were tracing you, I watched, wondering what he was up to," Nora said. "You may not believe me when I say this, but I regret my actions. I was a vengeful and jealous woman of the worst sort. I was foolish to the core. And I know you don't want to hear this, Claire, but I see myself in you. I know that you've been working through the night. I know that you're on some sort of mission. And I know that it will destroy you in the end if you let it. When your father died, my world went dark. I blamed myself; I still blame myself. Of course, that's one my victimization issues that I need to work through. I'm not responsible for Handel's actions, and neither are you."

The woman was rambling, and Claire couldn't listen to her voice any longer. She grasped the handle and pulled open the door.

"We need to work together if we want to fight him," Nora said, her voice growing fainter as Claire stepped into the hallway and hurried toward the stairs.

When she made it to her room, she stood in the doorway for several moments. Her breathing was erratic, and her entire body was shaking. She'd been set up. From the moment of her birth, she'd been considered an experiment. She didn't know if her father loved her mother or if her mother would have found a way to protect her. Since her parents died when she was ten years old, she was too young to have ever guessed the true cause.

Claire pulled out a duffel bag that Frances had left behind and stuffed a few items of clothing inside. Then she switched on her laptop, connected to Wi-Fi, and booked an airline ticket under a name that Frances had told her to create. Claire had chosen Kelly Anderson. Claire then added the laptop to the duffel, along with her fake identification. Finally, she grabbed all of her bottles of medication, taking one pill before zipping everything closed. The side pocket bulged, and Claire unzipped it. Frances had kept some emergency cash inside. American bills. Anything would help.

Next, Claire pulled out a case from beneath her bed—her personal sidearm. Nora had insisted that she go through weapons training and keep a gun. Now, Claire inspected the gun, grateful she had a skill that she might need. She pulled the harness from the case and strapped it on under her shirt, then slipped the gun into the holster.

Claire shouldered the bag and crossed the room. She looked back from the doorway. She'd found healing in this place, friendship, a purpose, even hope. But now it was time to be on her own. Nora had broken her trust, and in truth, she should have never had it. As a final act, Claire flipped off the lights that had been on since she arrived nearly four years before.

She walked through the silent corridors. Frances had been right. No one would stop her from leaving.

Claire took the staircase to the main floor, half expecting to see Nora waiting for her, arms crossed. Or even Irene standing in the foyer ready to talk her out of leaving. But no one stood between Claire and the front door. She turned the dead bolt and pulled open the heavy door. The door sighed on its hinges, but still no one came.

Claire set off down the long driveway that led to the security gate. The older man in the booth stepped out. His shaggy gray hair made him look more like a starving artist than the burly guard that he was.

Claire had never officially met him, but he said, "Hello, Claire, do you need transportation tonight?"

She hesitated. But his tone had been friendly, and he didn't seem surprised to see her. Claire was sure he'd been witness to plenty over the years.

"Yes, a taxi would be great," she said, her pulse drumming as she thought about what she was doing—leaving the safe confines of the château. The last time she'd been in public, she'd met Paul at the All Hails Pub.

The security guard went into the booth, made a call, then waited inside the booth. He didn't try to engage in a conversation, which was fine with Claire. The taxi arrived in under fifteen minutes.

She nodded to the driver, who was a thin man with a thick mustache, before she climbed into the back seat.

"Where to, ma'am?" the driver asked.

Claire wondered if this driver would tell Nora where he'd taken her. "The closest airport," she said. As the taxi pulled away from the estate, Claire's stomach flipped over. The interior was dark, and the only light came from the taxi's headlights illuminating the narrow road in front of them.

She turned on the small interior dome light above her seat, and the driver said nothing.

Then she dug into her duffel and took one more pill. Leaning against her seat, she turned her head and kept her attention on the trees and occasional farmhouses they drove past. In just a few hours, the sun would be up, and she could breathe more freely. In just a few hours, she'd be on a plane.

CHAPTER 35

THE SOUND OF dripping water made its way into Claire's subconscious, and although she couldn't quite open her eyes, she slowly became aware of all the sensations running through her body.

Her first thought: *I'm alive.*

Her second: *Paul and Handel are dead.*

Or ... Perhaps she wasn't alive, and the afterlife had dripping water. Paul wasn't dead. He hadn't bled out on the thick rug in the compound. Handel wasn't dead either, and she hadn't shot him and watched him collapse.

Claire forced her eyelids to move. They wavered but didn't exactly lift. A moan rattled through her chest. Was that her?

Or Nora.

What had happened to Nora? Claire had dragged the woman as far as possible. They'd made it to the corridor, right? But then there was the smoke.

Claire inhaled, and it felt as if tiny needles were pricking her lungs. Her hands lifted, moving freely, then finding her chest as if she could stop the pain with touch.

"Easy," a male voice said, one that was familiar. *Not Paul. Not Handel.*

A warm hand touched her arm, and the contact made Claire flinch.

"Don't try to move, Claire," the man continued.

The warm hand on her upper arm, her bare upper arm, now seemed too hot. Was he gripping her? Was he restraining her? She'd been able to bring her hands to her chest. Her breathing increased, and her lungs strained to take a full breath.

"Try to breathe as slowly as possible," the man continued. "Your lungs have sustained injury, but they're recovering nicely. The most important thing you can do is stay relaxed. It will stop the pain."

But the pain was only increasing. Every breath hurt more than the first one, and emotions that Claire couldn't name were flooding her body. That voice. She knew that voice. But she couldn't open her eyes.

And then she recognized it. *Dr. Raymond.*

She was a prisoner to her own body. Unable to move, she was once again at the mercy of the WAO. Handel might be dead, but here was Dr. Raymond carrying on the work.

She opened her mouth to scream.

"Claire?" Dr. Raymond said, his voice rising in volume. "You need to calm down! Claire!"

He was shouting now, and he was still touching her. Something sharp pricked her shoulder. Another drug. Another test.

Claire felt her body relax and her breathing even out. Perhaps it would be better this way. To just give in and stop fighting. She was so tired.

"Claire?" Dr. Raymond said, his voice simmering through her. This time she didn't panic; she merely waited for him to continue.

"The tear gas and smoke damaged your lungs," Raymond said. "I found you and Nora unconscious, but I was able to get both of you out."

Claire could hear him, although she had no strength or motivation to reply. Dr. Raymond had gotten them *out*—out of the corridor? Out of the compound?

"Nora is up and walking now, doing much better," he continued.

Nora is alive. She made it.

"But your health was already run-down," Raymond said. "Nora told me about how you've been living in hiding and the devastation you started for the WAO."

Here it comes. The threats.

"With Paul gone, and Handel gone, and Bethany disappeared somewhere, I think I'm the only one who can tell you about Paul."

What is he talking about? What about Paul?

"He and I had begun to put together a plan," Raymond said, his voice growing quieter. "Handel tried to have Paul assassinated. And you, you had your chance to kill Paul too, but you spared his life, even though you'd temporarily paralyzed him." He chuckled.

What does he find amusing?

"Don't you understand, Claire?" Raymond said. "Paul had turned against Handel. He wanted to work with Nora to help *you.* He wanted revenge on his stepfather. Paul was going to take you to your son."

The tingling started. But this wasn't the kind that made her lungs feel like they were going to burst. The tingling was like having carried a massive backpack up a steep mountain for days and days, and then suddenly, you set down the backpack, and your body came alive with a deep relief.

Claire opened her eyes slowly. The room was silver and turquoise, shimmering like a huge aquarium. Raymond sat in a chair near her bed. Beyond him *was* an aquarium. An entire wall of glass that seemed to undulate with life as fish swam in and out of rock formations and spiked plants.

"You're in my private home," Raymond said. "Nora will be back in a couple of hours. She's been quite resourceful, really. Helping with nursing you, preparing meals, and barking plenty of orders to someone named Genevieve."

Claire swallowed against the thick dryness of her throat and tried to speak. Her voice came out as hoarse, but audible. "My son."

Raymond nodded. "Yes, he's alive. Paul told me that he'd found the boy."

She blinked, and her vision bounced in and out of focus. But it didn't panic her. Whatever Raymond had stuck her with seemed to be keeping her very, very calm. "The address."

Raymond's brows lifted. "You have the address?"

Claire tried to nod, but every muscle in her neck protested. "Paul gave me the address," she croaked out. What other address could it be? No matter what anyone drugged her with, she'd never forget one letter or number of what Paul had written on that piece of paper and flashed to the infrared security camera.

"You have something to look forward to, Claire," Raymond said. "Try to rest and get better. You have a little boy to meet."

Claire watched in disbelief as Raymond rose and crossed the room. He went into another room, and she heard him moving about what sounded like a kitchen. The wall-size aquarium caught her attention again. The fish zoomed about, as if searching for something, but they kept making sudden turns, trapped inside their glassed-in world.

Claire felt the same way. She'd escaped from the prison of the compound only to be boxed in by the lies of the Amazon Sisterhood and, after, the need to hide from her true identity. And now her own physical body was refusing to cooperate.

Would she recover? Was she truly free? Or was Dr. Raymond lying to her again?

The sound of a door opening reached her, and then Claire heard voices. *Nora.*

"She's awake? And alert?" Nora said.

Raymond's deeper voice sounded. "I gave her a muscle relaxant. She was starting to panic because of the pain."

"All right," Nora said. "I'll check on her."

Moments later, Nora came into the room.

Claire stared at the woman. She was alive and looked completely healthy. Her hair was smoothed back into a twist, and she wore a touch of makeup.

"How are you feeling?" Nora asked, a smile blossoming on her face. She sat right next to Claire before she could answer and grasped her hand.

Claire didn't know how she felt about this woman touching her.

"I . . . I'm alive."

Nora nodded, her eyes filled with amusement. "I'm alive too, thanks to you. I'm glad you're awake so that I can thank you."

Claire searched the woman's eyes for any sign of recrimination. Claire had killed her husband, after all. "I didn't know what else to do."

The lightheartedness fled Nora's eyes. "You did the right thing. The only thing, really." She raised her chin slightly, her gaze determined. "I would have done the same if you hadn't pulled the trigger first."

"I—I'm sorry about Paul," Claire said.

Nora nodded, her eyes filling with tears. "I am too. He was a good man at the core. His stepfather certainly did a number on him, but those last few days, I could see his heart changing."

"Yes," Claire said in a soft voice. Between what Raymond had said and the way Paul had told her not to forget the address he'd found for her, Paul had made up for some of his earlier crimes.

Nothing could ever completely atone for Claire's destroyed life, but now there was new hope. "What's happening with the WAO? What's Raymond's role in all of this?"

"Everyone has scattered," Nora said. "Some have been arrested, but they are only being held as suspects. No charges have been formally filed, although it seems to be in the works according to the media. Apparently, an FBI agent from the States has been pushing things along and validating some of the information that was leaked." She looked pointedly at Claire.

"I thought it would all take longer," Claire said, suppressing the slight smile that was pushing her mouth up.

"The impact is global," Nora continued. "Fortune 500 companies are scrambling to explain their association with the WAO and its subsidiaries." She folded her hands together. "Major countries lowered their loan interest rates to keep the stock market viable."

"So there's no fall guy?" Claire asked.

"No," Nora said. "Someone started a fire in the compound. Bethany somehow got out—someone must have carried her, but I don't know if she survived. Raymond got us out." She looked down at her twisting hands. "Paul and Handel were identified along with a few others."

Claire paused. "They're really both gone?"

"Yes," Nora said. "It's been about five days since Raymond brought us here, and we were worried we didn't have the right medical supplies here to help you out." She leaned forward and lowered her voice. "I know you don't trust me, but I also know that I owe my life to you."

"I'm not going back to the Sisterhood," Claire said. It would be the easy way, she knew. But there were just some things she couldn't forgive. Handel's death was a testament of that. Nora might be a sweeter villain that Handel, but Nora had done too little, too late.

"I wish you would give us another chance," Nora said.

Raymond came into the room, carrying an electronic tablet. It was playing a news program. "The CEO of Hughes & Ross just resigned," he said. "And the DeStefano Financial firm is under federal investigation by the US government."

Claire watched the small screen as a picture of Robert DeStefano flashed behind the news anchor, who acted like she was delivering the most juicy gossip. Perhaps she was. Claire watched in silence for a few minutes as the news anchor went through the long list of company names. Then Claire said, "I'd like to sleep now."

CHAPTER 36

THEY WERE MEETING at a park. There was no paperwork, no legal contracts, but Raymond had assured Claire that the couple knew this day was a possibility. Not for the boy's mother to claim him, but for the boy's father. The couple had been told the mother had died in childbirth.

Handel Raine hadn't wanted the responsibility of a child on his hands, but if the child met the IQ tests, then Handel would have brought him into the WAO.

That had all changed now.

Claire had turned down both Raymond and Nora's offers to accompany her. She'd been staying in a hotel not too far from Raymond's home over the past few days. Claire was now an expert of sorts through the dozens of articles she'd read on adopted children, foster children, displaced children, and challenges such as attachment disorders and bonding with birth parents.

But ever since she realized that the address Paul had risked his life to give her belonged to her child, Claire knew she wanted to raise him. He might be in a wonderful home, with caring foster parents, but he was *hers*. And hers alone. He had no one else related to him in the world.

"Thank you, I should be back soon," Claire told the taxi driver. She'd thought about renting a car, but her head had been hurting all morning in anticipation, and her lungs were aching. They'd healed, mostly, but there was still a ways to go. Raymond told her that she wouldn't be able to live in a high-elevation city, so she wouldn't be returning to Park City. She'd picked out a location on the coast of Florida, although she hadn't shared any of the details with Nora or Raymond.

As supportive as they'd been to Claire, she had to completely free herself and become a new person. That meant another new identity. But that was fine. This time it would be for her son.

A couple sat on the park bench, and the jungle gym was empty save for a young boy perched on the top bars. School was in session, so other children weren't about, and it must be naptime for the younger ones in the neighborhood. Child development was another thing she'd read up on.

Claire walked slowly, her eyes glued to the small form. The first thought that went through her mind was his safety. Couldn't a kid his size fall off and break something? The second thought was that his hair was the same color as hers.

He looked up and met her gaze, not shying away at all, just curious. Claire liked that immediately. She didn't know what to expect of his personality and character, but he could very well become hysterical when he left his foster parents.

The man and woman now spotted her, and both of them rose to their feet.

"Jacob," the man said. "Come and meet someone special."

Claire glanced at the man and woman. The woman looked as if she'd been crying, and the man's jaw was set firmly. His eyes were kind, gentle, and that told Claire everything she needed to know. The boy had been well cared for and loved.

The boy said, "Coming," and scrambled down as if he'd done it a hundred times a day. So effortless. He hurried over to Claire, doing a half jog in that way that kids always seemed to be overflowing with irrepressible energy.

"Hello," Claire said when the boy stopped in front of her. His eyes blinked up at her, and Claire's heart soared. They weren't Handel's eyes. They weren't hers.

They were her mother's.

Relief swept through her.

Claire had wondered if her son would look like his father, the man she loathed, and the man she'd killed. She'd read about divorced women and how sometimes they struggled if their child reminded them of their exes.

"Hello," the boy said. "I'm Jacob."

"I'm Claire," she said, holding out her hand like she would in a formal situation. She supposed this was a formal occasion—she was meeting her son for the first time.

He put his small hand in hers and solemnly shook it. Then he smiled, keeping his eyes on her. "Mum and Dad told me about you."

The way he'd said *Mum* and *Dad*—affectionately—tripped her heart.

"Oh?" Claire said, feeling breathless. But she was going to stay in the moment and remember every word this child spoke while at the same time marveling that she'd created this human being. "What did they tell you?"

His foster parents remained by the bench, as if they wanted to give her some time alone with her son—and some privacy—before the arrangements had to be discussed.

Jacob shrugged his small shoulders. Claire noticed that

everything about him was small, but looking at him made her heart feel large. "They said you're my real mum. They said that I was going to live with you now."

He was staring at her as if he thought she was an interesting creature. He didn't seem to be sad or hysterical. It was as if he thought this was the natural order of his life.

"Yes," Claire said, her voice cutting out for a moment. "I *am* your mum, and I was very sick for a long time."

"And now you're better?" he asked, his face brightening.

Claire's throat tightened. "Now I'm better." She tried to smile but feared it was more of a nervous twitch. The boy was still staring at her, and she was staring right back.

"Would you like to live with me?" she asked him.

He didn't answer right away, and Claire's heart started to pound. She knew his foster parents wouldn't give her any trouble. Nora and Raymond had already made sure of that. The foster parents were to have previously said their goodbyes so that handoff wouldn't create additional trauma for Jacob.

"I think it would be okay," Jacob said at last in a thoughtful tone, as if he'd given it great consideration.

Claire's heart melted.

"Did you know I like dogs?" Jacob asked.

She blinked back the forming tears. "I like dogs too."

He glanced over at his foster parents, then he asked her, "Do you have a dog?"

"No," Claire said, thinking fast. "I thought I'd wait until you can help me pick one out."

The boy's face lit up. "She said we can get a dog!" he called out to his foster parents.

They smiled at him, and Claire wished she didn't have to break up this little family. She was grateful her son had been taken care of, that he was alive, that she'd never have to worry about him meeting his real father. But she'd been waiting for this day ever since he was born, never quite believing it would happen.

He turned back to look at her. "Will we get the dog in America?" he asked.

"Yes," Claire said. "I don't think dogs like plane rides."

"Okay," he said. "I already packed my clothes." He pointed to a small suitcase next to the bench. His entire six years of memories would be relegated to whatever fit into that case.

When he was eighteen, Claire would let him contact the foster parents again. But until then, she had to go off the grid. She didn't want to explain all of this to Jacob now.

"Where are we going first?" Jacob asked.

This was all moving very fast. "To the airport, and then we'll fly to America."

"*Then* can we get a dog?"

Claire nodded. "Then we'll get a dog."

Jacob grinned, and Claire's heart completely melted.

He ran over to his foster parents and hugged them. Claire walked closer, keeping her distance. The woman was crying, and the man looked like he was about to.

The man picked up the suitcase and handed it over to Claire. She could only nod her thanks, although there was so much more she wanted to say, but she couldn't form the words around the lump in her throat.

Jacob turned from the couple, seeming completely fine and happy. Claire knew that could change at any moment. From Jacob's viewpoint, he was going on an adventure. It all sounded fun right now, but he'd miss his foster parents. They were all he'd known for the first six years of his life.

She didn't know why she did it, perhaps it was an instinct,

but as Jacob headed toward her, she held out her hand. Jacob didn't hesitate and slipped his hand into hers. They walked toward the taxi waiting at the far end of the park.

Jacob asked her about what her favorite kind of dog was and if there would be a park by their new house.

"We'll go to the park every day if you want," Claire said. She was no longer on the run, no longer hiding. She could leave her house and go to the park. She could even go out in public . . . anywhere she wanted.

She found a smile tugging at her mouth, making her heart feel light, her step quicker.

When they reached the taxi, Claire buckled Jacob into his seat first, then loaded the suitcase. It was heavy but manageable. Claire felt only slightly out of breath. She'd promised Raymond that she'd take it easy for a few weeks. Once Jacob started school, she'd force herself to rest while he was gone during the day so that she could be more active when he was home.

Jacob was full of questions as they drove to the airport, and Claire discovered that he hadn't been much farther than the neighborhood he'd grown up in. She wondered if that was a stipulation from Handel.

He fell asleep about an hour into the flight, and Claire couldn't stop watching him. His dark eyelashes rested on his perfectly smooth cheeks. His small fingers clutched the airline blanket to his chin. Claire reached out and touched his hair, marveling at the color so like her own. He'd told her he had a wiggly bottom tooth and that he wanted to take swimming lessons again.

Claire hadn't told his foster parents which state they'd be living in, but she gave them an email address so they could communicate with her. They'd both looked a little shell-shocked at the park, and Claire really did feel for them. She did. But Jacob was her son, and even just sitting by him on the plane while he slept made her feel more whole than she had in years. Possibly since her parents' death.

CHAPTER 37

Claire dumped the last three anxiety pills into the toilet. She knew she could take them to the police station and dispose of them properly, but she had to get rid of them now.

It had been two months since Claire had needed to take any medication to make it through the day without a panic attack. Two months of living with her son and caring for him. It wasn't hard to love him—that she had done since before his birth—but she'd finally come to know him. And that had filled her life with a joy she never expected.

"Mom!" his voice rang throughout the house, bouncing off the hardwood floors. Being called *Mom* had taken some getting used to, and she'd schooled herself not to get weepy when Jacob did so. "I'm ready!" A bark echoed Jacob's shout.

Jacob had named the black Labrador Buddy. And it seemed to fit the dog. Buddy stuck by Jacob's side every minute that he was home, following him around and barking back when Jacob talked to him. It was like they were having a conversation. Buddy was a few years old and acted as if he were too tired to bother with anything when it was just him and Claire. But when Jacob was around, the dog suddenly had a ton of energy.

The three of them had settled in a small coastal town in Florida, and Claire loved it. In her last act before completely separating herself from every connection with the WAO, she'd laundered a healthy amount of money through a few accounts until it landed in her new account at the local city's credit union. She wouldn't have to worry about money for the rest of her life, and Jacob would receive a good chunk on his twenty-fifth birthday. For now, she'd work to make a difference in the life of her son and in the lives of other children in need—abandoned, neglected, or otherwise. She was already working on setting up a foundation to funnel money into deserving programs.

She'd let Jacob keep his name, and she'd altered hers to Clara Sorenson, keeping their last name as common as she could. So they were Clara and Jacob Sorenson. Single mother and son moved recently from England. Jacob's accent wouldn't change overnight, and it was easier to keep as close to possible to his actual roots.

Claire had no problem creating a fake birth certificate and the other documentation needed to enroll him in school. She'd put him in a private school, and even so, the first day saying goodbye to him at the front entrance was excruciating.

School was the only time they were separated, and Jacob had become her little buddy.

"Come on, Mom!" Jacob said. Buddy barked.

Claire smiled to herself. His impatience reminded her of herself at that age. It seemed anything that had involved her parents had taken forever. But now Claire realized that life moved at lightning speed—and she wasn't about to miss a moment more of Jacob's.

She'd pulled a sugar cookie recipe from Pinterest, and tonight they were cutting out the shapes, then later they'd decorate them. It was a random and fun activity. Something to do after school. Claire had read a dozen child development books, and this activity was hands-on, with unlimited creativity, and it involved the parent. Perfect.

Claire flushed the pills down the toilet, then carried the pill bottle to the kitchen where Jacob was sitting on a barstool and leaning on the island counter, his chin propped on his hands. He tapped his foot against the island.

"Can we make them green?" he asked as soon as he saw her.

Buddy ran up to her, and she patted the dog on the head. Satisfied, Buddy ran back to Jacob and sat at his feet, tail wagging.

Claire dropped the pill bottle into the kitchen trash, then turned to face her son. She loved his light hazel eyes, so much like her mother's, and the way that his hair was tousled, and how he was always a bit sweaty at the hairline because he never seemed to sit still for very long.

"Do you mean green frosting, or making the actual cookie dough green?" Claire asked.

He thought for a moment. She loved how he did that. He always considered her questions seriously as if his answer or decision were extremely important.

"If we make the cookie dough green, then the monsters will look scarier," he finally announced.

"Oh, so we're making monster cookies?" Claire asked. "What about flowers or butterflies?"

Jacob wrinkled his nose. "You can make your own kind like that, but I'm making monsters."

"All right," Claire said with a laugh. "Maybe your monsters will want to play with my butterflies."

He grimaced and shook his head.

Claire was glad her son wasn't afraid of monsters and that he'd never known a real one. She intended to keep it that way.

"All right, here's the recipe," she said, handing over the paper where she'd written down the ingredients. "Can you help me read what it says?"

Jacob smiled. He loved to show off his reading skills from school. They read through the ingredients together, and Jacob found most of them. When they had them all out on the center island, they got to work.

"Okay, read the first step of the recipe again," Claire said.

"I don't have to read it," he announced. "I already memorized it."

"But you only read it once," she said, looking at him as she unwrapped the butter.

He shrugged his small shoulders. "I can see it in my head still. We're supposed to soften the butter, then blend it with the sugar."

Claire stared at her son. "You can see it? Like a picture, or like words?"

"I don't know," he said. "I just know."

Claire went silent. Her son was gifted. For better, or for worse, he had her gift.

"How do we soften the butter?" Jacob asked.

She blinked. "Uh, we can try the defrost setting on the microwave." She went through the motions, her mind trying to comprehend what she's just learned about her son. It both thrilled and scared her. She had to tell herself over and over that the WAO was gone, finished, and would never be able to harm her son.

Once they had made the dough, Claire said, "Now it has to chill in the refrigerator so it gets hard enough to roll out."

Jacob seemed disappointed to have to wait even longer. "The recipe didn't say that."

"Trust me," Claire said. "The dough will be easier to roll out. Maybe we can go to the park for a little bit while we wait."

"Okay! Let me get my soccer ball." Jacob scurried out of the kitchen, Buddy running and barking after him. Within moments, all three of them were heading out the front door. Jacob gripped Buddy's leash in one hand and carried the soccer ball in the other.

Claire locked the dead bolt in addition to setting the alarm system. Out of habit, she always kept the blinds closed on the front windows of the house. They passed through the gate, which she also kept locked with a key. She didn't relish the idea of neighbors stopping by unannounced. She'd met the ones who lived close but had kept her distance.

Otherwise, Claire felt safe in the neighborhood, and she should. It was a gated community, and people stayed to themselves for the most part.

The park was also private and usually quiet. So it made for a nice place for Jacob to run around. He skipped ahead of Claire, and she loved watching his enthusiasm for life. It was contagious, and her heart swelled as she looked at the wonders of new things through his eyes.

Once they reached the park, Jacob ran to the slide first and climbed up the ladder. Buddy took off after Jacob and even enjoyed a trip down the slide before he came over to sit by Claire.

She sat on one of the benches beneath a shade tree. The Florida sun was that late afternoon color of orange-pink, and a few clouds had banked to the east, but nothing that looked like it would threaten rain.

Buddy didn't last long at Claire's side, and he ran around the park, then joined Jacob.

Claire's phone buzzed with an alert. She glanced at it to see that Riya had posted to Facebook. Claire clicked on the post and read that Riya was doing a fundraiser for her kids' school. Claire would make another anonymous donation later tonight.

She pocketed her phone, but moments later it buzzed again, this time with a text. For a while she ignored it. Not many people contacted her cell phone. Only the school had the number. It was with this thought that she pulled it out of her pocket.

Nora had sent a text. At first, Claire was surprised. They'd only communicated briefly after the first week she had arrived in the States. Alarm swept through her. Nora had said she wouldn't be contacting Claire unless it was important.

Claire opened the text and read through it quickly, her heart sinking.

By the time she'd finished reading it, she felt the memories rushing back.

Frances returned to us a few hours ago, and she's in pretty bad shape. We aren't sure what happened to her or where she went. She's mostly incoherent. But she does keep asking for you, so I thought I'd let you know in case you can think of something that might help her.

Claire reread the message and blinked back the burning tears that started. Frances was alive. Had she returned on her own? Or did someone deliver her? Claire closed her eyes for a few moments. What had Frances endured over the past years? If she was incoherent, was she strung out on drugs? Had she been beaten?

Claire's heart ached for her friend and whatever horrors she might have endured. She exhaled and opened her eyes. Jacob had his arms around Buddy's neck as they wrestled. Jacob laughed, and Claire let the sound wash over her. A child's laughter was perhaps the best balm to the soul.

She read the text again. Why was Frances asking for *her*?

Her fingers hovered over her phone as she debated what to type back.

She wanted to help, but how would that work? She

couldn't compromise her new identity, her living situation, her child's safety . . . Finally, she wrote: *Thanks for letting me know. I'm so glad she's returned safe. Perhaps we can arrange a phone call.*

She sent the text and turned off her phone. Jacob and Buddy had found a stick and were playing fetch with it. She tried to focus on their playing, but the text from Nora still invaded her thoughts.

Leave the phone off, she told herself. Later, she could check to see if Nora replied. She focused on her breathing and let the pulse of anxiety rush through her. She tamped down the irrational thoughts of buying a plane ticket. Taking Jacob with her to the Sisterhood. Visiting Frances. Helping her heal.

Frances is in capable hands. The Sisterhood will take care of her. I can't fight another person's battles. What could Claire really do to help that Nora wasn't already doing?

Claire's body felt numb, and she wished her mind would follow. She continued to sit, watching Jacob and Buddy play and letting normal surround her. The park. The warm breeze. The sounds of Jacob's laughter. Buddy playfully barking.

She wasn't entirely sure how long they were at the park, perhaps an hour, when Jacob came running over. "Can we finish the cookies now?" he asked, Buddy at his side, panting from the exercise.

Claire realized she hadn't been focused on Jacob or the dog for a while. Which was foolish. Not that she expected a kidnapper to be lurking around the corner of the neighboring house, but Claire prided herself on being continually aware of her surroundings.

"Sure," she said, and stood up.

Jacob slipped his warm and sweaty hand into hers. Claire's heart soared at the simple gesture. They walked back to their house, Buddy tugging on the leash as much as Jacob would allow. As they neared their house, Jacob released her hand, and he and Buddy ran toward the gate.

"Wait a minute," Claire said with a laugh. "I need to unlock it."

"It's open," Jacob said, and pushed the gate inward.

Claire's heart nearly stopped. She'd locked the gate; she always did. "Wait! Jacob—"

He released Buddy from his leash, and instead of bounding toward the front door, he stopped.

The dog emitted a low growl.

"What's wrong with him?" Jacob asked, going through the gate.

Claire caught up with Jacob and grabbed his hand. "I don't know," she said. "But we need to wait out here for a minute." She eyed the house. Without testing the door, she had no idea if it had been opened.

But she'd never heard Buddy growl like he was. And she *knew* she'd locked the gate. Hadn't she?

"Come on," she said, taking Jacob's hand. "Buddy, this way!"

The dog looked over at her, then back at the house.

"Now, Buddy. Let's go!"

Finally, the dog walked toward her, and she releashed him.

Claire hurried down the neighborhood street until they were back at the park. Then she called the alarm company.

"Nothing has been triggered," the service representative told her over the phone.

"Can you tell me the time of the last alarm activation at the front door?" she asked.

When the representative told her, Claire knew it was the same time she'd first left the house. It had been *her* activation. She thanked him and hung up.

"Mommy," Jacob said, tugging on her hand.

She looked down at him, feeling like her breath was about to cut out.

"You didn't lock the gate," he said.

Claire stared into his eyes. "Are you sure?"

He nodded. "Remember, Buddy tried to pull me off the sidewalk, and you grabbed the leash. So the gate shut. You didn't go back and lock it with your key."

Claire continued to look into his eyes as her heart rate began to slow. "Okay, you're right." How could she forget that? She didn't forget anything. Her mind had gone into hyperdrive when she saw Jacob open the unlocked gate. Perhaps with the text from Nora about Frances, Claire was being more paranoid.

"Okay," she repeated, mostly for her own benefit. "Let's go back. I was just worried for nothing, I guess."

Jacob only nodded, but he gripped her hand extra tightly on the walk back home. It was as if he knew she needed the reassurance.

When they reached their house, Claire tried not to let the panic rise again as she opened the unlocked gate, stepped through, relocked it, and crossed the yard. This time, Buddy didn't stop or growl. Perhaps he'd just been set off by her own panicked voice.

She disabled the alarm and opened the front door, and she and Jacob and Buddy stepped inside. Then she immediately reset the alarm. She couldn't help but scan the front room. All of the lights were on—how she'd left them. The house smelled and sounded normal.

"Come on, Mom," Jacob said. "Let's finish the monster cookies."

"I'll be right there," she said. "I'm just going to the bathroom for a minute. You can get out the bowl from the refrigerator."

She watched Jacob hurry to the kitchen and heard him open the refrigerator door. Exhaling, she stepped into the bathroom. She read through Nora's text one more time. Then she wrote: *Give Frances my best when she's coherent. I'm sorry that I can't help. I hope she recovers. But I need to stay dark for my son's sake.*

She hit Send, knowing that if she allowed herself to be swept back into the world she'd left, she wouldn't be able to protect Jacob. He was the most important thing in her life. He was her everything.

Before joining him in the kitchen, Claire went to the front room again. She peeked out of the blinds and watched the street for a moment. Then she checked the alarm system and read through the log of activations. She could confirm each one. She was safe. They were safe. She had to trust in that.

"Mom!" Jacob said. "Buddy wants to taste the cookie dough."

"No," Claire said, fighting a smile as she walked into the kitchen. She loved the normalcy that Jacob brought to her life. "Maybe he can try a cookie *after* we bake them."

Jacob laughed. Another thing she adored about her son. Laughing came easily to him.

She grabbed the rolling pin while Jacob dumped the dough out. As she rolled the dough flat, and Jacob kept telling Buddy how he had to be patient and wait for his cookie, Claire forced herself to focus on this moment with her son. Not to dwell on the past, and not to worry about tomorrow or the next day.

By the time the cookies had baked and cooled and Jacob had eaten five or six, and Claire had eaten her fair share as well, she started to truly relax. She felt good about her decision to keep Nora and the Amazon Sisterhood at arm's length. They were a group of talented and tenacious women. They didn't need her.

Jacob needed her.

"Come on, Jacob," she said, messing up his hair. "Time for bed."

"I'm not even tired," he said, then released a gigantic yawn.

They both laughed. "What did you say?" she teased.

"All right," Jacob said. "I guess I'm sort of tired." He slipped his hand into hers as they walked down the short hallway to his bedroom.

Claire's heart filled and overflowed at the simple, trusting gesture. They read a story together—a Sesame Street book about Cookie Monster—and Jacob hugged Buddy about four times before he let Claire lead the dog out of his room.

Rules for Buddy included that he couldn't sleep in one of their bedrooms. Buddy knew his routine and happily settled on the rug by the front door. Claire also went through her routine, checking all the locks on the doors and windows, then double-checking that the security system was set.

She liked to climb into bed early and read—usually articles and world news. In the safe cocoon of her bedroom, complete with her pale-blue bedspread, the outside world felt miles away. And that's how she liked it.

Before pulling up her usual website haunts, she turned her phone back on to see if Nora had replied. It wouldn't change her mind, but Claire was just curious.

There wasn't anything from Nora, but a text had come through from an unknown number. Claire's heart skipped a beat, and she told herself not to jump to any conclusions. It could be someone from the school, or a mom of one of Jacob's new friends. She'd given about four or five people her cell phone number.

But when she read the text, her breath stalled.

I won't blame you if you don't want to see me or talk to

me. I wanted to let you know I'm staying in your town. I hoped to have one last chance to apologize before I go underground. I'm sorry for everything. —Paul

CHAPTER 38

Claire stared at the word *Paul.*

Someone was screwing with her. Someone who knew which town she lived in. Someone who had her cell phone number.

Claire pushed the covers aside and climbed out of her bed. She couldn't think. She couldn't breathe. She dropped the phone onto her bed and leaned forward, resting her hands on her knees, trying not to pass out. *No. No. No.*

She'd have to relocate. She'd have to uproot Jacob. Change names. Change everything.

Claire's eyes stung with tears as she thought of how stupid she'd been. How much danger she had put Jacob in. Maybe she should have left him in England with his foster family. Traveling with a kid was so much more complicated. Even as Claire thought of giving up Jacob, she knew she could never do it. She might as well cut out her own heart.

She picked her phone back up and with trembling fingers opened her contact list. Claire didn't even bother to consider whether or not Nora might be asleep.

"Claire?" Nora answered, her voice very much alert. "What a surprise."

"Is this a secure line?" Claire asked.

"Of course."

"Mine isn't," Claire said, unable to keep the hysteria out of her voice. "Someone found my number and is trying to intimidate me."

"Slow down," Nora said. "What happened?"

"I have to know one thing," Claire said. "And please, please tell me the truth. Is Paul Raine alive?"

The pause at the end of the line infuriated Claire.

"Nora!"

"Calm down," Nora said in a firm tone. "You don't know what you're asking me to do."

Claire hurried into her bathroom, feeling like she might throw up. The fluorescent lighting of the bathroom showed her a woman with crazed eyes looking back at her in the mirror. "Tell me. Right. Now."

"Look, I don't have clearance—"

"You told me you would help me with anything I needed," Claire spat out. "You told me that you would always have my back, my *best* interest. A few hours ago, you asked for *my* help with Frances."

Nora remained silent on the other end of the line.

"I hate you," Claire said. "*I hate all of you.*" She pressed End on her phone and slid down the bathroom wall. She wrapped her arms about her legs and started to sob.

Her phone rang. *Nora.* Claire ignored it.

Ten minutes later, it rang again. Claire ignored it.

When Nora called the third time, Claire pressed Accept but said nothing.

"Paul's alive," Nora said in a faint voice. "He was supposed to go underground completely. He cut ties with everyone and everything—he insisted on it." She paused, and when Claire still said nothing, Nora said, "Now tell me what happened."

Claire exhaled and wondered if she could even find her voice. "Someone texted me claiming to be Paul. He said he was in my town. He said he wants to apologize."

"Impossible."

"Obviously it's not impossible, seeing as *he's not dead.*" Claire couldn't keep the bitterness out of her voice. Her emotions were starting to pitch again. Paul was alive, and everyone had lied to her about it. Raymond. Nora. Who else knew?

Nora spoke. "Paul's the one who—he made me promise to never tell anyone, especially you."

Claire squeezed her eyes shut. "Then why did he text me? Or was it someone else—someone who knows he's alive, and now they're after me?" Her voice was growing hysterical again.

"Come back to the Amazon Sisterhood," Nora said. "We can protect you here. I can send a bodyguard to your place right now to escort you. We'll hire a private tutor for Jacob."

"No," Claire shot out. "I'm going to find a way to put a stop to this—to all of this." She breathed in, breathed out. "Give Frances my best, but just know this is the last time you'll hear from me." She hung up without letting Nora reply.

Claire dragged herself to her feet and nearly staggered to her bedside table. Inside the locked drawer was a 9mm. She pulled it out, then left her bedroom and walked into the front room. Buddy lifted his head from where he was lying by the front door, on alert.

"Come on, boy," Claire said, leading him to her bedroom. "Stay in here for a while." She shut the bedroom door and returned to the living room. Looking through the blinds, she surveyed the street. Everything looked normal and quiet.

She lifted her phone and pulled up the text. The words were still the same. Now that she knew Paul was alive, she read it differently—if the text really was from Paul.

She typed back a reply, then hit Send before she could change her mind.

Call me.

Twenty seconds later, her phone rang. *Unknown Number.*

The ringing phone shot adrenaline straight to her heart. She clicked Accept and brought the phone to her ear.

"Claire?" Paul's voice.

It was him. It was Paul. She'd had his voice memorized for years. She'd also watched him die.

"How could you?" she said, her voice breaking.

"Let me explain," he said. "I owe you at least that."

She couldn't answer, not right away. "Where are you?"

"About a mile away."

She exhaled. Inhaled. "How did you find me?"

"It's what I do."

Right. "Were you at my house earlier?"

"Yes." He paused. "I'm sorry if I scared you."

"Was the gate unlocked?"

"Yes. I left everything the way I found it. I knocked on the front door, but no one answered."

She stared into the darkness of the living room that was cut by the faint glimmer of a night-light in the kitchen. "You came to my neighborhood, where you know I'm trying to build a life with my son, and you *knocked* on my door?"

"I don't always make the best decisions," he said.

Claire didn't know whether to laugh or cry. Or stay numb.

"How is he?" Paul asked.

Jacob. "He's . . ." Her voice caught. "He's beautiful."

"Yeah, he is."

She heard the emotion in Paul's voice too, and it wasn't helping her stay calm, collected. The silence extended between them.

"Can I see you?" Paul asked in a low voice.

Claire wanted to say no. She wanted to scream at him. But mostly she wanted to see him. If only to say goodbye, because that was all that could happen now. If she was to forget her past, she had to forget Paul. "For a few minutes. How soon can you be here?"

"Ten minutes."

It took him eleven.

Claire watched through the blinds as a car slowed and stopped on the other side of the street. The streetlight a few houses down did little to illuminate the man who climbed out of the nondescript car.

Her heart thundered as she watched him cross the street, no hesitation in his step, as if he'd been to her house before. Which of course he had. She recognized him, even in the dark, and even at this distance. He looked leaner than she remembered, though. She supposed living life on the run had burned some calories. He wore a dark shirt, and his hands were shoved into his pants pockets. As he neared the gate, the light from her porch reached him enough that she could see that he hadn't shaved in a few days, and his hair seemed longer.

He reached the gate and found it locked.

Claire had left it locked.

He waited, keeping his gaze on the front door. It was as if he could see through it, could see her on the other side. He was waiting for her to make the first move. To let him in.

Claire crossed to the front door, taking one deliberate step after another. She unlocked the door, then opened it. Paul didn't move, didn't react, but she could feel his gaze on her.

She stepped out onto the porch and paused, focusing on her breathing. Then she stepped off the porch and walked along the short walkway to the gate. Paul's eyes were on her, but she wasn't looking at him yet. She wasn't quite ready to meet his eyes. Using her key, she unlocked the gate and swung it open.

Paul walked through and stopped.

Again, Claire didn't look at him as she shut the gate and locked it again. She turned and headed back to the house. Paul didn't follow immediately, but when he did, she heard his footsteps. They echoed the rapid beat of her heart.

She reached the front door, which she'd left ajar, opened the door wide, and stepped through. Once she'd cleared the threshold, Paul came inside. The only light was coming from the porch light, filtering through the blinds, and a night-light in the kitchen, so the living room remained dim.

Paul remained close while Claire shut and locked the front door. She turned to see him watching her, standing right next to her.

"Claire," he began.

She reached up and slapped him.

His dark eyes narrowed, and he brought his hand up to press against his cheek.

She'd hit him pretty hard, but not hard enough to draw blood. She couldn't believe he was alive—and that he hadn't told her. That he'd let her believe all this time she'd left him to die. New anger coursed through her. Anger because he'd deceived her. Rage because she'd grieved over him, and seeing him now made her realize how much she'd mourned. How much guilt she'd carried.

"Claire, listen—"

She reached up to slap him again, but he caught her hand this time. They stood together in the near dark for a moment, her hand suspended near his face while his hand gripped her wrist.

His dark eyes searched hers, and in them she saw remorse, she saw compassion, and she saw a man who'd almost given up his life for her. Who, according to police records, had been found burned to death in the WAO compound fire. She saw a man who, with his dying breath, had given her what she wanted most. If he hadn't led her to Jacob, she wouldn't have him now.

She raised her other hand, and this time he didn't try to stop her. But she didn't strike him. Instead, she touched his cheek. His stubble was both soft and rough as she slid her fingers along his jaw. He didn't move as she slipped her hand behind his neck as she stepped closer.

Breathing in his familiar scent, she felt heat rush through her body at his nearness. He released her wrist, and she moved her other hand to his shoulder.

Paul held completely still, as if he were afraid to move.

Perhaps she'd always wanted to do this, and perhaps it would only happen once. But she wanted it to happen. Now. She pressed her mouth against his. He seemed to freeze. She'd made a mistake, she decided. She was about to pull away, but then his hands skimmed down the sides of her body, and he grasped her hips. He started kissing her, his mouth moving against hers, warm and insistent.

She kissed him back, and he pressed her against the wall so that she was pinned between the wall and his body. The heat from his mouth seemed to reach her very toes. She ran her fingers through his hair, and he drew away for a split second, only to start kissing her neck.

Paul was alive. He was holding her in his arms. His heart was beating against her chest.

"Claire," he whispered. "I am so sorry."

His mouth left a trail of heat wherever he kissed her. She didn't know where this was going or what tomorrow would bring, but touching Paul, here, now, was fulfilling something deep inside of her that had been missing for a long time, possibly forever.

"I'm so glad you got out of there," he said, resting his forehead against hers. "When I woke up, I thought I'd lost you."

"How did you get out of the compound?" Claire asked, trying to catch her breath.

Paul stepped away from her. "Let's sit down . . . I need some space—to explain, to think clearly."

They moved to the couch, and Claire sat on the opposite side from him. She pulled her knees up and wrapped her arms around her legs. She was trembling, and she wasn't sure why.

"Are you all right?" Paul asked. He didn't miss a thing.

"I don't know."

"Come here," he said, holding out his hand.

She moved closer, and he linked their hands together. Then he reached over with his other hand to smooth back her hair.

"I don't entirely trust myself with you right now," Paul said. "This is nice, though. I think I can behave if we stay like this."

She looked up at him. "I'm the one who kissed you."

His gaze went to her mouth, and heat shot through her again. "I'm glad you did. It gives me hope that you don't hate me."

"I do hate you—I mean, I'm mad at you," Claire said. "But I also missed you, and I'm glad you're alive and—"

"Shh," he said, wrapping an arm around her and pulling her close. He pressed a kiss on her forehead.

Claire closed her eyes and allowed herself to relax against Paul.

"I wanted to tell you everything as soon as I woke up," he said. "Raymond pulled me out of the compound the same time he rescued you and Nora, but he took me to another location. When I realized how close I came to death, and the fact that my death had already been reported, I thought it would be safer if I broke all ties."

"Safer for who?"

"You, Jacob, Nora, Raymond . . ." he said. "Handel might be dead and the WAO destroyed, but there are still people out there who I don't want to ever bother you. If I'm out of the picture, then I can protect you anonymously."

Claire exhaled. "Bethany."

Paul nodded.

She wrapped her arm about his waist, and he pulled her closer.

"What happens tomorrow?" she asked.

When he didn't answer, she looked up at him. "You can't disappear again."

"I can't risk something happening to you or Jacob." He trailed his fingers along her jaw.

"Life is a risk."

His mouth lifted into a half smile. "That sounds like a billboard."

"You'll love Jacob," she said. "He's an amazing kid."

He dropped his hand, skimming her arm. "Like his mother."

It was Claire's turn to smile, but then she sobered quickly. She had to know what Paul was really planning, if tonight would be the last time she'd ever see him. Even if he stuck around and met Jacob in the morning, would that be the end?

"You're thinking too hard," Paul said, as if he could read her mind. "Should I be worried?"

"Jacob is really thriving here," Claire said. "But there's always a chance that something will be compromised, and we'll have to pack up and relocate. Change our names, start over."

Paul nodded. "That's true, although you've been really careful. It took me some work to find you. I couldn't even crack Nora."

"I was thinking . . ." She watched him closely. "Relocating three people wouldn't be much different than relocating two."

Paul's gaze didn't waver, but she still didn't have a clue as to what he was thinking.

"The risk is much higher, though," he said. "With me added to the mix, there are more chances that one of us could be tracked."

Claire tilted her head. "I never thought you'd back down from a challenge, Paul Raine."

He raised his brows. "Is this a challenge?"

"Will it make a difference?"

Paul leaned down and kissed her. Instead of the frantic passion of moments before, he kissed her slowly, tenderly. "I'll make you a deal," he whispered when he drew back. "I stay, and you have to promise to follow my security measures."

"Like what?"

"You need surveillance cameras installed around the yard," he said.

"All right." Claire slid her fingers along his neck. "What else?"

"Jacob needs a GPS tracker on his person at all times, maybe in the form of a watch."

"Okay."

"Our phones need to be linked so that we get the same messages and phone calls," Paul continued.

"Are you flirting with me?" Claire asked.

"This is serious," he said.

"I know, and that's what I love about you," Claire said, then she stilled. Had she just said that? She hadn't meant to make any sort of declaration.

"You need a newer-model car," he said, his breath warm against her neck as he lowered his head. "Something with four-wheel drive."

"Okay, what else?" Goosebumps rose along her skin.

"Target practice twice a week," he continued.

"Only if you come with me."

"Done."

She pulled him into a tight hug. He buried his face against the hollow of her neck. "Thank you for coming back to me," she said.

"I couldn't stay away," he murmured. "Believe me, I tried."

Claire closed her eyes and let the warmth of his arms envelop her. Paul was here, with her, and she was going to make the best of it. With Jacob, and Paul, she would live for every day the future might bring.

ACKNOWLEDGMENTS

As always, there are many who had a hand in helping to bring this book to fruition. I'm grateful for the early feedback on this story from Grace Doyle, as well as my agent Jane Dystel. In addition, I'm ever grateful for my beta readers who read more than one revision of this book. They're as passionate about plot and characters as I am, and it was wonderful to be able to have so much feedback. Many thanks to Patti Hansen, Laura Charchenko, Katie Judy, Shannon Henderson, Julie Finlinson, Susan Bangerter, Heidi Robbins, Melanie Wilkerson, Barbara Kappen, Susan Rowser, Corey Pulver, Karen Tuttle, Kathy Haggard, Lorraine Gwilliam, Autumn Needs, Lisa Gile, Tamera Westhoff, Julie Smith, Kathy Douglas, Tabitha Valencic, Andrea Plotner, Kathleen Brebes, Katie Williams, Kathy Bennion, Abby Holt, Jessica Cottam, and Mary Beaumont.

Finally, many thanks to copyeditor Haley Swan and her diligent editing.

ABOUT H.B. MOORE

HEATHER B. MOORE is a *USA Today* bestselling author of more than a dozen historical novels and thrillers, written under pen name H.B. Moore. She writes women's fiction, romance and inspirational non-fiction under Heather B. Moore. This can all be confusing, so her kids just call her Mom. Heather attended Cairo American College in Egypt, the Anglican School of Jerusalem in Israel, and earned a Bachelor of Science degree from Brigham Young University in Utah.

Sign up for Heather's email list: hbmoore.com/contact
Website: HBMoore.com
Facebook: Fans of Heather B. Moore
Blog: MyWritersLair.blogspot.com
Instagram: @authorhbmoore
Twitter: @HeatherBMoore